A Rob Wyllie paperback
First published in Great Britain in 2020 by Rob Wyllie Bo

CW00431710

RobWyllie.com

A Matter of Disclosure

Rob Wyllie

PROLOGUE

It was parked opposite the main entrance of the building, taking no notice of the fading school safety zone markings painted on the street. For several months now, the school had run a largely ineffective campaign to stop their cadre of entitled, high net worth parents parking their Range-Rovers, BMWs and Mercedes in the zone at drop-off and collection time. But today, the prime spot was taken by an unremarkable white van sporting the anonymous logo of one of dozens of parcel delivery firms that have sprouted like crazy in this Amazon age.

3.15pm on a sunny September afternoon and a shrieking multi-cultural mass of Year Ones and Twos streamed into the playground in their neat white polo-shirts and grey trousers and skirts. Outside the gate, a troupe of expensively-dressed yummy-mummies, many with toddlers in arms, talked of designer brands, reality TV stars, property prices, hopeless husbands and fantasy lovers, as was their daily routine. The fathers, fewer in number, talked Fulham, Arsenal, Chelsea and made politically-incorrect observations under their breath about the attractiveness or otherwise of the mothers assembled at the gate. Then gradually the Lucys, Milos, Nikitas and Aarons began to emerge on to the pavement, some scanning the street for their mothers or child-minders, others reluctant to leave behind their playmates. Before long the throng had spilled into the street, in a scene that was repeated here every day as in countless primary schools up and down the land. Such an easy target.

No-one noticed as the driver of the white van started her engine and gently slipped the gear selector into Drive. It sat idling for a few moments as she gave thanks to her god for choosing her for this important work, and then there was a roar from the engine as she jammed the wooden stake against the accelerator pedal and a screech of tyres as the brake was released, sending two and a half tonnes of metal careering across the road at a frightening speed. There were no screams at first, the ghastly horror being played out in silent slow motion, young bodies tossed into the air like skittles, pushchairs transformed into unrecognisable masses of twisted plastic and aluminium, a dozen or more lives crushed out of existence in an instant under the wheels of the van or against the sturdy stone wall of the school. It was all over in a heartbeat.

Except it wasn't over. As a stunned crowd began to gather around the scene, unable to even begin to comprehend the enormity of what had just happened, the electronic timer crudely taped to the dashboard counted down the last few seconds of its life. Five...four...three...two...one...zero.

Across the street, a safe distance away, the hooded driver gave a smile of satisfaction before slinking away un-noticed into the leafy backwaters of Notting Hill.

Chapter 1

She had awoken a full hour before dawn, bounding out of bed bursting with excitement about what lay ahead. *The most important day of her career, ever.* Not for the first time in recent months, she left behind an empty bed, for that day Philip was to be show-boating for the international media in the Lebanon, pretty much a normal day for this rock-star of the human-rights industry. Checking her phone, she saw he had sent her a text. *'Big day! Best of luck, tough case but hope it all goes well p.s. in Jerusalem tomorrow, back Friday.'*

No kisses, and not exactly an optimistic tone, but defending a child-murdering terrorist bomber was never going to be easy. And tough case, that was the understatement of the decade. Pulling on her dressing gown, she crept quietly into Ollie's bedroom, kissing him lightly on the cheek without disturbing him. There was just time for a quick shower before getting dressed. But at least this morning there was no need for Maggie to do what she had done almost every morning for the last two or three months. Opening the doors on her husband's side of their fitted wardrobe, slowly and methodically, working from left to right, searching through the pockets of Philip's suits. Because yesterday, after over one hundred days of drawing a blank, she had found what she was looking for. *Evidence.* A payment receipt from The Ship, which she vaguely knew to be a trendy gastropub in Shoreditch, just round the corner from Philip's office. Two hundred and sixty-nine pounds - about the going rate for dinner for two at that over-rated establishment. And the date on the slip - two weeks ago on Thursday, recent enough for her to remember that evening he came in after midnight, trailed by a faint but discernible scent of perfume. Expensive perfume, because Philip wouldn't be cheating with some cheap tart. He said he had been in a client meeting all evening. He was always in client meetings, according to him. *Liar.*

She sank down on the edge of her bed, briefly covering her face with her hands. Glancing up, she caught sight of her reflection in the wardrobe mirror. Forty-two years old, the shimmery bloom of youth now gone. Was she still attractive? On a good day perhaps she was, but she had to face it. If she wasn't quite in the autumn of her years, it was definitely late summer. But she wasn't going to cry, not on this day of all days, a day she hoped would turn out to be special. *The breakthrough*. She had to shut everything else out of her mind. Keep calm and carry on.

Running downstairs to fix a quick coffee, she was momentarily surprised to find Daisy already up and about. Most days her niece - more accurately, Philip's niece, the only daughter of his twin brother Hugo and currently employed as their temporary nanny - would not surface until well past 7.30am and then there would be a frenzied explosion of activity compressed into ten minutes or less as Ollie was dragged from his bed then dressed, breakfasted and ushered into the old Fiesta for the frantic three-mile drive to school.

'Morning,' Daisy mumbled, distractedly stirring a mug of instant coffee with one hand whilst scrolling her phone with the other. Maggie noted that her niece's usual sullen mood was present and correct, but that she was already dressed, looking uncharacteristically conventional in a pretty Boden print dress, her unruly mass of red hair neatly held back with a cheap faux tortoise-shell clasp. Then she remembered that for Daisy too, this was going to be a special day.

'Good morning Daisy dear, you look nice. Of course, you're going to visit your dad today, aren't you, I've just remembered. Will you be ok?'

'Of course, why shouldn't I be?' Daisy said. 'It's no big deal.'

Actually it is a big deal, thought Maggie, visiting your father in prison for the first time, but there was nothing to be gained from expressing that view right now. Daisy was angry, angry with the world. Angry because she had lost her addict mother when she was only ten, the wound still open and raw. Angry with her activist father for continually putting his pathetic causes ahead of the needs of his vulnerable young daughter. And especially angry with her aunt for failing to get him off the manslaughter charge. It hadn't been her finest hour, Maggie had to admit, but there was only so much a defence barrister could do in the face of overwhelming evidence, and a guilty verdict had been inevitable no matter what she had said. He was damn lucky not to have been charged with murder and damn lucky to get away with an eight-year sentence, considering the seriousness of the offence, that was Maggie's blunt view. Hugo Brooks had been -still was - an arse and fully deserved everything that he got, but no, you couldn't very well say that to your nineteen-year-old niece.

Instead she said, somewhat uncertainly, 'Well, as long as you are going to be alright. There's money in the drawer for a taxi, and of course you need to be there on time or else they won't let you in, so just allow plenty of leeway. But you know that already. And remember, you don't need to worry about collecting Ollie from school today, he's going back with Felicity Swift to play with his friend Tom.'

Daisy didn't look up from her phone, her thumbs tapping out a message to an unknown recipient. An angry message, if the ferocity with which she smashed down on the keypad was any guide. 'Yeah, as you say, I know all that already. I'll be fine'.

Maggie's Uber arrived at 6.15am as arranged, and was soon threading its way through the quiet streets of Hampstead on the wet and gloomy April morning. By 7.20 am she was at her desk. Yesterday, she had printed out the email and its attachment and was now reading it for what must have been the ninth or tenth time. Explosive, to say the least. With the trial set to resume at 1.00pm, she only had the morning to decide what to do. Five hours before what was almost certain to be the most important moment of her career, if she had anything to do with it.

Her mind drifted back to that weird day three months earlier, when, returning from yet another car-crash of a court hearing, she had found Nigel Redmond, the scheming Clerk of Drake Chambers, lurking by her desk.

'Nigel. This is an unexpected pleasure. To what do I owe this great honour?'

'Eh bah gum lass, you look thoroughly hacked off.'

He did it every time they met. The crass mockery of her Yorkshire roots, evidently believing that it was amusing. But it wasn't.

'Another tough day on the coal-face of justice my dear, am I right?'

He had got that right at least.

'Stupid stupid police,' Maggie said. 'The two moronic cops on my case turn up all suited and booted and then suddenly one says to the other, *I thought **you** were bringing the evidence file?* Can you believe it? Of course, the judge goes ape-shit and re-schedules the trial way out to November. And now my slime-ball client goes free and I've just lost three days' work. Justice, don't make me laugh.'

Redmond was under no illusions as to why many of his learned colleagues had decided to practice law. For them, it was all about the remuneration, handsome and bountiful, and he liked to use that knowledge to his advantage.

'Well, don't worry young Maggie,' he had said in an obsequious tone, 'because I'll make sure you still get paid for today.'

And then, quite out of the blue, he had dropped the bombshell. 'And anyway, you're going to be in the money big-time because haven't I got a *beauty* of a brief for you. You're going to just *love* this.'

Then without a further word of explanation he had passed her *Crown verses Alzahrani*. Passed to Maggie Brooks, she of the exceptionally low-flying career, little miss distinctly average, not yet a QC despite nearly twenty years as a barrister. And if she was being honest, that wasn't just because she was a female working-class northerner swimming in a sea of white male public-school dickheads. That didn't help, but in occasional moments of honesty she forced herself to consider the possibility that maybe, just maybe, she really wasn't that good. But whether that was true or not was at this moment immaterial, because now, quite improbably, she was defending the notorious teenage terrorist. Finally she was in the spotlight, the big break she had always dreamed of but which until now had always eluded her. Later today she would be centre stage at the Old Bailey, and she was determined to do everything in her power to win. That was all that mattered, win at any cost, do or die, and then the big briefs would start to come in, when she could expect to clear at least one hundred and fifty grand a year, maybe more. Then she might be invited to apply to take silk. At last. Maggie Brooks QC. Or maybe it should be Maggie Bainbridge QC? Actually, she preferred her maiden name. It tripped off the tongue rather nicely, she thought.

But there was no time for idle daydreaming when she was due back in court at one o'clock sharp. Which meant she had only the morning in which to decide what to do about the Khan report. She perched her reading glasses on her nose and began to leaf through her scribbled notes, refreshing herself on his background, cobbled together from internet searches and a helpful article from the online edition of the Lancashire Evening Chronicle.

Dr Tariq Khan. British Pakistani, raised in Blackburn, Lancs. Grandfather arrived in the UK in the early fifties, worked as a bus driver, had four children including Khan's father Imran. Tariq born in 1970, eldest of four siblings. First member of his family to go to university, wins place at Cambridge to study physics. Graduated with first in 1993, then did PhD, subject unknown. Research scientist at Rutherford Appleton Laboratory in Oxfordshire for seven years. Father Imran active in community - Imam at local mosque.

He had done well, this Dr Khan, considering his modest background, and now it would appear he was occupying a very senior position at the Government Communications Headquarters up in Cheltenham. She turned to her laptop and clicked on the folder she had created just two days before, then opened an image file. The photograph was a typical end-of-conference group shot, showing Khan to be in his early-to-mid forties, bearded and smartly dressed in a three-piece suit but otherwise of unprepossessing appearance. It had been taken three or four years earlier in Denver in the US, at something called the *Third International Symposium on Automatic Recognition Technologies*. A further internet search had turned up the conference agenda, which listed him as Dr Tariq Khan, Head of Recognition Technologies, GCHQ, England. The subject of his presentation had been *The Future of Automatic Facial Recognition in Civil Society*. It looked as if he knew his stuff all right.

So the big question had to be, why in hell had he decided to write this damn report? A report, if she had interpreted its densely-written technical arguments correctly, that could blow the prosecution case out of the water? The obvious answer was that as a Muslim, he sympathised with the terrorist Alzahrani and this was an effort to see her freed. With a start, Maggie pulled herself up, recognising the lazy racial stereotyping thinking that it was. Tariq Khan was as English as she was and probably as proud a Lancastrian as she was a proud Yorkshire lass. Besides which, he worked for GCHQ for goodness sake, and he wouldn't have got through that door without the most intense scrutiny of his background and politics. So no, it had to be something else, surely?

The email had come in just three days earlier from an organisation calling itself *British Solidarity for Palestine*. She had found a website, poorly-designed and amateurish in construction, the home page stridently condemning Israel, the US and Britain for what it called their war crimes. There were a smattering of celebrity endorsements, the usual suspects, including, they claimed, the present Prime Minister Julian Priest. No surprise there, given his long-standing support for the cause, although it seemed unlikely that he would be involved with such an unprofessional outfit. She had asked Philip if he knew anything about them and he said he had never heard of them, his verdict being they were probably a bunch of wanky virtue-signalling sixth-formers jumping on a bandwagon. This, from the king of wanky virtue-signalling himself.

But whoever they were and whatever their motivation, there was little doubt in her mind that the report was genuine, and she found it hard to suppress her excitement. This was going to be the giant coup, the big high-profile victory against impossible odds, the win that would make her reputation. Then the work would surely come flooding in and with it, the fat fees and everything you could do with it. Things like dumping a cheating pig of a husband. And then maybe in a year or two she could take silk. God, she wanted that so badly.

Of course, she knew exactly what was the right thing to do next. She should tell the judge about the report, get the police to track down Dr Khan, call him as a witness and let the estimable British justice system take its course.

But she wasn't going to do any of that, because she had a *much* better plan. Not entirely her own idea it was true, but brilliant nonetheless. For the final time, she checked that sentence in the email. No, she hadn't misread it. There it was, absolute dynamite, the phrase that she had carefully underlined in red pen.

We have evidence that the prosecution has had Khan's report since the start of the trial, perhaps earlier.

Perhaps earlier. She leaned back in her chair and smiled to herself. Just for a moment, she had forgotten about the crumpled credit card receipt in her pocket. And about her cheating husband, a man she was unsure if she had ever really loved. But sod him, she was on her way.

Chapter 2

The armoured Foxhound, still incongruously painted in its desert camouflage, was parked around sixty metres away, close enough to get a clear view of the suspect vehicle, a nondescript silver-grey Peugeot, but not too close to make them vulnerable should the car bomb choose to detonate. At least this time there had been a coded warning. It had taken the skeleton team of PSNI officers the good part of an hour to clear the immediate area. Even at four-thirty on a dank and misty April Saturday, the street had been busy with shoppers, each resolved to take full advantage of Easter weekend bargains by turning up in person rather than relying on the internet. The Explosives Ordnance Disposal team had arrived whilst the police were still on their loud-hailers repeating 'we have had a bomb warning, please clear the area. This is not a drill, this is not a drill' over and over again. Armed officers in flak jackets and cradling Heckler & Koch MP5SF semi-automatics were positioned every thirty metres or so, nervously scanning the horizon for an unseen enemy.

'Bloody hopeless sir, don't you think? Those PSNI lot I mean.'

Captain Jimmy Stewart took another draw on his cigarette before answering. 'Aye well Naomi, the problem is they've not yet come to terms with the fact that the troubles are back. They can't believe that Northern Ireland is going back to the seventies, who does? Nobody wants it, but the local politicians hope if they ignore it, it will just go away.'

Naomi Harris, his young sergeant, was just one month into her first deployment with 11 EOD&S Regiment, the army's bomb disposal outfit. An Essex girl, she had spent her first three years' of service over in Afghanistan, dismantling and packing up all the kit the Army had left behind when the fighting men and women had come home. When the opportunity to retrain as a technician in the Explosive Ordnance Disposal and Search Regiment came up, and with it promotion, she jumped at the chance and here she was, just one year later, alongside one of the army's most experienced bomb disposal officers - experience that was soon to be lost to the military, because Jimmy Stewart, at thirty-two years old and with ten years' service behind him, had little more than three more months in uniform before hitting civvy street.

'You were there at that terrible thing in London weren't you sir? That school in Notting Hill.'

'Aye, I was.'

It wasn't something you were likely to forget. Just like Helmand all over again, except the victims weren't young squaddies but innocent little kids. And just like so often out there, his disposal team had arrived too late to do anything about it. Not that it mattered whether it was a Taliban IED or a Palestinian nutter with a white van and two kilos of cheap IRA Semtex, the carnage was just the same. He hoped that girl who did it would be locked away for life. Pity they didn't have the death sentence still.

'There wasn't any warning, was there sir?'

Jimmy was beginning to get irritated by Harris's prattling, but he recognised it as an involuntary reaction to her fear. First time in action. He could remember how it felt.

'No there wasn't. So let's just concentrate on the job in hand, shall we?'

He hadn't meant for it to sound as harsh as it did. She fell silent for a moment before the nerves got the better of her again.

'So just remind me again sir, which one's Catholic and which one's Protestant, Rangers or Celtic? I don't really follow football.'

A broad smile spread across his face. 'Christ sake Harris, that could get you knee-capped over here. Rangers are the Protestants, Celtic the Catholics. The clue's in the colours. Celtic, green, shamrock in the badge and all that.'

Of course unlike him, Naomi hadn't grown up in a city where the curse of Protestant-Catholic sectarianism was everywhere. How could she be expected to know? And every Glasgow generation were taught the same old tired prejudices, the same stupid songs, *The Sash My Father Wore* and the Irish rebel songs celebrating an uprising that was nearly a century old. Now here on the streets of Belfast it was back, in its deadliest form. Brainless beyond belief.

The radio crackled into life. *'EOD 12, are you in position?'*

'Affirmative Control' Jimmy replied. 'How are we doing with the phone sweeps?'

'Just awaiting the information from Vodaphone. They're the last one. They have given us an ETA of 17.05. Just a few minutes to wait then we can put all the info together and see where we are.'

'Thanks Control, not too long to wait then. And they're all lined up to do the call blocking once we've had a look?'

'*Affirmative EOD12. Should only take a few minutes to get that implemented, that's what they're telling us.*'

'Ok thanks Control. So just keep us in the loop, will you? Over and out.'

Thirty years ago, the scene would have been swarming with soldiers, but now security was in the hands of the local police force, the Police Service of Northern Ireland. With still no devolved government sitting in Stormont, the province was once more under direct rule from Westminster and ministers were reluctant to provide any further provocation to dissidents on both sides of the divide by once more having troops on the streets, although looking at the cop's quasi-military garb, it was hard to tell what difference it would make.

At ten past five there was still no update from Control on the phone scanning. 'Just have to wait,' groaned Jimmy, taking another cigarette from the pack. 'We need to know if there's a phone in that car, 'cause if there is, it's ninety percent certain that's going to be the trigger mechanism, and also, it probably means we're being watched by the bad guys. They'll want to do more than just blow up an old motor, won't they?'

They only had to wait a few minutes for the report to come through.'*EOD12, four devices have been detected within the area in question.*'

'Four? Bloody hell! Probably means some of these half-wit cops have left theirs switched on. Ok Control, we'll just have to assume that one of them is in the suspect vehicle. Let's just get on to the telecoms guys and get them to block all incoming calls to these cells. We can't risk some lowlife setting it off with a nicked Galaxy 10. Over and out.'

'More waiting sir?'

'Afraid so sergeant, nothing else for it.'

After a few minutes she broke the silence. 'Sir, our guys in Didcot are saying that the explosive used in that Notting Hill bomb was Semtex, and it was probably supplied from here. I thought all that stuff was supposed to have been turned in as one of the conditions of that Good Friday agreement?'

'Aye, and if you believe that you believe in the tooth fairy. They'll have kept a big stash somewhere, you can bet your backside on that.

They've probably got a wee e-commerce site on the dark web too, and making a nice living out of it. And they'll still have all the old contacts in Libya and Iran in their wee books, so no problem finding customers.'

Still there was nothing from Control.

'So what are you going to do when you leave the army sir, if you don't mind me asking? Any ideas?'

'Well yeah, got a few ideas kicking around, but not really settled on anything yet,' he replied. 'Maybe have a nice wee holiday, and then I'll start looking around for something.'

In actual fact, Jimmy Stewart didn't have a clue what he was going to do when he left, but what he did know was that it couldn't come too soon. Then maybe the nightmares and flashbacks might fade or even go away for good. Because the truth was, it was screwing him up, big time. In Afghanistan, OED were always first on the scene after an Improvised Explosive Device had gone off. It was the Taliban's prime modus operandi, and in the early years, even the most amateur of bombs ripped the inadequately-armoured personnel carriers into pieces like coke cans. You never forgot the carnage, the stench of burning flesh, the scattered body parts, the pathetic moans from the mortally wounded and all the time you were thinking - is there another one waiting for me? And now, nearly four years after he had left Helmand, it was starting all over again, right here in the UK. No, he couldn't wait to get out. And maybe he could concentrate on what he really wanted to do. Rebuilding his shattered marriage.

'OED12, we have confirmation from the telecoms guys. Incoming calls are now blocked.'

'Right Harris, we're good to go,' Jimmy shouted. 'Let's get the Dragon out the back and get cracking.'

He prodded a button on the dashboard and with a loud whirring sound, the bottom-hinged tailgate began slowly to descend, forming a steep ramp down to the roadway. A few moments later the Dragon Runner Remote Control Vehicle powered up and began to inch down the ramp under Naomi's remote guidance.

Her eyes were focused on the bright LCD screen of her control pad. 'The Dragon's on the road now sir. I'll just bring it round to the front, do a few checks and then we can start moving it up to the target.'

Manipulating the joystick, she spun the Dragon round one-hundred and eighty degrees on its tracks then piloted it forward until it sat directly in front of the Foxhound. With a click on the keypad, the articulated manipulator arm which gave the device its name began slowly to extend, the hydraulic control rams emitting a soft hiss as it achieved its full reach of nearly two metres. At the tip of the extended arm was the dragon's head, fitted with a powerful high-definition video camera with a three-hundred-and-sixty-degree field of vision.

'Good, everything seems to be working ok. So I'm going to prime the Small Explosive charge sir, do you think we'll need that today?'

'I don't know, we might. Let's just move her up to the target and have a wee nosey with the camera first. Although I doubt whether they would be so stupid to leave the bomb in full view, but you never know our luck. These New IRA lads haven't been doing this for long.'

It had begun to rain, spraying a fine mist on the pillar-box windscreen of the Foxhound, making visibility even more difficult than it already was. Jimmy narrowed his eyes and peered out along the wide street towards the Peugeot. He caught sight of a young police officer standing in the doorway of a department store, no more than thirty or forty metres away from the suspect car. 'Crikey, he's a bit close,' said Jimmy, shaking his head. 'Sixty metres we said. Bloody amateurs.'

The silence of the evening was broken suddenly by the shrill wail of a car alarm. It was the Peugeot, its bright hazard warning lights flashing in syncopation with the alarm.

'Oh-oh,' Jimmy said, 'what's this?'

After about a minute, the alarm stopped. 'Might be something interfering with the car's electronics sir?' Naomi said enquiringly. 'Like the signal from a radio transmitter?'

'Aye, might be. Let's get the Dragon up there sharpish.'

'Ok sir'. She pushed forward the joystick, setting the track-wheeled robot trundling along the roadway. It had only moved a few metres when the car's alarm went off again, and then suddenly a figure came into view on the remote's screen. Horrified, they watched as the young policeman stepped out of the doorway and began walking tentatively towards the car.

Naomi screamed out a warning. 'Stop! Hell, what is he doing? What is he doing?' Tossing the control pad onto Jimmy's lap, she shouldered open the heavy door and jumped down on to the pavement.

'Harris,' Jimmy screamed, 'what the hell are you thinking! Get back in the truck, get back into the truck! That's a bloody order!'

A second later, the still evening was disturbed by the crack of a high velocity rifle. A sound only too familiar to Jimmy Stewart from his service in Afghanistan. Then the bullet smashed into Naomi's face, her head exploding as if in slow-motion, splattering a torrent of blood, flesh and bone against the windscreen of the Foxhound.

He sat transfixed, paralysed with shock. *Please, not another one, please, not another one.* And then he started to weep, sobbing inconsolably, the cumulative pain and anguish of loss finally too much to bear. He was still weeping ten minutes later when the backup team finally arrived.

Chapter 3

Maggie re-read her summing-up for the fifth or sixth time, tweaking a word here and there, testing a theatrical pause or two at the critical points. This was just for backup, she reminded herself, because if the day panned out as she expected it to, there would be absolutely no need for a defence summary. But best to be prepared, just in case. It had briefly crossed her mind that if the Khan report was to be believed and the identification evidence was really flawed, then maybe Alzahrani was actually innocent as she had claimed, and that maybe her case wasn't so hopeless after all. But this wasn't the time for self-doubt. The plan was good and she was resolved to stick to it.

She had made the decision, rightly or wrongly, not to tell her client about the existence of Dr Tariq Khan's report. Well, to be honest, she knew it was wrong but she didn't want Alzahrani screwing everything up at the last minute. Ethically a bit suspect, to say the least, but Maggie was not interested in the opinions of a terrorist like Dena Alzahrani. All that mattered was the outcome of the trial. Hopefully, when they had their final meeting this morning she wouldn't do anything stupid like deciding to plead guilty. It was unlikely, because she hadn't said more than two words in any meeting they had had so far.

Finally satisfied with the summing-up, she gave a thumbs-up to her junior Ricardo Mancini and soon they had gathered up their documents before setting off down Giltspur Street. A few minutes later she was striding across the immense oak-panelled entrance hall of the Central Criminal Court in her wig and flowing robes, trailed by Mancini, who had charge of the several thick buff folders containing the case notes. The beautiful building, more commonly known as the Old Bailey after the street on which it stands, was erected in 1902 on the former site of Newgate gaol. In the early Victorian era the gaol was the scene of the public hangings that were a popular public entertainment. Today, there was to be no hanging, but the interest in this modern-day case was equally intense, the public gallery jam-packed and the press out in force for what was expected to be the final day of the Alzahrani trial.

On the way, Mancini had still been nagging on about the damn report. 'And you're sure we're good about this Maggie?' he had asked for the fifth or sixth time, as they threaded their way through the buzzing throng of morning commuters. It was evident he was not going to let it go without some resistance. 'This is our last chance, isn't it?'

'I've told you, just leave it please Ricardo,' she had replied, more than a hint of exasperation creeping into her voice. 'We're making this into more than it really is you know.' You are, was what she meant. Now she was glad she hadn't told him about it until the very last minute possible. He was a nice guy but not very imaginative, and actually, a bit of a prig too. She knew he wouldn't approve of what she had planned, of that she had been certain, and worse still, if he'd known about it from the start, he might well have turned whistleblower and that would really have buggered everything up. So it had definitely been the right decision to keep him in the dark.

'In the scope of things it's probably not that important,' her words the exact opposite of the truth. It was important, but not because of the actual content of the thing, since she had no idea whether the dramatic conclusions of Khan's report could be trusted or not. No, it was important simply by the fact that it existed at all.

Generally, she was nervous before the final day of a trial, no matter how weak the case against her or how unconvincing the evidence, but today she was calmness personified. Her opponent Adam Cameron QC was absolutely premier league when it came to advocacy, that was her opinion, with a string of high-profile victories to his credit. Hadn't he made her look stupid in the Hugo Brooks trial, a humiliation she wasn't going to forget in a hurry? If she hadn't considered herself strictly second division before that monumental failure, then she had no option but to face up to that fact in the aftermath. But now, like a minor league football club on an extended cup run, she was playing in the premier division. The only problem was, she was certain the jury had already bought Cameron's version of the case hook, line and sinker. It didn't matter that there was just one piece of evidence, some suspect and grainy video footage that when analysed with the fairy dust that was automatic facial recognition software, had claimed to identify Alzahrani. AFR, as the experts called it, was absolute catnip to judges and juries alike. Couldn't be argued with. Besides which they just didn't like her client, and who could blame them? But that was all going to be irrelevant now once she had enacted her master-plan. At least she hoped so.

She met Cameron in the entrance hall just as they were preparing to enter the courtroom, where he greeted her with a fake bonhomie that was entirely in keeping with his character. No doubt he had been waiting for her, lurking in the shadows, waiting his opportunity to unsettle his opponent, like a sledging cricketer at the start of an important test match. It was a tired old tactic, but perhaps it revealed he wasn't so confident about the outcome after all. Or maybe he had a secret to hide. *We have evidence that the prosecution has had Khan's report since the start of the trial. Perhaps earlier.*

'Maggie darling, I'm surprised you've even bothered to turn up today,' he purred. 'Nothing for you to work with of course, but really, I thought you might have put up at least a bit of a fight. In the interest of justice and all that. At least give the jury something to think about in return for giving up a month of their lives. Put on a bit of a show, eh?'

'Piss off Adam darling,' she answered, good-humouredly. The smug git wouldn't be laughing in an hour or two if she had anything to do with it.

'Ha ha, no-one likes a bad loser,' he said, but then, strangely, 'so, no last-minute cats waiting to be pulled out of bags, I hope?'

Was it her imagination or was there a hint of nervousness and uncertainty behind the confident veneer? Damn, that would ruin everything.

***

'I'm your barrister, and it is my job to advise you. And my advice is once again, please don't wear your headscarf in court.'

She didn't expect to get an answer, and she wasn't disappointed. All through her custody and right up to the moment she was charged, Dena Alzahrani had given a brusque 'no comment' to every question she had been asked, and she had been no more forthcoming with Maggie since she had taken on the case. In the witness box, she had simply denied everything, coldly and dispassionately, in a manner guaranteed to get up the noses of even the most liberal-minded juror. And that damn headscarf. Maggie fully respected her right to wear it of course, and she was equally sensitive to the possible accusations of racism that might be directed at her for trying to dissuaded her. But the jury, now that was another matter. To say that it lacked diversity was the understatement of the year, and she didn't want to play to its prejudices any more than she had to. But all of that was going to be immaterial because she'd realised early in the relationship that her client was going to be immune to any coaching or guidance as to how to behave in court. It was normal for some sort of relationship to be formed between barrister and client, because even the most obtuse defendant knew that their fate was in the hands of their lawyer, and they all wanted to get off -usually. But Alzahrani was different. For a start, they didn't even know her true identity. She'd entered the country on a fake Jordanian passport stamped with a fake student visa, but other than the fact that her accent marked her as Palestinian and that she looked around nineteen or twenty, they knew no more about her.

'Ok, well it's up to you.'

Suddenly Alzahrani asked,

'What do you think will happen to me?' For the first time, Maggie saw fear in her eyes, the mask of defiance finally slipping, albeit briefly. *So she is human after all. Ten minutes before we're due back in court. Don't tell me she's going to plead guilty at the last minute. Hell, that's all I need.*

'Well, we will be hoping for the best of course, but I think, honestly, it's highly likely that the jury will find you guilty. You will then be held in custody for several months and then we will come back to the court for sentencing.'

And they'll lock you up and throw away the key, was what she didn't say.

'Ok, as I said it's up to you. But my advice is lose the scarf, look like a scared and vulnerable young girl exploited by evil men, and you might just persuade one juror to give you the benefit of the doubt.'

In an instant, the default surly mask returned. She was as stubborn as she was stupid, this young woman. Maggie had known that much from the start. The only pity was if her plan worked, then her client, almost certainly guilty, would walk free. But that was simply collateral damage. What was important was the victory, the triumph of a case won against the odds.

Today, that was all that mattered.

***

'All rise.'

Judge Margo Henderson QC was presiding, peering up over her half-rimmed glasses at the public gallery as she walked into court.

Aside from the spectacles, she was in many ways the antithesis of the stereotypical high court judge. Not grey-haired, not male, decidedly glamorous, and about the same age as Maggie. Their age was the only thing they had in common, Henderson's career trajectory having been as meteoric as her own had been mediocre. Although possessed of a needle-sharp sense of humour which was deployed frequently to deflate the more pompous of the QCs who stood in front of her, she was no soft touch. Today her mood was serious, the gravity of the crime dictating a sombre tone and the defendant if found guilty could expect a sentence as stiff as the law would allow. Dena Alzahrani had been taken to the dock a few minutes earlier, handcuffed, and then, as throughout the trial, she sat slouched in her chair with a defiant expression on her face. And wearing that bloody headscarf. The judge thanked the Clerk then prepared to explain to the jury how this, the final day, would pan out.

Maggie might not have regarded herself as much of a barrister, but she thought she knew how to read juries and always kept notes about the reaction of each of the twelve as a trial progressed. And almost to a man or woman, this lot had already made up its mind. Perhaps she had her doubts about the twenty-something crop-haired girl who, quite without evidence, she imagined to be central-casting's go-to left-wing activist. *She* wasn't going to be swayed by the charms of a smarmy toff like Adam Cameron, but she was the exception, and Maggie doubted if even Miss Crop-Hair could hold out in the jury room when under pressure from eleven fellow citizens pressing for a guilty verdict. No, this was already a done deal. But that didn't matter, not if her plan worked as she expected it to.

Now the judge was speaking.

'Members of the jury, I will give both prosecution and defence one final opportunity to present evidence or summon witnesses, although I think we heard yesterday that they had both concluded their respective cases. Then you will hear the summing up from both sides, and I urge you to listen carefully to the points that my learned friends will make before finally deciding on your verdict. It is important you do not allow your decision to be swayed by any judgement you make on the character of the defendant, nor by the undoubtedly serious nature of the crime.'

Some hope of that, Maggie thought. And in any case, other than

Miss Crop-Hair, they had already decided.

'Instead you must base your verdict only on the strength of the evidence that has been laid before you,' the judge continued. 'I hope that is clear. So firstly Mr Cameron, do you have any final matters you wish to bring before the court?'

A long silence. Five seconds...ten seconds...fifteen seconds...thirty seconds. Hell, don't tell me he's going to bring it up *now*. Surely not, not at this late stage?

'Mr Cameron?'

Finally. 'No m'lady, the Crown is ready to sum up.' Relief.

'And you, Mrs Brooks?'

Maggie did have a matter to bring up, but she was going to hold back that little bombshell until Adam Cameron had done his summing-up. Maximise the humiliation, maximise the theatre. And then boom - light the blue touch-paper and take cover.

She gave the judge a prim smile. 'Nothing more m'lady, thank you.'

'Very well Mrs Brooks. Mr Cameron, please proceed.'

Getting to his feet, he slotted his reading glasses into his waistcoat pocket then strolled over towards the jury, smiling his trademark obsequious smile.

'Good morning ladies and gentlemen. Well, Judge Henderson has summed up admirably what are your duties today, and I know you will perform them to the very best of your ability. You have sat and listened diligently through the twenty-one days of this long and complex trial, and no doubt many of you will already have made up your mind about the guilt or otherwise of the defendant. My job today is simply to remind you of the case against Dena Alzahrani, which I believe to be overwhelming. I do not think you will need to be reminded of the dreadful crime itself...'

And then of course, he proceeded to remind them. The cold-blooded murder of eighteen innocent people, ten of them little children under the age of ten years old, their young lives cut short, blown to pieces by an indescribable act of violence by the young woman who now sat in the dock. If the jury hadn't been convinced before, they would be now, but Maggie wasn't in the least concerned. Because it wasn't going to make any difference to the outcome no matter what Cameron said.

She scanned the jury for signs of a reaction. It would have been nearly five weeks since the terrible details of the crime had been described to them and Cameron would not want to take the risk that its impact had diminished through the simple passage of time, although there was little likelihood of that, given the graphic horror of the attack. No doubt he was now going to spell out the evidence, and in as simple terms as possible. No fancy legal jargon and critically, no more than two or three facts for them to take in. But this case wasn't even as complicated as that. Automatic facial recognition had identified the perpetrator. AFR, the new DNA. That was all they needed to know.

First however, he was going to remind them of the character of the accused, lest any misguided juror should be harbouring even a morsel of sympathy for her. Perhaps he had sized up Miss Crop-Hair and didn't like what he was seeing.

'You will remember you saw a video where Alzahrani boasted of carrying out a *spectacular*, right here in London. For that, we must thank the clever men and women from our cyber warfare teams and of course their CIA counterparts, for their splendid work in breaking into what I believe is known as the Dark Web - and forgive me if my terminology isn't quite correct. In that video, she was very specific about the attack being here in our city, and very specific about the date on which it was to take place. It was of course the eleventh of September last year, the day of the terrible atrocity in Notting Hill. I do not need to remind you, ladies and gentlemen, of the significance of that particular date. *Nine-eleven*. The most infamous date in our recent history, and chosen quite cynically by the defendant to maximise the publicity that her atrocity would command. An atrocity, ladies and gentlemen, for which she herself was wholly responsible.'

Very good Adam, Maggie thought, but you've still got to prove that, haven't you? Judge Henderson evidently shared her view.

'Mr Cameron, that is your case to make, it should not be stated as if it is a fact.'

'My mistake m'lady, you are quite right,' he said, smiling, 'I apologise.'

Unperturbed, he continued. 'Now you will remember a chilling phrase from that video...' he took his reading glasses from a waistcoat pocket and read from his notes... *'I will make those infidel children burn in hell.* Appalling, horrifying and savage, undoubtedly. But what I would like you to focus on is the fact that the defendant had full knowledge of the act in advance, both its location here in London and the exact nature of the planned attack. *I will make those infidel children burn in hell* - her intention could not be more clear.'

He stole a quick glance at his watch. Yes thought Maggie, about three minutes so far. Keep it brief and to the point, that's what you're doing, don't want the jury falling asleep with boredom.

'But of course the fact of Dena Alzahrani boasting that she would carry out the act does not in itself constitute proof that she actually did it - although you might well conclude, ladies and gentlemen, that so specific was her threat that you might on the balance of probability find her guilty on that alone.'

Judge Henderson raised an eyebrow, but on this occasion decided against intervention. Maggie smiled to herself. She had to hand it to him, he was damn good, and now he could go in for the kill. It was just such a shame for him that it was all going to be in vain. So here it was. What he was describing as the concrete evidence.

'You will remember that we heard from the key witness Mr Wojciech Kowalczyk - I think I have pronounced that correctly...' - drawing a smile from several members of the jury, but not Miss Crop-Hair - '...who saw a hooded figure jumping out of the driver's door of the lorry and then running along Princedale Road towards his parked van. Mr Kowalczyk is a Polish plumber - a very rich man' - more smiles from the jury - 'and as you have heard, was sitting in the driver's seat talking on his phone having just completed a job in a nearby property. He had started his engine and as a result his dash-cam device had began to record. That dash-cam, ladies and gentlemen, caught in full view the escape of the defendant on video, and despite her being hooded and wearing sunglasses in an attempt to prevent identification, the police were able to use automatic facial recognition technology to identify the fleeing figure as Dena Alzahrani.'

That had been a pretty stupid mistake, not to know that the authorities kept a database of digitised facial images of all visitors from so-called 'countries of interest' and that Jordan was on the list. It was a school-girl error, but then Alzahrani wasn't much more than a school-girl herself. They had picked her up that same afternoon, blithely sitting at the back of her UCL classroom as if it was a quite normal day.

'Now as we heard from Professor Walker, the Crown's expert witness, there is no doubt at all about the identification of the accused. The new DNA, that's how Professor Walker described this clever technology. A memorable and apt phrase, I think you will agree.'

Maggie gave a wry smile. This case wasn't going to tax the mental powers of the jury very much, of that she was sure. The new DNA, they would remember that, and DNA evidence was full-proof, wasn't it? Except that Dr Tariq Khan, world-renowned expert at GCHQ, disagreed. Adam Cameron knew that and keeping it to himself was going to be the biggest mistake of his career. But then unexpectedly, a wave of uncertainty swept over her. Because there was absolutely no proof at all that the email she had received was genuine. And even if it was, all it had said was that the *prosecution* knew about Khan's report. That didn't mean that Cameron himself had seen it. She knew something of how these things worked and it wasn't beyond the bounds of possibility that it had gone direct to the Crown Prosecution Service where some public-spirited official had decided it would be better if their famous QC didn't get to know about this little inconvenience. If that was the case, then her carefully-conceived plan was about to go up in smoke.

Cameron was now standing motionless as if in an act of meditation, his eyes closed, breathing deeply, his hands clasped in front of him as if in prayer. Amateur dramatics it was true, but effective because the jury was giving him its full attention. Lady Justice Henderson was less impressed.

'Can I take it then that your summing up is complete Mr Cameron?' she said sharply. 'If so, we will have a short break before asking Mrs Brooks to take the floor.'

'Eh? - ah, no,' he blustered, 'eh - I was just gathering my thoughts.'

'Well, please gather them up quickly, and continue.'

'Yes, thank you m'lady.'

Maggie shot her an admiring smile as Cameron, momentarily deflated, pressed on.

'Now in a moment I expect you will hear the defence claim that Miss Alzahrani is no more than an immature fantasist who is not capable of planning and carrying out a sophisticated crime such as this. It is true that no evidence was found that showed her to be the bomb-maker, but that is irrelevant to this case. What is unarguable is that she was positively identified leaving the scene, not by a pair of fallible human eyes, but by infallible state-of-the-art automatic facial recognition technology. The new DNA. We may not like how it is creeping into our everyday lives. We may well be uneasy that it threatens our privacy, but today, we see how it can be a fantastic force for good. Ladies and gentlemen, Alzahrani is no fantasist. She is a calculated cold-blooded killer, driven by the pursuance of a distorted strain of Islam, a grotesque agenda that bears no resemblance whatsoever to the true meaning of this peace-loving religion. She was clearly identified on camera leaving the scene of the crime, leaving no doubt whatsoever that she was the perpetrator.'

Several jurors were now nodding their heads in involuntary agreement, including Miss Crop-Head, outwardly at least giving the impression of a late conversion to the prosecution camp. That was it as far as he was concerned. Job done.

'I said at the start that our duty, yours and mine, is to see that the victims and their families get justice.' A few more affirming nods from the jury. 'I think you will agree that only a verdict of guilty will deliver that justice... a justice they so richly deserve. Thank you, ladies and gentlemen. Thank you m'lady.'

A good performance thought Maggie, but watching as he returned to his seat, she was taken by the complete absence of emotion on his face, not even the slightest smile of satisfaction. He wasn't a modest man by any means, and she was expecting to see the usual self-satisfied expression, rather like the one she had to suffer three months ago when she had lost the Hugo Brooks trial. But today he looked distracted, relieved, furtive even. Rather odd. *He knows.* She was sure of it now.

Judge Henderson was now speaking.

'Thank you Mr Cameron. Mrs Brooks, given that the Crown's summing up was commendably short and to the point, are you ready to present the defence summary without a recess?'

'Thank you m'lady, but I'm afraid a matter has arisen which I need urgently to bring to your attention.'

The judge peered at her over her spectacles, an expression of mild irritation on her face. She did not like it when a barrister disrupted the smooth running of one of her trials.

'Very well Mrs Brooks, let's hear it.'

'If you would, m'lady, I think this is matter which I need to discuss with you in private.'

Another sigh of irritation and a glance at her watch.

'Is this absolutely necessary Mrs Brooks?'

'Absolutely necessary I'm afraid m'lady. It's a matter of disclosure.'

Maggie caught sight of Cameron out of the corner of her eye. He sat motionless, the colour visibly draining from his face.

He knows.

'Very well. Ten-minute recess.' The judge turned to the Clerk, 'John, can we get some tea in my chambers, thank you. Come with me, both of you.'

Chapter 4

'A matter of disclosure you said Mrs Brooks?' Judge Henderson peered over her glasses as she stood up to pour tea from the elaborately-decorated china pot. 'Sugar Mr Cameron?'

The judges' chamber, a large room not far off half the size of the courtroom itself, was elaborately panelled in oak, carpeted in a luxurious thick patterned Wilton, expensive when new no doubt, but now rather threadbare in patches. Around the room hung portraits of former Lord Chancellors, going back all the way to Sir Thomas More who had held the post more than five hundred years earlier. Maggie and Adam Cameron sat on opposite ends of a large mahogany desk, perched on the edge of their chairs like naughty pupils up in front of the head teacher

'No thank you m'lady'. As he leant forward to pick up the saucer, his shaking hand causing the cup to rattle loudly. It wasn't just the teacup that was rattled.

'Well, tell all please Mrs Brooks, tell all.'

'M'lady, the defence has reason to believe that the Crown has in its possession a technical report from the government's own leading authority on automatic facial recognition that states quite unarguably that the reliance on such technology for the identification of my client is in this case unreliable. And I'm sure I don't need to tell you m'lady the significance...'

'Mrs Brooks, please forgive me,' interrupted the judge, 'but that was quite a sentence, so let me be clear on what you are saying...'

'Sorry m'lady, put simply, the government's leading expert, a Dr Tariq Khan, is saying that is not possible to be certain that it was Alzahrani in that dashcam video. His report says there is an eighty-six percent chance that she was identified in error.'

'I thought we were led to believe that this technology was the new DNA and therefore infallible. Am I given to understand that this is not the case?'

'In this instance m'lady, it does seem that way, yes.'

Henderson stroked her chin in contemplation and took a sip of her tea. 'And you say this was known to the prosecution when?'

'We believe that the Crown has had the report in its possession since before the start of the trial m'lady,' Maggie replied. 'A few days before, is my information.'

And then the bombshell. 'And so I'm concluding that they chose not to disclose it to the defence because they knew it would weaken if not destroy their case.'

'Quite so Mrs Brooks, quite so. And you had it when?'

'Just three days ago m'lady.'

'And how did it come into your possession may I ask?'

'It was emailed to my chambers by an organisation that claimed sympathy to the Palestinian cause, m'lady.'

'And you did not think you had a duty to immediately bring this before the court?'

Maggie had been expecting this one. 'I don't think it was a defence responsibility, no m'lady. It was a leaked document, of uncertain provenance supposedly sent to us by a group about which little is known. My junior has carried out some cursory investigation work in the short time we had available and we believe it may be genuine, but of course we do not know how it came into being. For that you must ask Mr Cameron.'

Through all this Adam Cameron had sat in silence, staring at his shoes, his discomfort manifest, with the look of a man about to mount the scaffold. And now the executioner was speaking.

'Mr Cameron, what do you say to all of this?' Henderson leaned forward as if to hear the explanation more clearly.

'Eh, well we discussed the matter...' He sounded nervous.

'We? Who is we?'

'We? Yes, the CPS m'lady. When the report was passed to us, obviously we discussed it in some depth but in the end decided it was not material to the case.'

'Really,' she said, 'and pray tell me, when exactly was this report passed to you, as you put it.'

He was clearly fumbling for an answer. 'Eh... when?... eh, I'm not exactly sure.'

'Well let me simplify the question Mr Cameron. Was it passed to you before or after the start of the trial?'

This will be good, thought Maggie.

'It eh... I think it was around the start of the trial, but I'm not sure, I would need to check.' It was not convincing.

'Let me repeat my question. Before or after, Mr Cameron?'

He crumbled. 'Before m'lady. We had it before. Just a few days before it started.'

The judge paused to make some notes in the ring-bound pad that she had taken earlier from a desk drawer.

'So let me get this clear. The trial is just about to start after several months of careful preparation, then along comes an inconvenient piece of late-breaking evidence and you decide to dismiss it there and then. Tell me, did you even bother to try and speak with this Dr Khan?'

'M'lady, it wasn't like that...'

Henderson's irritation was obvious. 'Mr Cameron, did- you- try- to- speak- to- Dr- Khan?'

'Not personally, no m'lady. I believe he was interviewed by some of my senior Crown Prosecution colleagues, but no, I did not speak to him myself at any point.'

'And so you, as the Queen's Counsel for the Crown, did not think it important that you should meet with this individual and judge for yourself whether his evidence was indeed material? A key witness, with the potential of undermining the whole case, and you did not seek to speak with him yourself?'

Cameron looked as if the noose had been placed around his neck and Margo Henderson was about to pull the lever that opened the trap door.

'No m'lady, as I said, I believe he was interviewed by CPS lawyers and it was felt that it was not relevant to the case. But perhaps on reflection, yes, I probably should have spoken to him myself.'

'Perhaps you should have reflected a bit sooner, Mr Cameron,' she replied.

'M'lady, may I raise a point?' Maggie said, and without waiting for an answer, 'It would be good to know how the report came into the hands of the CPS in the first place.'

Henderson did not seem offended by the interjection. 'Yes, a good point Mrs Brooks. Mr Cameron, I assume you can help us with this?'

Still he did not look up, instead mumbling something inaudible under his breath.

'What? Speak up Mr Cameron.'

'I believe it came via a government department m'lady.'

Maggie could not hide her astonishment.

'Government? What do you mean government?' Henderson asked.

'Who in the government? The Home Office, the Department of Justice, MI6, who?'

'I don't know. It just came to me via the CPS.' If he had access to the lever, he would have opened the trapdoor himself.

'You know, I am finding this rather hard to understand. I say it again - you Mr Cameron, as the QC for the Crown, did not think it important to understand the source of this report? Frankly I'm astonished, I cannot think of any other way to put it.'

She glanced down at her notebook, nodding slowly, her lips pursed.

'So, I have to say this is a grave matter, very grave indeed. Frankly it's not the first time in recent years that I have had to deal with the police and the CPS failing to disclose material evidence...'

'M'lady, honestly, it wasn't like that...'

'Mr Cameron, I'm not finished. Please do not interrupt again. As I was saying, this is not the first occurrence of this reprehensible behaviour, and I'm getting very fed up with it, very fed up indeed. I would go so far as to say that I fear it is becoming somewhat of a trend. And in this case, it seems we may have government interference too. That is something I thought I would never see in this country in my lifetime. This is very serious, you must know that Mr Cameron.'

She did not wait for his answer.

'Look, I need to consider this very carefully before deciding what I'm going to do. For now, I'm going to suspend the trial so I can take advice and consider the next steps. I will see you two back in this room, let's see, in three days' from now. Clerk, could you please inform the court room and ensure the jury are reminded again of their obligation not to discuss the case with anyone whilst they have been stood down.'

With that, she picked up her notebook and swept out of the room followed by the Clerk, leaving Maggie and Cameron alone. Now he was angry. Very angry.

'You bastard.' He was visibly shaking and looked close to tears. 'This will ruin me, you know that. You bastard.'

'You ruined yourself Adam,' Maggie replied, getting up to leave. 'Both sides have an obligation to disclose all material evidence. That's law school one-oh-one, as our American friends would say. You should know that, you've been at it long enough. See you on Friday.'

As she left, she gave a quiet smile of satisfaction. *This was it. At last, the career breakthrough.* Just a couple of days to wait, and then, welcome to the big time. Maggie Bainbridge QC. It sounded rather good.

***

Three days later, they were in the anonymous Victoria Street building that housed the Office of the Attorney General, a measure perhaps of how serious the judge was taking the disturbing news that had been revealed on the last day of the trial. Lady Justice Henderson kept them waiting for over forty minutes, a receptionist shepherding them on arrival into a stark waiting-room furnished with cheap plastic chairs most of which had seen better days. Maggie and Adam Cameron sat in opposite corners of the room, having exchanged nothing but a cursory 'good morning.' She, relaxed and confident, he still wearing the demeanour of a condemned murderer.

Finally a smartly-dressed young woman appeared and announced 'Lady Justice Henderson will see you now'. Today Maggie had chosen a slim tailored skirt and crisp white blouse, since this wasn't a courtroom appearance and therefore there was no need for the stuffy wig and robes. Margo Henderson too was dressed informally in navy trousers and a lavender cashmere cardigan over a white tee-shirt. Cameron by contrast had decided to play it safe, opting for a standard barrister-issue three-piece navy pinstripe suit.

'Good morning Mrs Brooks and Mr Cameron.'

They answered in unison. 'Good morning m'lady.'

She sighed as if to underline the seriousness of what was about to be discussed. 'You both know very well why you are here. As I said on Tuesday, it's a grave matter, a very grave matter indeed.'

'Yes it is,' Maggie said.

'Grave,' Cameron agreed.

'So, as you might expect, I have consulted widely with learned colleagues and with the Attorney General herself. I have also been able to find out more about Dr Khan from his bosses in Cheltenham. Coming to that first, it may interest you both to know that I spoke at length with the Director of his division, a Dr Jane Robertson, on Wednesday afternoon. Firstly, it should be said that Dr Robertson was not aware that Dr Khan had written his report, and she stressed that it had not been commissioned by any legitimate authority that she knew of, certainly not within GCHQ or any of the security services.'

'So who did commission it?' Maggie asked, her tone sounding more blunt than she intended. A flicker of annoyance crossed Henderson's face.

'I was coming to that Mrs Brooks. Dr Robertson interrogated Dr Khan on Wednesday morning on that subject. It seems quite simply that he had been following the case in the media and was uneasy when he heard that Professor Walker was to be the Crown's expert witness. Dr Robertson promulgated the view that Dr Khan may have been driven by professional rivalry. He apparently does not recognise Professor Walker as an expert in the field, and says that they have crossed swords in the past on what she calls the conference circuit.'

'So that's all it is?' Maggie said, surprised. 'Just some geek's ego trip?'

'Apparently so Mrs Brooks,' Henderson said, 'but Dr Robertson did yesterday discuss Dr Khan's report with other senior scientists in his department and there was a unanimous view that if Dr Khan questioned the Walker testimony, then it must be flawed. They have great faith in his technical expertise, and if he believes the identification of the defendant is not reliable, then it must be so. I don't have to remind you Mr Cameron, that it is upon that evidence which your entire case rests.'

He was evidently not sure if he was expected to comment on this so remained silent.

'But do we know m'lady how the report got to the prosecution?' Maggie asked. 'Mr Cameron thought it may have come via a government department or agency.'

'I said I thought the CPS got it that way,' Cameron said. 'I personally had no direct interaction with any government agencies or officials.'

'Well I think I can answer that,' the judge said. 'It seems Dr Khan simply searched for the email address of the Head of the Crown Prosecution Service, and then sent a copy through to Lady Rooke's office. Elizabeth Rooke claims that her officials passed it on to the case director without looking at it, a claim I am inclined to believe. I have also spoken to the Attorney General and to the Home Secretary...'

'You spoke to Lucinda Black and Gerrard Saddleworth?' Maggie said, surprised.

'Naturally. In a trial of this importance, I would expect both to be constantly kept up to date with developments, but it seems in this case, the CPS team did not deem to share the information with them.

Neither the Head of the CPS, the Attorney General nor the Home Secretary were aware of the existence of this report. I cannot help but think this will be highly damaging when it reaches the public domain, to both the CPS and the government.'

Great, thought Maggie, but what are you going to do about the case itself? She did not have to wait long for an answer.

'So, this has really been a shambles from start to finish,' Henderson said. 'I cannot really put it any other way. But what is absolutely clear to me is that the Crown does not have a case without reliance on what is now seen to be the highly unreliable facial recognition evidence obtained from the tradesman's dashcam. Had the Khan report been properly considered I have little doubt that the case would not, indeed could not, have been brought before this court. In mitigation, I do accept the fact that the report was not available when the case was being prepared, but only surfaced after the pre-trial and plea submission. That is an explanation but not an excuse. I am given to conclude that this, and not for the first time in recent years I must add, is a serious attack on our justice system. I cannot and will not allow this reprehensible trend to continue.'

This is it. This is it.

Henderson peered over her half-rimmed reading glasses, her gaze fixing first on Maggie and then on Adam Cameron. Now, it seemed, it was time for her verdict.

'So I have consulted with Ms Black, Lady Rooke and Mr Saddleworth and have informed them that I will have no option but to declare a mistrial.'

A mistrial. Maggie had hoped against hope for that outcome, but for it to come true was beyond her wildest dreams.

'They are understandably dismayed, but agree with me that the integrity of our justice system is bigger than any individual case. I will return to the court at two o'clock this afternoon where the jury will be dismissed and the defendant will be free to go.'

Now Maggie was struggling to conceal her elation. It was the result she had longed for more than any other. Her client was to be freed despite impossible odds, and she now had the big win she had hoped and prayed for, but never really believed could happen.

Adam Cameron bowed his head, stunned into silence. Maggie, misjudging the mood, said with a smile. 'Thank you m'lady,' and stood up as if to leave.

'Sit down please Mrs Brooks,' Henderson said sternly. 'I'm not finished with you two yet.'

And then slowly and forensically, Maggie's whole world, her very future, was crushed into extinction by Lady Justice Margo Henderson QC.

* * *

She did not remember anything about the journey home that evening, so deep was her distress, and was relieved that Daisy had already put Ollie to bed by the time she got back. All she wanted to do was sleep, sleep for a week, sleep for a month or a year until it all just went away. She filled her wine glass to the brim and drank it in two gulps, then, shaking, she stumbled over to the fridge and filled it once again. *Sleep, please, please let me sleep.*

But she could not sleep that night and as she lay tossing and turning, question after question filled her mind, gnawing away, hour after hour. Why oh why did I think I could get away with it? So bloody stupid. Adam Cameron, the smooth Old Etonian, gets off with a light wrap on the knuckles, whilst inept but anonymous CPS lawyers take the bulk of the flak. *A serious collective error of judgement, but with no deliberate intention to pervert justice.* That's what the judge had said. Not great from Cameron's point of view, but hardly ruinous.

And then, like a bolt from the blue, Henderson casually dropped her bombshell, leaving Maggie stunned, disorientated and broken. Information from an authoritative source, identity not disclosed, proving that the defence team, and by implication Mrs Maggie Brooks, had in fact received the Khan report more than six weeks ago, not just in the last few days as they claimed.

It was a damn lie, of course it was a lie. It had been scarcely more than a week since she had seen the damn report for the first time. What authoritative source, and what information? Henderson wouldn't say, no matter how much Maggie pleaded with her. This was turning into a complete nightmare.

And now she was to be referred to the Bar Standards Board, accused of, what was it, *conduct likely to diminish public confidence in the legal profession or the administration of justice.* A stunt, Henderson had called it, a blatant attempt to circumvent the jury system. Worse, she stood accused of lying to the court about the timeline of the report. Lying to the court, about the worst offence a barrister could be accused of. Now she faced a fine or perhaps more likely a long suspension. That was bad enough, but what it really meant was that her career in all practical senses was now over.

She sat up and peered groggily at the clock by her bedside, having finally accepted that sleep would not come. It was 4.30 am. She picked up the TV remote and pressed the standby button bringing the set to life. The BBC was broadcasting its interminable rolling news, leading with the murder of a young woman soldier in Belfast who had been shot through the head whilst attending a suspected bomb incident.

Following closely in the running order was the freeing of Alzahrani and the sensational collapse of the trial. Lady Justice Henderson was not scheduled to release her report until 10.00am the next morning, but already it was leaking like a chocolate teapot. The BBC's legal correspondent was talking about 'another failure to disclose evidence by the CPS,' and that the judge's report 'is expected to be particularly critical about the role of inexperienced defence barrister Mrs Maggie Brooks.'

This was not how it was meant to be. Now the anchor was saying 'Now let's take a look at tomorrow's papers'. There was Alzahrani, pictured on the front page of the *Chronicle* under the headline 'Notting Hill Bomber to be Freed'.

Then, eventually, they cut to other news. In a dusty refugee camp a few miles from the Syrian border their Middle East correspondent was interviewing the famous human rights lawyer Philip Brooks. Alongside him, looking like bloody Lara Croft in combat trousers and a tight-fitting *Action for Palestine* tee-shirt, was the dark Mediterranean beauty Angelique Perez, one of his firm's up-and-coming Associates. He had told Maggie he was travelling alone.

Chapter 5

A mistrial. The celebrations were muted of course as they had to be, since they knew that it wasn't seemly to be exultant over the release of a child-murdering terrorist onto the streets of the capital. But family is family and that's what always comes first for anyone, no matter who you are, no matter how important your position in life. It's family first and everything else is secondary. The plan had been crazy and audacious, and none of the group had given it a hope in hell of success - except its conceiver, who through sheer force of conviction persuaded them to go with it. Trust me, that's what the conceiver had said, and in the end, but not without considerable reservations, that's what they had done. And without knowing, little Maggie Brooks had played her part to perfection. Naive, vain, stupid. She had been the perfect choice.

Now they sat in the quiet committee room just off the Central Lobby, sipping on stiff gin and tonics and reflecting quietly on a job well done. All neat and tidy and consigned to history, and it would stay that way as long as everyone kept their mouths shut. And even if they didn't, there was always Plan B.

Chapter 6

Penelope White didn't much like coming into the office these days. Admittedly there was seldom the need, given that all her copy could be submitted electronically, but the less she saw of Rod Clark, her editor at the *Chronicle*, the better. For she was the award winner, the controversialist, the bona-fide journalistic superstar. It was her opinion that poxy editors didn't have the right to mess about with her copy, but Clark still liked to try. He seemed to have difficulty in understanding that it was her who sold the damn papers, not him.

But even she could see that today was different, which is why she had set the alarm for the god-awful hour of 6.30am and braved the tube to get to the Kensington offices for 8.30am. Too bloody early.

'Morning Penelope, this is indeed a rare pleasure.' She knew Clark would have already been in for hours, if indeed he'd actually gone home the previous evening. He lived and breathed the paper, to the detriment of every other relationship in his life. As did she.

'Morning Rod. I hope you've got the coffee on.'

He smiled. 'All ready to go, and brewed just the way you like it. Nice and strong.' He resented the amount of arse-licking that White demanded, but was prepared to put up with it in return for her genius. For now at least.

She was holding a copy of the first edition. 'So, this was your work then was it Rod? The best we could come up with was *Bomber Disappears after New Evidence Emerges*?'

'You weren't around for the website deadline. I got Yash Patel to knock it up. He's a bright lad, great future.'

Her expression suggested she didn't agree with his assessment. 'I suppose it qualifies as accurate reporting, if nothing else.'

He ignored her sarcasm. 'That's why I asked you to come in. There's a lot of angles on this story and I wanted to ask your advice on how to play it. Any thoughts?'

Of course she had thoughts, she had scarcely thought of anything else since Henderson had declared the mistrial. She would have to be careful of course, after attending that dinner with Gerrard and Philip and Dr Kahn, but that shouldn't be too difficult.

'As you say Rod, lots of angles. But you know my mantra, it's got to be about the players. Readers are only interested in the human side.'

'Got that, yep. Brilliant.' As if he didn't know, having clocked up thirty years in the industry.

'So there's a lot of people with shit on their shoes after what's happened. Adam Cameron, that smoothie QC, he's been made to look like a complete tit for a start.'

Clark pursed his lips. 'Well, I suppose so, but he's one of ours, don't forget.' What he meant was Eton and Oxford, solid establishment. 'Might not get the universal approval of our loyal readership if we make him look stupid.'

She rolled her eyes. 'Not that it would be difficult, but I agree.'

'There's Margo Henderson too,' Clark said. 'The judge. It was her that actually let Alzahrani walk after all, even though the police wanted her held in remand. We could run a nice line about the out-of-touch judiciary.'

'No. Apart from the minor problem that the police didn't have any evidence to support their demand, we've run the judge-as-enemy-of-the-people story more times than I've forgotten.'

He knew she wasn't going to accept any of his suggestions, and he didn't mind. Unlike her, he didn't run on ego. This was just a ritual mating dance, the display of brightly-coloured feathers before they got it on. It was only a matter of how much foreplay she would tolerate before they settled on the idea she had had from the start.

It seemed as if the foreplay might be running on a bit longer. 'So, my first thought was to do something on the CPS and the disclosure cock-up, but make it personal. *Really* personal. Elizabeth Rooke - *Lady Rooke* - she's the boss, as I'm sure you know...'

White's tone suggested that she knew he didn't. She was right.

'...and the general consensus is that she has been way over-promoted. I talked to a few people and found out that she's been married three times and, listen to this, she's recently invested in some top-of-the-range cosmetic surgery. Tits, face, arse, the whole package.'

His eyes narrowed. 'That sounds interesting Penelope. Though I'm sensing a but.'

'Yeah Rod. It's a good story alright, but I think it's got limited shelf-life.'

'So maybe I'll give it to Yash to run as a side story. Page seven or eight, something like that, he'll make a good fist of it. And I can tie it into my editorial.' He knew how to wind her up, and he liked doing it. Very much.

For once, she didn't take the bait. 'Whatever, you're the boss. So I also thought about the government's role in all of this. What I mean is the Home Office and the Justice Department have sat on their backsides for years whilst the CPS and the police treated the rules of disclosure as a minor inconvenience.' She knew that would tick Clark's boxes and ring all his bells at the same time. Because he couldn't afford to miss a chance to put the boot into the administration. Not because he was a supporter of HM's opposition himself, although she assumed he was, but because those were his instructions from the paper's owner.

But for the story to be any good, it had to be personal, and that meant attacking the Home Secretary. The Right Hon. Gerrard Saddleworth MP. Dear Gerrard. Her current lover. No, that wasn't going to happen.

Clark was sensing another but. 'Perhaps we can slip that one into the online edition for the subscribers if you don't want to front-page it.'

She shrugged. 'Yeah, give it to Yash. Anyway...'

He relaxed his shoulders and gently rapped on the table. It was time. 'So Penelope, let's have it.'

'Maggie Brooks and Dena Alzahrani. That's the angle.'

She picked up her phone and showed him the photograph she had got from Philip. One that showed Maggie at her very best, but with perhaps just a hint of smugness and entitlement in her expression. At least, that's how White intended to describe it.

Clark raised an eyebrow. 'She's quite an attractive woman. I didn't know that.'

'Exactly,' White replied. 'Attractive but useless. So, it's quite simple. We cast her in the part of the villain. Smart-arsed lawyer, completely out of touch with the public mood, pulls a stunt and a vile killer walks free.'

'Some might say she was only doing her job,' Clark said. 'Everybody is entitled to a fair trial.'

'Sod that Rod, this has got nothing to do with justice, you know that. This is about selling papers and that's what you want, isn't it?'

She knew he would have no answer to that, and she didn't wait for one.

'So right on the top corner of the front page, we put a huge big counter. That shows the number of days that Alzahrani has been walking free on our streets, and we print it every day until she is caught. Centre stage we put a big picture of Maggie Brooks and day after day we pile on the pressure. Drip, drip, drip, drip. We write about the previous cases that she lost. We talk to grieving parents of the victims who tell us they are disgusted with what she had done. We question her marriage, suggest that all is not well in that department. We even go back to her school and find out that she was a horrible little creep that nobody liked. In summary, we pile on the shit. Standard stuff really.'

Clark nodded. He'd known from the start that he would have to agree with whatever she came up with, but he always tried to retain some semblance of dignity. 'Ok Penelope, but just make sure you check anything contentious with legal first, alright?'

'Of course I will Rod,' she lied. 'By the way, I've got tomorrow's headline.'

She picked up her pen and scribbled a few words on her notepad, and then spun it round so Clark could read it.

Maggie Brooks - the Most Hated Woman in Britain?

It looked good alongside Brooks' photograph. And this was only the first day of Alzahrani being on the loose. Give it a couple of weeks when they still hadn't tracked her down and there would be no need for the question mark. Penelope White would see to that.

Chapter 7

Jimmy Stewart lounged back in the battered armchair, idly flicking through the day-old newspaper. The Chronicle's garish banner headline declared it their 'One Hundred Day edition'. One hundred days since the Palestinian Dena Alzahrani, to the deep embarrassment of the security services, had disappeared into thin air. After having been whisked away from her trial in a black limo. The infamous black limo. That had really pissed off the papers, qualities and tabloids alike. Especially when just four days later, the anti-terrorist boys had come up with some new evidence. On a whim, some junior forensic geek had decided to have another look at what was left of the van. And had found some DNA. Dena Alzahrani's DNA, only it was nine months too late. Embarrassing for the Met, since the teenage terrorist had disappeared into thin air, causing an almighty stink. Since then there had been nothing. No leads, no sightings, nothing. He saw too that the paper was still sticking it into the hapless barrister who had engineered her release. Maggie Brooks, the most hated woman in Britain. The label had stuck, and there she was again on the front page. Very pretty, but goodness, what must it be like to live with all that crap being thrown at you.

Tucked away in the inside pages, they were breaking the news of the discovery of a huge stash of bomb-making materials in an anonymous warehouse in Pinner. Nearly one hundred thousand disposable ice-packs, containing enough ammonium nitrate to blow up Wembley Stadium. A forty-six-year-old Iranian with suspected links to Hizbollah had been arrested. Why he had been allowed to roam the streets of London unchecked in the first place was the subject of much outrage in the article, a viewpoint with which Jimmy agreed.

He was in the mess room of RAF Northolt, his EOD team having been permanently transferred to London a fortnight ago after the discovery of the Pinner bomb factory. Nearly three months to the day after the Belfast attack. He dreamt about it every night, a recurring nightmare on top of all the other recurring nightmares, this the worst of all. The pretty face of Sergeant Naomi Harris smiling at him, earnest and eager, eyes sparkling with love for life. 'So what are you going to do when you leave the army?' she asks, over and over again. And then the crack of the bullet from the gunman's rifle, smashing her head into little pieces.

'Penny for them sir.'

Private Alex Marley, straight out of training, fresh-faced, brimming with enthusiasm. Jimmy groaned inwardly. *Bloody hell, not another one.* Why did they keep sending him these bloody novices, he wasn't a bloody babysitter. And after what had happened in Belfast, for Christ's sake. For once it would be nice to get some grizzled old hand, someone who had been round the block a bit, with a bit of street smarts. Problem was, not many of the EOD&S guys made it to veteran status. The 'killed on duty' stats weren't good, and if you survived that then the PTSD got you. Only mugs like himself tried to carry on, and where had that got him?

'Just daydreaming Marley. My Euro millions numbers have come up and Scotland have won the World Cup.'

'Woman or men sir?'

'Sorry?'

'The woman's football team or the men's. Your woman's team is actually pretty good sir.'

'And the men's is pretty rubbish,' Jimmy laughed. 'Yes, I know, that's why it's only a dream. You're interested in footie then?'

'I am sir. I play a bit too. I'm hoping to make the joint services team this year.'

'Well good luck with that, hope you make it. No Scottish blood in your background?'

'Not as far as I'm aware sir. Jamaica and Catford I'm afraid. Although I'm told I did visit Carlisle once with my grandmother, when I was three.'

'Marley, I think you'll find that's in England actually, but it's probably close enough for you to qualify.'

Out of the blue, his personal radio cracked into life. *'Captain Stewart, I think we have a live incident'.* A glance at the wall-mounted television, permanently tuned to Sky News, confirmed his worst fears. Their breaking news was of a suspected terror attack at a Hampstead primary school. Grainy pictures of the scene, evidently captured on the phone of an eye-witness, showed a large white van jammed against the gates of the school. The flashing blue and green lights of the police cars and paramedics were eerily reflected by the film of autumn rain that had fallen earlier that day.

'Shit,' Jimmy said, 'c'mon Marley, we need to get down there quick.' He had been briefed on the earlier Notting Hill attack, and this already had all the hallmarks of a copy-cat operation. That time there had been a bomb, and it was surely odds-on that there would be one again today. The technicians had already got the Foxhound's engine running when they reached the garage, the postcode remotely programmed into the vehicles military-grade sat-nav system.

'Control, what's the status?' he barked. Marley swung the heavy vehicle in behind the police escort waiting on West End Road. It set off at pace, its sirens wailing, clearing a path through the busy traffic.

'*Reports of an on-board IED. Incident Commander has ordered police, fire and ambulance personnel to clear the area. There are multiple impact casualties at the scene, and a woman trapped under the front wheels of the van.*'

All these kids and mothers, seriously injured and no way for the paramedics to help them until his bomb squad gave the all-clear. He shuddered at the thought, the agony they were suffering, lying alone and terrified. Here they were in London and the nightmare was starting all over again.

It took nearly eighteen minutes for them to arrive at the school. He knew that would be too late for some victims who would already have died as a result of their injuries, victims who might have been saved if the paramedics could have got to them sooner. Commander John Rufford was waiting for them as they approached the crime scene barriers. Jimmy jumped down from the cab and shook his hand warmly.

'Captain Jimmy Stewart, EOD&S. I can see where the van has ended up. We'll get started right away but please make sure you keep everyone at least a hundred metres back.'

'Roger and good luck Captain,' replied the Commander. 'We won't get in your way, but at the risk of stating the bleeding obvious, the quicker the better'.

'I know sir, we'll do everything we can.'

Jimmy had now been joined by Private Marley, looking pale and frightened. It was her first live incident and it was slowly dawning on her that this job was going to have to be done without the help of the Dragon or any of the other high-tech machinery in their extensive armoury.

'What are we going to do sir?'

He heard the fear in his colleague's voice, and he liked that. Bravery and over-confidence got you killed in this job, and with just two weeks' service left, he was not about to have the loss of another young life spinning round his brain in the small hours.

'You Marley, are going to stay right here by the Foxhound and keep in touch with Control. Do not move from the vehicle unless I specifically tell you to, understand? I want you to watch all the video that I send back from the helmet camera and let me know if you spot anything, anything at all. I need you as my second pair of eyes. Got that?'

'Yes sir, but...'

'No ifs or buts, that's procedure and we're playing this one by the rule book'.

Except it wasn't quite going to be played by the rule book. The rule book would dictate working down a long check list before putting any EOD lives in danger. The rule book would mean first sending in the Dragon to do a thorough video survey, and then waiting until Control had reviewed the footage and made its recommendations. The rule book would mean more people would die. Jimmy was going to rip up the rule book.

He slung the heavy toolkit onto his back and sprinted down the road to where the van lay, its windscreen smashed and bonnet crumpled where it had crashed into the heavy stone gatepost. As he approached, he began to hear the moans and cries of the injured. A little girl, her neat uniform ripped and splattered with blood, lay on her side, crying for her mummy. Beside her, a boy of about the same age. Already it looked too late for him. The young woman trapped under the wheels of the van looked in a bad way, but was still clinging to consciousness. She saw Jimmy approach and let out a faint 'help me,' but he couldn't help her, not at this moment. This was like Afghanistan all over again, except the wounded weren't professional soldiers who were paid to put their lives in danger day in day out. These were innocent civilians, woman and children caught up in a conflict they knew little about and about which they cared even less.

You had to steel yourself, tell yourself that the only way to help these people was to do your job and disarm this bomb, but it was damn hard and today Jimmy knew that he'd come to the end of the road. Just this one more operation, that was all he had in him. He just had to get out while he still could.

Come on man, think. The chances were that the bomb's trigger mechanism would be in the van itself, rather than being detonated remotely. Probably a motion or vibration sensor or just a simple electronic timer. If this was another Palestinian attack by the same group responsible for the Notting Hill incident, then it was logical to think they would use the same tried and tested method as before. Besides that, it was not easy to prime a motion sensor without blowing yourself up in the process, and this lot did not seem intent on joining the ranks of the suicide bombers. And then he noticed that the driver's door was closed. *Yes.* That meant that the attacker must have shut it behind him when he fled the scene, most probably an unthinking automatic reaction. So that almost certainly ruled out motion or vibration sensors. Good- then it had to be a timer. Only problem being that it might be programmed to go off in the next two seconds. Not so good.

He clicked on his two-way communicator and pulled down the helmet-mounted microphone.

'Ok Marley, I'm going in now, ok, just keep your eyes fixed on that video.'

'Ok sir, I'm on it.'

The timer was easy to detect, being stuck to the front of the dashboard in full view and attached by double-sided tape. It was nothing more sophisticated than a simple electronic stopwatch, costing no more than two quid on Amazon - cheap and deadly. He looked at the rapidly-changing display, calibrated to the millisecond. Only six minutes before it went off. *Oh-oh.* Examining it, he saw that eight or nine coloured wires sprouted from below the device, leading to an open storage cubby-hole on the passenger side. There it was, slotted into a large manila envelope - half a kilo of prime IRA Semtex, packing enough stored explosive energy to blow a twenty-metre-wide crater in the roadway below. He examined the package closely, counting the number of wires going in - eight of them, and just one that, when snipped, would disarm the detonator. It was like Russian roulette, but with the odds stacked eight to one against you.

'Shit, shit, shit.'

'Sorry sir?'

'I think we're buggered here Marley. There's just so much decoy wiring, there's no way I can risk mucking about with it.'

'I can see that sir. Could you not try and dismantle the timer, see if you can figure out how it's wired?'

'I thought of that, but I'd bet my arse that it will have some sort of anti-tamper mechanism. Remove the cover and boom, up it will all go. That's not going to work I'm afraid.'

The sweat was now pouring down his brow as he began to comprehend the sheer hopeless of his situation. *C'mon, think man, think*. But there was nothing, absolutely nothing they could do. And procedure, the book, dictated that he now withdrew to safety. Right away. No room for sentiment or mindless valour in the army. Nothing could be done for the wounded, so get out whilst you can, saving a valuable human asset to fight again. Leaving the gravely injured to their fate, waiting until the timer ran down and the bomb wreaked its terrible carnage. That's what he had to do.

Suddenly the radio crackled into life.

'Sir, I think I might have an idea. I'm not sure if you will like it though.'

'Go on.'

'We think it might be IRA technology in the bomb sir, don't we, same as that Notting Hill one? So that probably means that it was delivered to the terrorists as a complete package. All wired up and ready to go. And probably fairly stable, no motion detectors or suchlike in the bomb itself.'

'So?'

'So maybe you could take it out of the van as a whole package too.'

Clever. Why hadn't he thought of that? It was because it was a stupid plan and still way way out of procedure. There was only five minutes or so left, and it might take him as long to disentangle the bomb from the van. One slip, a wire gets broken and it goes off, meaning certain death for him, and probably not even saving the victims either. And let's face it, he didn't want to die, and no-one would condemn him if he got out there and then. It was definitely a dumb stupid plan. If it went wrong, they would probably court-martial him. Posthumously. For thirty seconds he sat rooted to the spot, his mind in turmoil, a morass of indecision. The bloody army, they could only expect so much of a man, and hadn't he done more than his fair share over the years? Surely this was a step too far. Get out man, whilst you still can.

'Sir? Sir, we don't have much time.'

'I'm just thinking Marley, give me a minute.' But they didn't have a minute.

'Oh screw it, look, I'm going to give it a try. Can you get on to the Commander and make sure they clear everyone at least another sixty metres outside the cordoned zone. Oh, and just one more thing Marley.'

'Yes sir?'

'Does your plan say what we should do with the bloody thing once we get it out?'

'No sir. Sorry sir.'

'Thought not. Over and out.'

He set to work, taking off his backpack, placing it on the passenger seat and opening the top flap. Good, there was plenty of room in there beside his tools for the device. Next, he carefully prised the little timer off the dashboard, taking great care not to put any tension on the wiring. Fortunately, there was enough play in the wires to allow him to put the timer straight into the backpack. So far so good, now for the bomb itself. Fairly stable was what Private Marley had said, but he wasn't taking any chances. He managed with some difficulty to slide the package part-way out of the cubby-hole, but then for no obvious reason, it refused to go any further. *Shit.* He tried to squeeze his fingers into the narrow gap between the bomb and its receptacle, probing to see if he could find out what was jamming it, but it was just too tight for him. *Come on, come on, come on.* He stole a glance at his watch. Only about four minutes to go. *Shit, shit, shit.* His heart was pounding in his chest, his head throbbing with pain. Feverishly he began rooting around his backpack, looking for the long yellow-handled screwdriver that he always carried with him. Where the hell was it? But finally he located it, deftly pulling it out of the bag then carefully inserting it between the bomb and the side of the cubby-hole. It seemed to reach all the way to the bottom, but no matter how much he wriggled or probed, he just couldn't budge it.

'Sir, we're running out of time.'

'Do you think I don't know that Marley, for Christ's sake.'

He tried again one more time to free the package, tightening his fingers around the protruding edge and tugging with as much force as he dared, but still it refused to move. Shit, this was all going tits-up.

And now he had just a few agonising seconds to make the decision. Live to fight another day, that was official policy. Get the hell out of there whilst you still could. Leave the wounded, you can't do anything more for them, that's what they drummed into you in all these Sandhurst courses. Easy enough to say when you were sitting in a warm classroom.

'Sir...' Marley's voice was anxious. 'What's happening sir?'

There wasn't time to answer, but then what was he going to say? Then he had a sudden thought, the surging adrenalin clearing his mind. *Ninety seconds, that's all I'll give it, and then I'm out of here.* He grabbed a pair of wire-cutters from his toolbag and dived under the steering column, searching for the wiring leading to the ignition switch. Red... green... blue, yep there they were. Snip the red one, snip the green one, then strip the coating away to expose the bare wire. Done. Now twist them together, see what happens. He looked up to see the dashboard ablaze with warning lights. Yes, we have ignition. Jumping into the driving seat, he stabbed the start button. The big diesel began to turn over. *Rah-rah-rah-rah.* Come on, fire will you! He let the starter motor spin a few more times but still the engine would not start. But just as he was slamming his fists on the dashboard in frustration, the comms channel crackled into life.

'Maybe you could move it on the starter motor sir?'

'Private Marley, you're a blooming genius.' He rammed down the clutch pedal, crashed the gearbox into reverse and pushed the start button once more. As soon as the starter motor began to churn, he released the pedal, causing the van to shoot backwards a few metres. *Keep it going, keep it going.* He managed to reverse it about ten metres before the battery finally gave up the ghost, but at least that was something. He pushed open the door of the van and jumped down onto the road, and as he did so, his eyes met with those of the young woman who had been trapped under the wheels, still conscious and surely in unimaginable pain. To the left of him lay the little schoolgirl, no more than five or six years old, covered in blood and still crying for her mother. *Leave the wounded, you can't do anything more for them.* With just seconds left before the timer ticked down to zero, there was no time to save them, of course there wasn't. *Leave the wounded, you can't do anything more for them, that's procedure.* Live to fight another day, preserve the asset.

In a split second he had made the decision. He scooped up the little girl in his arms then, without a backward glance, ran for his life to the shelter of the school's sturdy stone wall.

Chapter 8

So it had been a hundred days? That's what the headline in the *Chronicle* was saying and she had no reason to doubt its accuracy, although to Maggie, it felt more like a hundred years. She still came into the office every day, but that was just through force of habit, the inexplicable human desire to cling to routine in times of difficulty. There was no work for her of course and their Clerk Nigel Redmond had barely spoken to her since the trial let alone brought her any briefs, not even the crappy ones she was used to. Colleagues avoided her in the corridor and it went strangely silent around the water-cooler whenever she came into view. The most hated woman in Britain was evidently no more popular in Drake Chambers, as if mere association with her was enough to taint their own precious reputations. And she thought they had been her friends.

As she sipped her lukewarm coffee, the same question went round and round in her head. *Who could have done this to me?* But done what? She had checked her inbox a dozen times, and it was absolutely the case that Khan's report had arrived just three days before the last day of the trial. She was no IT expert and she wondered if perhaps it had been *sent* weeks earlier and had somehow got lost somewhere in cyberspace, but a thorough Google investigation had ruled that out. The sender's timestamp was just a few seconds before she had received it. This was no mix-up, and so whoever had told the judge that she had it earlier was lying. But the question remained unanswered. *Who and why?* It didn't make any sense. To make matters worse, the organisation that had purportedly sent her the report had vanished into thin air. The website of *British Solidarity for Palestine* had disappeared and their email address returned a *mailbox unavailable* error. There was nothing to show that they had ever existed.

In twenty-three days' time she would be in front of the Bar Standards Board when her only defence would be -what? It would be her word against Lady Justice Henderson, and that verdict was only going to go one way. She hoped they would finally tell her who it was who had made the assertion that she had that report more than six weeks earlier than she had actually received it. Because otherwise, how could she be expected to get a fair hearing? But deep down, she knew that wasn't going to happen. They would all close ranks against her because who really cared about the fate of a second-rate barrister who had been too much in the public eye for their liking?

Not her husband Philip, for a start. Their marriage had been in trouble before all of this had happened, she knew that, but now he was spending the whole working week away, and at weekends if he did come home, he was cold and distant. It was only Ollie, her sweet precious Ollie, that kept her sane. He was only six and she wondered if he could feel the tension between his mummy and daddy, both of whom he loved unconditionally. For his sake if nothing else she thought she should keep the marriage together, but with each passing day that seemed to become less and less likely. Now she was spending more and more time working out how she would adjust to life as a single mum. There would be enough money for her to buy a small place, obviously nowhere as grand as their Hampstead home, but it would be more than fine for the two of them. She would not be able to practice at the Bar, but she could easily go back to the more mundane side of her profession. Wills and probate, property conveyancing, it was hardly thrilling but it would pay the mortgage. They would be ok, she was sure of that.

She looked up to see Redmond standing in front of her desk. From his expression, she could tell that there was something badly wrong.

'Maggie, there's been an attack on Ollie's school. A van. It's been driven at the school gates. The BBC is saying there are casualties. I think you'd better get there. I'm sorry.'

Instantly, her heart was crashing, her stomach churning as she tried to process what he had said. *Please, please, please let him be ok.* Through the fog of confusion she realised that Redmond was still speaking.

'Look, I can order a taxi, it will be the quickest way. Do you want anyone to come with you?'

'What? No, no I brought my car in today. I'll be ok.'

She grabbed her coat and rushed through the door leading to the stairwell. It had been a spur of the moment decision to drive in that day, but now she was glad she had, as she ran through the dark underground car-park to where her Golf was waiting. At least she would be in control, because she just had to get there, as fast as she could. She fumbled around in her handbag, searching for her gate pass. Hell, why was that barrier always so slow? She screeched out into the narrow street, attracting a barrage of horns as she recklessly threaded her way through the late afternoon traffic. These damn traffic lights, why were they never at green?

As she drove her head was swimming with emotion, her mouth dry, her eyes moistening. If anything happened to Ollie, she would die, she knew she would. Then suddenly, she thought about Daisy, her niece. She would have been standing at the gates waiting to collect Ollie. This was all too hard to bear.

As she battled along City Road the phone rang. It was her mother calling from home in Yorkshire. She could tell from her wavering voice that she was already beside herself with worry.

'Maggie, I've just seen the news. Is Ollie safe?'

'I don't know mum, I don't know, I'm just trying to get to the school now.'

Without warning, a pensioner in a Honda Jazz pulled out of a side street then proceeded to dawdle along at twenty miles an hour, neck craned forward peering through his windscreen.

'Get out of the way!' Instinctively, Maggie jammed her foot hard on the accelerator to overtake, narrowly missing an oncoming delivery van. The driver gesticulated wildly, mouthing an obscenity and blaring his horn.

'Maggie, are you ok?'

'London traffic mum. Look, I need to go, I'll call you as soon as I hear anything. I'm sure Ollie will be ok.' How she hoped against hope that this would be true.

Soon she was on the Holloway Road, where the traffic was moving at a snail's pace as the tail end of the school run clashed with early commuters on their homeward journey. Then the phone rang again. This time it was Philip. His voice was frantic, desperate, close to breaking down.

'I've just heard. I've been trying to call the school but it's constantly engaged. Can you get up there right away and see if he's all right?'

'I'm on my way Philip. I've not heard anything more than they're saying on the news.'

'Look, I'm going to catch the earliest flight back I can. Angelique has been looking and we can get the 5.30, should get us through Heathrow by 7.00. I'll get there as fast as I can. And call me as soon as you have

news.'

Angelique. What the hell was she doing there? He was supposedly there for an important two-day meeting with the Scottish First Minister and her Justice Minister. Why would you take a junior associate to that? But there was no time to think about that now, she had to get to Ollie's school. *Come on, come on!* A long queue of vehicles was backed up at the junction with the Seven Sisters Road, seemingly grid-locked. She blasted her horn at the driver in front who was texting on her mobile, oblivious that the car in front of her was now moving. Then she saw the red sign that had been placed at the road side. Shit, it was road-works, and of course the temporary traffic lights which controlled them were at red. They always were. She banged the steering wheel in frustration, then jabbed the phone icon on the Golf's touchscreen. Scrolling down the phonebook, she chose Felicity Swift, mother of Ollie's friend Tom, but it went straight through to answerphone. Hardly surprising in the circumstances. And then a cold shiver passed through her as she remembered that Felicity was one of the many rich stay-at-home mothers who were able to collect their children from school each day. She would have been outside the gate, laughing and joking with the other mums and nannies. Like Daisy. *Please no.*

The lights had finally changed and she accelerated through the junction, moving to the outside lane and, ignoring the speed cameras, driving as fast as she dared. Then up Highgate Hill and onto Hampstead Lane. At last, nearly there.

She arrived at the school to a scene of frantic activity. Dozens of armed police and soldiers were on patrol, guarding the formal crime scene which had been established around a two or three hundred metres radius from the school gates. Tents had been erected and a string of ambulances were parked along the roadside, blue lights flashing through the gloom of the damp autumn afternoon, waiting to take the injured to the nearby Royal Free Hospital. Maggie abandoned her car in the middle of the road and ran to where two police officers, one male, one female, guarded a gap in the red-striped perimeter tape.

'Stop there madam please,' the male officer said sharply.

'I'm a parent,' Maggie cried. 'I need to see if my little boy is all right.'

'I'm afraid we will need to search you first,' the other said, more kindly, adding unnecessarily, 'This is a terrorist incident.'

'Please, as quickly as you can,' Maggie pleaded, almost in tears. 'Please.'

But the policewoman was not to be rushed. With painful precision she checked each arm in turn then filleted inside Maggie's coat with her hands, progressing down her back and over her bottom.

'Can you remove your boots please madam,' she ordered.

The policewoman stood impassively as Maggie removed her boots, leaving her stocking-footed on the cold tarmac. But at last the search was completed and she was directed to a tent to the left of the gates where teachers were trying to help the dozens of parents that had rushed to the school when they heard the news. Immediately she saw Miss Roberts, Ollie's young class teacher, armed with a clipboard and talking animatedly with a number of agitated parents.

'Look, it's really hard to get information, we can't get in the way of the emergency services and keep asking them for updates. I have a list of my class here and thankfully most of them have been accounted for.' *Most of them.* 'Please, please, that's all the information I have at the moment. Your children have all been taken to the school hall where they are being looked after by members of staff.'

In the crowd, Maggie spotted Felicity Swift and she could tell immediately that something was terribly amiss. She went over to her and gently took her arm.

'What's wrong Felicity?'

'It's Tom. He's not on Miss Roberts' list, and I've been to the hall and he's not there either. She thinks he may be one of the injured, I'm just waiting for my Jules to arrive and then we can go to the hospital.' Her voice was frantic with worry.

'I'm so sorry Felicity,' Maggie said quietly. 'I don't know what to say, but I'm sure he will be ok, little boys are so tough.' She wrapped her arms around her friend and squeezed her gently. 'It will be alright, it will be alright.'

'I saw Ollie in the hall,' said Felicity through her tears. 'He's ok. You should go and see him. I'll be fine, honestly.'

Thank god. Maggie took her phone from her pocket and texted 'Safe' to Philip and her mum. Now she must go to Ollie, hold him in her arms and never let him go.

She became aware of Miss Roberts approaching her.

'Mrs Brooks. Look, I'm afraid I've got some bad news. It's your niece, Daisy isn't it? She was... well, it seems she was hit by the van and was trapped beneath the front wheels for some time.'

She could see the young teacher was struggling to hold her emotions in check.

'They've taken her to the Royal Free. I think it's quite serious. I'm so sorry.'

***

They sat in the cold corridor alongside the trauma unit, not speaking. From time to time they stood up to look through the window where Daisy was lying unconscious, wearing an oxygen mask and connected to a barrage of high-tech monitoring equipment. It was nearly a week since the attack, during which time the highly-skilled medical team had fought tenaciously to save her life. She had multiple broken bones and serious internal injuries, and already she had endured three major operations, with more to come. The doctors were cautiously optimistic. She was young and the young possessed remarkable powers of recovery. That was the message of hope they were giving the family. She was going to be ok, that's what they were saying.

Along the corridor, holding hands, sat Felicity and Jules Swift, their faces pale and drawn, eyes bloodshot from the crying. Their son had been in a coma for five days now, and privately, the doctors had given up hope, but the parents had been given the same assurances as the Brooks. *Tom was a child and children possessed remarkable powers of recovery*. It was not convincing but whilst he clung onto life, there was hope, and hope was all they had to sustain them.

The surly guard who had escorted Hugo Brooks from Belmarsh prison had sloped off for a coffee and a cigarette. A bit of a risk and he shouldn't be doing it but he considered it unlikely that his charge would try an escape in the circumstances.

'You don't have to stay Maggie,' Hugo said. 'I'll be fine, honestly. And Philip is coming back later, you should go and get some sleep if you can.'

She could really do with some sleep, that was for sure. She was dog-tired, but she didn't want to leave him. Although they had never got on, even before his trial, she did feel terribly sorry for him, as you would for anyone in his dreadful situation. In appearance, he was exactly like Philip but he possessed none of the magnetism that had so attracted Maggie to his brother. Whereas Philip was smooth, urbane and driven, Hugo had been content to potter around in his comfortable little world of progressive activism, getting by on his English teacher's salary and spending his weekends with his placards and banners on the demo frontline. And all the better if there was to be a bit of ruckus with the police, the chance to call them fascist pigs and hopefully get filmed by the BBC as you were dragged away struggling. Until it had all gone wrong when that young policewoman had died.

'No honestly Hugo, I'm fine. I'll stay for the next couple of hours then go and collect Ollie from school.'

It was the children's first day back, only five days after the attack, it being the view of the psychologists that it was best for kids to get back to normality as quickly as possible. Maggie's mum had been staying with them to look after Ollie whilst he was off school, but this morning she had returned to Leeds to look after Maggie's ailing father.

She looked at her watch - just coming up to half-past-twelve. Her mum should be home by now. Time for a quick call.

'Mum, how was the journey?'

'Fine darling.' She sounded strained, hesitant, not like herself at all.

'Mum, what's wrong?' asked Maggie, alarmed. 'Is it dad?'

'Maggie, have you seen the news?'

'No mum, what is it?'

'I've just seen it on the BBC News website. You should look at it now. It's bad news I'm afraid.'

Maggie pulled up the news app and read the headline. It hit her like a sledgehammer, her spirit crushed in an instant as she processed what it meant. The first reaction to a shock as big as this was usually denial, but this couldn't be denied, because there it was in bold type, unmissable and unequivocal.

Freed Alzahrani set to be named as Hampstead Bomber.

Suddenly a loud piercing alarm came from the heart monitor, and almost instantaneously, an amber beacon started flashing and a deafening siren shattered the quiet calm of the trauma wing. Within seconds, Daisy's bed was surrounded by a scrum of doctors and nurses, pulses racing, working in frantic unison to try and save the young woman's life. There was no time to pull down the blinds that screened the trauma room from the corridor, and Maggie watched in a daze as the electrodes of the theatre defibrillator were attached to Daisy's chest, her body involuntarily convulsing as the high-voltage charge was fired. Again and again they tried, but the heart monitor did not respond. A powerful injection of adrenaline was prepared and plunged into her chest, but still no response, and now there was a change in the atmosphere, something in the demeanour of the medics that told her that it was already too late.

Hugo was wailing uncontrollably, alternatively calling out his daughter's name, then clasping his hands in prayer, repeating 'Please god please god' over and over again.

'I'm sorry Mr Brooks, we did everything we could'. The consultant placed his hand on Hugo's shoulder, his voice steady, exuding warmth and professional compassion. *Multiple organ failure caused by the trauma of the accident. Difficult to diagnose or treat. We did everything we could.* Of course, what else would they say, could they say?

Along the corridor, six-year old Tom Swift's life-support machine was finally switched off. He died peacefully with his mummy and daddy and his favourite teddy bear by his bedside. *We did everything we could.* Dena Alzahrani had claimed two more victims.

And it was Maggie Brooks that had set her free.

* * *

Only one thought had occupied her mind. She had to get home, as fast as she could, to bury her head in her pillow, to drink until she could remember nothing, to just make it all go away, even if for only a moment. She would call Philip, make him leave his damn office early and go and collect Ollie for once. She had raced down a busy corridor towards where she thought the exit was, only to end up instead in the packed waiting room of the Blood Test clinic. Damn, these hospitals were like a maze. Eventually, she had spotted an ill-placed exit sign suspended from the ceiling which pointed her in the opposite direction from where she had come. Weaving through a crush of medical staff, porters, patients and visitors, she had eventually reached the heavy revolving doors of the entrance. Outside, she had breathed in a gulp of cool air then joined the long queue waiting at the parking machines to authorise their tickets. *Come on.*

The traffic around the hospital had been its usual nightmare but at last she had reached her quiet Hampstead street, where she had been surprised to see Philip's navy blue Range Rover parked outside.

In the kitchen, she had found Angelique Perez, dressed in one of her husband's striped shirts, her hair wrapped in a towel. A few seconds later, there was Philip in the white dressing gown she had bought him for his birthday. She would never ever forget his words on that day. *It's over Maggie, I should have told you before.* That was all he could find to say, on that day when her world was collapsing, where she desperately needed someone to help and comfort her, when she thought she would die. All he could say was *it's over,* whilst Angelique Perez looked on. So young, so beautiful, so bloody triumphant.

It had taken her just five minutes to get to the school, and only a few minutes more to reach Ollie's classroom. 'Mrs Brooks, you can't just march in here during class,' Miss Roberts had tried to protest, but sod that, Ollie was her son and she could do what she wanted. 'Where are we going mummy?' he had asked again and again, but she hadn't answered, because she didn't know. She just had to drive, anywhere, just keep driving, for hour upon hour - north, south, east, west, it didn't matter where.

She had not really been conscious of driving onto the level crossing or stopping the car so that it straddled one of the railway tracks. She vaguely remembered the sound of bells, which later she supposed had been the signal that the barriers were closing because of an approaching train. From the back seat, she thought that she may have heard Ollie crying but it was distant, detached and it did not disturb the feeling of peace and calm which had now blissfully enveloped her. At last, it would be over, the pain would be gone and everything would be okay. And then a dull thud as the articulated lorry rammed the back of the Golf, pushing it to safety. Seconds later, an altogether more violent crash as the Brighton express, travelling at ninety miles per hour, smashed through the lorry's trailer, sending debris flying in all directions.

PART TWO
One Year Later

Chapter 9

She watched him from across the room, transfixed, as he mooched around the neat exhibition stands, picking up a brochure here and exchanging a few words there with eager recruiting officers from the big names of the profession. What's he doing here, she thought, surely he's not hoping to get a training contract dressed like that? Perhaps just looking for an internship, but he's too old for that, isn't he? At least late twenties, no, older, early thirties at least. Scruffy and unshaven, with unkempt dark hair touching his shoulders, dressed in skinny black jeans and a crumpled black T-shirt bearing a washed-out AC/DC logo - and was that really cowboy boots he was wearing? But tall, ripped and good looking. *Very* good looking, a fact that had not gone unnoticed by her rival recruiters, both female and, it should be said, male too. A pretty young redhead from Addison Redburn, the distinguished City firm where Maggie's own career had started, glided up to him as he wandered past, gently placing a hand on his arm to arrest his progress, whilst drawing his attention to the contents of a glossy flyer that she held in the other. She was clearly intent in luring him to the confines of Addison's elegantly-furnished stand, where a high-pressure hit squad would take over, tasked with selling the ethereal prize of a glittering career at the bar to naive recently-minted graduates. Modern slavery more like, thought Maggie, although a bit better paid. But he was seemingly not to be ensnared, smiling ruefully and raising his hand to decline the young woman's offer, but accepting the leaflet as if in way of apology, even feigning to read it as he continued along the gangway before disappearing out of sight behind another stand.

In her peripheral vision, she became aware of a figure heading towards her, and in a split second she was drowning once again in the horrible emotional mash-up of hopelessness, fear and anger that had been her constant companion in the dark months since her perfect life had been turned upside down. The man, grey-haired, late forties, be-suited, marched onto her stand, brandishing a letter in his hand, demonstrably agitated. Trailing a few steps behind was a striking woman of around thirty, immaculately dressed in Armani and tottering uncertainly on a pair of expensive red stilettos.

'What the hell is this Maggie? What the hell is this? A custody hearing? You know, you are a seriously deluded bitch if you think a judge is going to let a nut-job like you anywhere near my son. That's not going to happen. Never. Not on my watch.'

Maggie had been expecting a reaction but not so soon, not here and not with *her* in attendance.

'Our son Philip, Ollie is our son. And you know very well I'm getting my life back together. I've got a job and a home...'

'You call this a job? What the hell do you know about investigations? And a home? Yeah, some seedy little bedsitter in Clapham is what I'm hearing. But what I'm really interested in is what the hell you are going to say to the judge? *Oh of course m'lud, I know I tried to murder my son last year, but honestly, I promise not to do it again, honest I do.* That's going to be an entertaining day out, that's all I can say.'

'I need to see him Philip. I need to see Ollie.'

She knew she should remain in control of her emotions, but her voice cracked as she struggled to get the words out. She stretched out her arm to steady herself against the pillar of the exhibition stand, waves of nausea threatening to overwhelm her. Pathetic, broken, she hated herself for what she had become. But she wasn't about to start begging to *him*.

'I know I won't get full custody, not after...not after what happened. But a child needs his mother, and you can't cut him off from me completely, it's so cruel. So I'm going to fight for this with every bone in my body. I'll never give up, no matter how long it takes.'

He moved slowly and deliberately, so that his face was almost touching hers. And then, speaking as if spelling out each word. 'This is the most stupid thing you've ever done, and that's saying something for a stupid bitch like you. So you can try what you like, but you won't be seeing *my* son, not now, not...'

'Hey, what's going on here pal?'

The voice was West of Scotland, working-class. Surprised, Philip Brooks swung round to confront his interlocutor.

'Sorry, are you talking to me?'

'Oh my, are you from Glasgow or something? I've not heard anyone say that for years. Mind you, by the look of you I don't think you would last five minutes on Sauchiehall Street.'

He extended a massive hand towards Brooks. 'Stewart. James

Stewart. My pals call me Jimmy'. It was ignored.

'I was just having a private conversation with my wife,' Brooks said, his composure partially regained. 'Really, I don't think it's any of your business.'

Jimmy gave a disarming smile. 'Well in my neck of the woods pal, men don't go around threatening women. So I'm making it my business, ok?'

And then, recognition.

'Hang on pal, I know you. That *Question Time* program on the telly, *that's* where I've seen you before. The human rights guy. And Julian Priest's pal. Yeah, I remember you now.'

'What of it?'

'Well I don't see much human rights going on here,' Jimmy said. 'Happy to talk the talk but not walk the walk, is that what it is? So my suggestion is you take your human rights and get the hell out of here before I shove them up your backside. And believe me, if you don't take my advice, it will be the most stupid thing *you'll* have ever done. And I also guarantee it.'

It was evident from Brooks' expression that he wasn't used to being spoken to like this. He stood motionless as if weighing up his options. But finally he turned to his companion.

'Ok Angelique, I think we're done here.' His tone suggested he was anything but finished, but the intervention of Captain Jimmy Stewart had clearly prompted a change of plan. But as they walked away, he suddenly spun round and making no effort to hide the bitterness in his voice, shouted, 'You've not heard the last of this Maggie, believe me. I said it before, and I'll say it again. You are not getting within a million miles of my son. Understand that.'

Maggie was vaguely aware of an arm being gently wrapped around her shoulder and of her being led to a wickerwork armchair at the back of the stand. She sat down, head bowed, whilst her rescuer struggled to rip the cellophane off a pack of paper tissues.

'Bugger, why do they make these things bloody impossible to open?'

'Th..thank you,' she said, her voice barely audible, and then to her surprise, came a quite unexpected sliver of a smile 'Yes, they are impossible to open aren't they? But thank you so much for helping me.'

Finally he had managed to rip open the pack but with such force that the tissues sprang out and spilled across the carpeted floor of the stand.

He laughed. 'That always happens, doesn't it? Bugger it. Come on, let's wipe away these tears and see if we can clean up some of that scary mascara, shall we? Would that be ok?'

Without waiting for her reply, he kneeled down in front of her and started to dab the tears from under her eyes. His touch was kind, gentle, caring, considerate and for Maggie, simply overwhelming. She threw her arms around him and buried her head in his shoulder. Then started to cry.

'There, there, let it all out, just let it all out.'

And for nearly ten minutes she did let it all out, the former wannabe hotshot barrister and soon-to-be former wife of the UK's highest-profile human-rights brief crying her eyes out on the shoulder of the man the papers had christened the Hampstead Hero.

***

Jimmy placed two polystyrene cups of tepid milky coffee on the table. 'Do you take sugar? I hope not, since I forgot to get any.' They had repaired to the scruffy little cafe that sat adjacent to the entrance hall of the exhibition centre. Maggie had made an effort to pull herself together, and now the tears had gone but she could not stop shivering, although she knew the room wasn't cold. She had draped her coat over her shoulders and pulled down the sleeves of her grey cardigan to warm her hands. She thought she must look like a refugee on one of these black-and-white Second-World War newsreels.

'No, just milk please. And thank you so much for helping me. Jimmy, isn't it?'

'Aye, it's Jimmy and that's about the tenth time you've thanked me in the last ten minutes. No more required now please, I get the picture fine. You're grateful for my intervention.' This accompanied by a broad disarming smile that she would come to love.

'No, I mean yes but... well I don't know what would have happened if you hadn't come along when you did. So thank you...' she smiled, realising what she had done '...sorry, sorry, I can't help it.'

'Not surprising, after all you've been through. Your husband seems like a right pig, if you don't mind me saying. Mind you, I'm not surprised, because he always comes across as a pompous idiot on the telly.'

'You must know who I am then, I suppose?'

'Well, you don't exactly need to be Sherlock Holmes to work it out. I've seen your picture in the papers. *'Is this the most hated woman in Britain?'* I think that's how the *Chronicle* described you. Of course I know who you are - you're the infamous Maggie Brooks.'

She laughed. Hell, she had actually *laughed*, despite the fact that she knew, without doubt, that she did not deserve to laugh ever again in her life after everything she had done and everything that had happened.

'Yes, I'm afraid that is me. The most hated woman in Britain.' It was true, more than a year on, and no easier to come to terms with despite the time that had passed.

'So what are you doing here?' Jimmy said.

'I was going to ask you the same thing. I was watching you earlier, you know, before Philip turned up.'

'Ooh, a stalker too are you? Only joking. Actually, I'm looking for a job Maggie, same as everybody here.'

'Dressed like a half-stoned rock singer? That's a novel approach, I must say. You certainly stand out from the crowd.'

'I wasn't expecting to be interviewed today. I was just doing a bit of a high-level survey of the market, collecting a few brochures, looking at what's on offer, etcetera etcetera.'

'If you don't mind me saying so, aren't you a bit old for a graduate recruitment fair?'

'And if you don't mind me saying so, I'd guess I'm still quite a bit younger than you.' Again, delivered with the same devastating smile that instantly defused any potential offence. 'No, after Uni, my future as a lawyer was all talked about and planned, but I gave it up for music and the Free Electric Band.'

'Excuse me?'

'It's a line from an old song from the seventies by Albert Hammond. The Free Electric Band. Sorry, lame joke. My old man really wanted me to become a lawyer but I didn't fancy it so I joined the army instead. Did twelve years, Iraq, Afghanistan, Belfast, the lot. Got demobbed about twelve months ago and been bumming around ever since trying to figure out what to do next. Well, to be honest, I did have a few wee problems to sort out but nothing that I couldn't deal with. It was a wee bit tough, but I'm good now.'

She was half-expecting him to elaborate, but he didn't, so for a while they sat without exchanging a word, toying with their coffee cups, immersed in private thoughts of pain, loss and despair. It was Jimmy who finally broke the silence.

'Goodness, what have I been going on about? We've only just met and I'm banging on about my pathetic little troubles. And after all you've been through. I feel a right idiot. Look, I'll shut up right now.' Once more, the captivating smile.

She took a sip from her coffee. 'No no, please don't worry about it. Everybody's pain is real to them, it's not a competition.'

'You say that, but I've no idea how you've coped with everything.'

The truth was she hadn't coped at all.

'You just well -*cope*, you have no choice.' That, also, was not true. You can decide not to cope, not to carry on with your wrecked life, to put an end to the agony for good, like she had so nearly done not much more than a year ago. It was this memory more than any other that made sleep so difficult to attain, and it was this nightmare that shook her awake on the rare nights when she did manage to drop off.

'But look, I mustn't keep you any longer. The fair closes soon, you'd better carry on with your job hunting. Thank you again for helping me.'

He groaned. 'Aye, and welcome to the end of Jimmy Stewart's short but sweet hippy dream. Time to put on the suit, get a haircut and knuckle down to the nine to five. Time to get a proper job like my big brother.'

'Is he a lawyer?' Maggie asked.

'No, a copper. Detective Inspector actually, here in London somewhere. I don't know exactly what he does, except he works in some dodgy department or other. Detective without portfolio he always calls himself. To be honest, I think there might have been some incident a year or two back, but I'm not surprised because he's a complete nutcase and a piss-head into the bargain'. The tone was affectionate.

'He sounds interesting, but talking of proper jobs, they probably won't start handing out offers until early in the new year at the earliest, so you've still got a bit of time left as a rebel without a cause.'

And then from nowhere, she had a crazy idea.

'Jimmy, now honestly please tell me right away if I'm being an idiot, but well, the reason I'm here is... I'm looking for an associate for my new business. I can't pay very much, not much more than minimum wage to be honest, but well, maybe it might tide you over for a few months and you could still apply to the big firms at the same time. And it might help you, you know, put some experience on your CV...'

He laughed. 'That would be very beneficial. 'Experience: I spent six months working for the most hated woman in Britain'. No but seriously, that actually might not be such a bad idea. What exactly will the work entail, if you don't mind me asking?'

She rummaged in her handbag for a few seconds, eventually emerging with a business card that she placed on the table. It read *Bainbridge Associates - Investigation Services to the Legal Profession* with a contact phone number and e-mail address.

'In case you're wondering, Bainbridge is my maiden name. You see, I had no option but to start my own firm after...well, after everything that has happened. Nobody's going to employ me as a lawyer now, are they, let's be honest, and my friend Asvina says I need a job and an income and be able to show some stability in my life if... if I'm ever going to convince the courts to let me see Ollie again.' Once more she struggled to hold back the tears. 'I'm sorry Jimmy, look, just forget I ever raised this, it was a stupid idea...'

He evidently did not agree.

'No, not at all Maggie. You know, this might not be such a bad plan. For a start, I could certainly do with earning a few quid whilst I'm trying to figure out what to do in the long term. Go on, tell me more, I'm interested, honestly.'

'Well, it's very dull work. We're not like the private detectives on telly, in fact we're not private detectives at all. We just do all the boring leg-work that needs doing in every big case but that the law firms can't justify charging their clients five hundred pounds an hour to do. So we check bank statements, verify the value of assets, do some basic internet searches on the other parties, that sort of thing. Mainly in the family law sphere, divorces, probate, property disputes...'

Maggie knew all about the work of legal investigators, having used them plenty of times in the past, but at this moment her own firm could best be described as embryonic, a fact she did not try to conceal.

'... I've made it all sound rather grand, but we've... I've only just started up and I don't actually have any paid work as of yet. But Asvina wants me to help her on a big divorce case she's about to kick off. In fact, I'm supposed to meet the client tomorrow for the first time. You could come along if you want, no obligation or anything, just to see if maybe it's something you would like.'

'I'll do it,' he grinned, 'but do I need to get a haircut?'

She smiled. 'No, but lose the AC/DC T-shirt if you don't mind.'

'No worries, I washed my Zeppelin one yesterday. I'll wear that. No, don't worry I'll find something. Just text me the address and I'll see you tomorrow.'

And so they shook hands on the deal, a strangely formal act considering the remarkable intimacy of what had gone before. An announcement over the tannoy signalled that the fair was scheduled to close in ten minutes. Maggie closed down her laptop, slipped it into its leather case and prepared to return to her cold lonely flat. But tonight, if only imperceptibly, something felt different, better. For the first time in over a year there had been ten minutes of her life when she wasn't thinking about Ollie and she wasn't thinking about the van crushing the life from her beautiful niece. It wouldn't last, she knew that, that would be too much to expect, but tomorrow after the client meeting she would at last sign off on the divorce - she knew she must, despite all the pain that it brought. Sign the damn form and wipe the slate clean. Encase the past eight years in concrete and try to forget.

Then Asvina Rani would explain her plan for the custody hearing. Her one true friend Asvina, the most brilliant family law solicitor in all of London, and the person who had single-handedly kept her sane -just - throughout her trauma. Asvina would have a plan, a brilliant plan and soon, Maggie and Ollie would be reunited.

Chapter 10

Jimmy spotted her a few feet away in the crowd as he emerged into the street from the concourse. 'Morning Maggie, blooming nightmare this, isn't it?'

True to his word, he had made an effort to smarten up. His hair looked freshly-washed and was tied back in a neat pony-tail. He wore a crisp light blue shirt with button-down colour and smart black jeans. The cowboy boots were still extant, but had been cleaned and polished and were relatively discreet, tucked under his trouser-leg.

'Yes, it's this Palestinian peace thing, what a laugh that is. Philip and all his mates will be there of course, virtue signalling like mad. Arseholes.'

They had agreed to meet up at the DLR station in Canary Wharf, five minutes' walk from the swish glass palace that housed the distinguished international law firm of Addison Redburn. It was approaching nine o'clock and the station was still packed with commuters, but today they were joined by the unsettling presence of heavily-armed police officers. This time it was just an exercise, in preparation for the conference that was due to take place in a few weeks' time, but it was still unnerving for the worker-ants as they scurried about their business. Critics considered the conference a complete waste of time, nothing more than a vanity project by a dying administration, given that the US, the United Nations and, most conspicuously, Israel were not to be officially represented. This had not seemed to discourage Prime Minister Julian Priest, who was rolling out the red carpet for his old friend Miss Fadwa Ziadeh, the glamorous and charismatic new leader of Hamas.

The law firm occupied all thirty- two floors of the waterside tower block and as befitted her status, Asvina Rani had been allocated an impressive south-west facing suite on the second-highest floor, commanding a view in one direction over the river to the picturesque Royal Borough of Greenwich, and towards St Pauls and the City in the other. Her personal office had all the trappings of corporate success, some might say excess; upmarket furniture, tasteful wall hangings and on two sides, wall-to-ceiling windows. Outside her door, a small army of junior lawyers, paralegals and personal assistants beavered away to keep the whole lucrative show on the road. The need to keep this army fed was one reason why the services of Ms. Rani did not come cheap, but her results were often spectacular and few clients complained.

A young PA had been sent to meet Maggie and Jimmy from reception and the high-speed elevator had taken less than a minute to deliver them up to Asvina's suite.

'Miss Bainbridge and Mr Stewart,' she announced in broad Cockney, pushing open the door.

'Thanks Mary.' Asvina got up from her desk and walked across the office to greet them. 'Using your maiden name again Maggie I see. That's a big step forward.' The friends hugged warmly.

'And you must be Jimmy,' she said, extending a hand.

'That's me,' he agreed, giving her the opportunity to witness his heart-melting smile for the first time.

Mary returned with coffee and they took their seats around a large glass-topped conference table.

'Asvina, I can't thank you enough for giving me this opportunity to get my firm up and running,' Maggie said. 'You know how important it is to me, with the situation with Ollie and all that.'

'You don't need to thank me, I'm just pleased I can help.'

Jimmy laughed. 'I've known her less than twenty-four hours and she's thanked me fifty times already. That's what she does.'

Asvina nodded. 'I know, she's lovely, isn't she? Anyway, let me tell you both about the case.'

She pushed a brown A4 folder across the table, spinning it round so that they could read the label on the front.

Maggie looked surprised. 'Saddleworth verses Saddleworth? Not *Gerrard* Saddleworth surely?'

'The same,' Asvina said. 'The Right Honourable Gerrard Saddleworth, HM Government's esteemed Home Secretary. But actually it's his wife Olivia who's my client, not her husband. You'll get to meet her in ten minutes or so once I've given you some background. That's assuming you haven't met her before?'

'I've been to one or two events the Saddleworths have also been at, I'm pretty sure of that,' Maggie said, wrinkling her brow, 'but I don't think I've actually spoken to her or been introduced. It's Philip and his brother Hugo who are old friends of Saddleworth and Priest, not me. From their university days.'

'They move in high circles don't they?' Asvina said, smiling. 'But I assume you've read the tittle-tattle in the papers about Mr Saddleworth's affair with a journalist?'

Jimmy nodded. 'Aye, with Penelope White of the *Chronicle*, I remember seeing the story somewhere. But hang on, wasn't it her who went for you big-time Maggie? The most hated woman in Britain crap, that was her doing.'

'Yes it was,' Maggie said. And perhaps it was no more than she deserved, because there was no denying the fact that she and she alone had been responsible for the freeing of Dena Alzahrani. Setting the notorious Notting Hill bomber free to repeat her heinous crime, just one hundred days later. Setting her free to murder her beautiful niece Daisy. Setting her free to condemn Jules and Felicity Swift to a life of unimaginable pain. Set free by the stupid selfishness of Maggie Bainbridge.

Jimmy was the first to notice her eyes moistening.

'Look, I'm sorry. I didn't mean to bring back the bad memories.'

'Come on, let's get to work,' Asvina said, sensing the mood. She removed a sheaf of papers from the folder and spread them across the table.

'This is what I have on the couple so far. So just for the record, they have one daughter, Patience, nineteen, and currently studying modern languages at Cambridge. Naturally, her future welfare is Olivia's priority. And this,' she said, pointing to a densely-printed spreadsheet, 'is the financial disclosure that we've got from her husband. Just one current account with Nat West, in joint names, that gets his parliamentary salary and a few thousand a year from his occasional guest appearances on an Andrew Neil TV show. About eighty grand in savings, mainly in bog-standard high street ISAs and NSI bonds, and a few thousand pounds' worth of Footsie shares. And of course there's the future value of his minister's pension, at about forty grand a year for life, guaranteed against inflation. No other significant income declared on the register of member's interests, other than acting as trustee for a couple of charities, for which he received only expenses. The house in the constituency is in joint names, worth about £450k but with over £100k mortgage still on it. His London flat, allegedly the regular venue for carnal activity with one Penelope White, journalist, is rented. He's from a modest background, so no big fat inheritance to look forward to and no other significant assets to speak of. As I said, bog-standard and squeaky-clean. He's comfortable, but not a rich man by any stretch.'

'So that all seems quite straightforward,' Maggie said, who had been listening intently, 'but there must be something else, otherwise why would you need us?'

Asvina nodded. 'You're right. But I'll let Olivia tell you about that herself. I can see she's just arrived.'

There was a knock on the door, Mary opening it just enough for them to make out her disembodied voice.

'Mrs Saddleworth's here Asvina. Shall I bring 'er in?'

Olivia Saddleworth was tall and slim but of rather plain appearance, although dressed head-to-toe with the expensive good taste of the prosperous country lady. Maggie estimated her to be in her early to mid-fifties, registering the Harris Tweed skirt, Barbour checked shirt and gilet, a pair of brown Duberry riding boots and the Mulberry handbag that she knew must have cost a thousand pounds or more. It seemed a bit out of place in central London and probably no less so in her husband's working-class South Yorkshire constituency.

Asvina quickly dispensed with the introductions then said, 'Olivia, I've just been bringing Maggie and Jimmy up to speed with your situation. They're going to help us with the investigations into your husband's financial status. As I told you on the phone, their job is to find evidence of undisclosed financial assets but I don't want to hold up too much hope because it is a very difficult task. You know we can't force banks and other financial institutions to disclose their clients' private affairs, only the courts can do that. And we have to be as certain as we can be before asking the court to intervene, because if we're wrong they'll award costs against us, and it'll negatively prejudice any future applications.'

'I understand Asvina,' Olivia said. 'I'll need to take that risk.'

Asvina raised an eyebrow in Maggie's direction.

'Olivia, I'm not sure you understand the level of costs we could be talking about here. I'm afraid you don't have the level of assets to survive a negative award. We are totally dependent on Maggie and Jimmy uncovering strong evidence if we are to make a court challenge.'

Jimmy directed his smile at Mrs Saddleworth. 'No pressure then.'

'So Olivia, perhaps you could tell Maggie and Jimmy why you are suspicious,' Asvina said. 'Specifically, the matter of the deposit box.'

Olivia Saddleworth settled back in her chair, her expression suggesting she had been looking forward to this opportunity for some time.

'I expect you all know about his... his affair with Penelope White. I'd confronted him about her, but of course at first he denied everything, so I started opening all his mail,' she said, matter-of-factly. 'It was quite easy, with him being in London all week. I wasn't sure what I was looking for, I don't suppose she was writing him love-letters or anything, but well... I just needed to do something.'

'I can understand that,' Maggie said. She knew all about powerful men who had decided to trade in their wives for a younger model. She also knew that tampering with mail was illegal and therefore whatever Olivia was going to tell them might not be able to be used in court.

'So, a week ago I found this.' From her leather attaché case she withdrew a glossy estate agent's brochure, the kind they only produce for their top-end properties, and placed it on the table. 'Hampstead Heath. And do you see the price? Three and a quarter million pounds. He can't afford that on his salary.'

'We can assume he is buying it jointly with White though, can't we?' Jimmy asked. 'She must be earning a good whack, national newspaper journalist and all that.'

'Yes she will be,' Asvina agreed, 'but low six-figures at best I would guess, still not enough to buy that sort of place, I wouldn't have thought.'

'That's true,' Maggie said, 'but I suppose just because he has asked for a brochure, it doesn't mean he is planning to buy it. Do you have anything else Olivia?'

'Yes, well...I know... I know it sounds terrible but I've been going through all his pockets and some of his private files and well, I did find some things...'

Maggie smiled. 'Been there, done that.'

Mrs Saddleworth rummaged again in her attaché case and brought out two brown A4 envelopes. She shook out the contents of one of them onto the table.

'Receipts for the type of hotels and restaurants that he never took me to. I assumed he was there with that bitch.'

'Do you mind if I take a look?' asked Maggie softly. She knew from her own experience how hard this must be for her. Sifting through them, she saw there were more than a dozen large bills from some of the most fashionable, and in her opinion, most over-priced establishments in the country, mostly in London but some in the provinces too. Over five grand in total.

'I don't suppose these could have been incurred on government business?' Jimmy asked.

Asvina laughed. 'I don't think so, there'd be a taxpayers' revolt if this got out.'

'And there is this too.' Olivia removed a crumpled letter from a second envelope and passed it to Maggie, who took it and began to read aloud.

'*Dear Mr Saddleworth, Thank you for continuing to choose Geneva Swiss Bank for your private banking needs. May we respectively bring to your attention that the annual fee for your secure deposit box service is now overdue. If you have already paid, please ignore this letter, and thank you once again for choosing Geneva Swiss.*'

She noticed the date printed on the top left hand side of the letter. 'But this was nearly eight years ago, is that right?'

'Yes, that's right.'

'And I assume your husband had some explanation for it?' Maggie said. 'Otherwise it would have turned up in the disclosures that Asvina showed us earlier.'

'He played it down,' Olivia said. 'He claimed it had been set up on the advice of a financial adviser he was using at the time, who said there would be tax advantages in taking some of his fees for public speaking engagements in cash.'

'Tax avoidance more like,' Jimmy said.

'Exactly. And so he says he had second thoughts about how wise that was for an MP and didn't go through with it.'

'Did you believe him?' Maggie asked.

'No, but the bank won't reveal any information so of course there's no way to check it.'

Clutching at straws, thought Maggie. 'Olivia, is there anything else you can think of that might help us?'

'I don't really know. I suppose maybe he is facing up to the fact that his party is going to lose the election, and at his age, he's never going to become Prime Minister.'

'So you think this is some kind of late mid-life crisis?' Jimmy said. 'That might explain the relationship with Penelope White?' Not surprisingly, he had struck a raw nerve.

'White is a bitch,' Olivia said in an indignant tone. 'All that female empowerment crap she spouts when she's just a cheap tart like all the rest.'

'Gerrard has a history of this then?' Maggie asked softly. 'Affairs, I mean.'

'Oh yes. I'm pretty sure he has had several liaisons over the years, but I've stupidly just put up with it, because I've never thought he would ever leave me, especially not for a woman like her. You know how black and white the Labour party can be. There are large sections of the party that would never forgive him for running off with a Tory.'

A woman like her. The right-wing warrior Penelope White, attractive and at least ten years younger than Olivia Saddleworth. The outspoken scourge of the political-correctness movement, a climate-change denier and the woman who had ran a year-long campaign to destroy Maggie Brooks' reputation. *The most hated woman in Britain*. That was Penelope White's work, and she despised her for it. But perhaps thanks to this case, she might finally get the chance to meet her, where she would tell her to her face what she felt about her. But as far as Gerald Saddleworth was concerned, it seemed obvious that he was at a turning point in his life, and had decided quite clinically to dispose of his old life and start afresh with a new one. New life, new wife. Maggie knew all about that.

'I've no idea what he sees in her, or her in him, and I don't really care,' Olivia was saying, 'but I expect he'll tire of her soon enough, like he seems to have tired of me.' Maggie felt it was said in hope rather than expectation.

'I expect you're right,' she lied. 'But let's see if we can put you in the very best possible position for the future. Our focus is to uncover as much as we can about your husband's finances, and I think we have enough to get started on. Jimmy and I will review it first thing tomorrow and come up with a plan of attack. Rest assured we'll leave no stone uncovered, and we'll be in touch as soon as we have anything.'

It sounded convincing, but with very little to go on, the truth was Maggie had not the faintest idea at all where to start. It wasn't surprising considering she had never done anything like this before.

***

'What do you think to that then Jimmy?' Maggie said, when the meeting was over. 'It didn't seem to take you long to get into the swing of it. Anybody would have thought you'd been doing it for years.'

'Aye, it was great. I really enjoyed it actually. Looking forward to getting stuck into the case and nailing that swine.'

'What about innocent until proven guilty?'

Jimmy shrugged. 'He sounds about as innocent as Stalin in my opinion, but fair enough, I suppose we do need to find some evidence.'

'Ok, well if you're absolutely sure you can cope with working with me, then we'll start tomorrow at 9am sharp, in my offices.'

He looked surprised. 'You've got an office?'

'I do. It's one of these serviced places down near Fleet Street. I rent one tiny room with two desks and it costs three times a month what I pay for my flat. It's called Riverside House, although it's nowhere near the river - you can Google it for the address. Turn up tomorrow - I'll arrange for Elsa to give you a pass card and a user code and password for one of the desktop computers. She's the receptionist for the facility, a very nice Czech girl - you'll like her.'

And she will like you, thought Maggie, what woman wouldn't? She couldn't really afford the office, but Asvina had argued that without it, it would be harder to convince a court that the business was respectable and therefore capable of providing a stable income. One that could pay for a decent home in which to bring up a child. Because that was the ultimate goal. Start off with a modest aim, one afternoon a month, then maybe even go for one or two days a month of supervised access and then take it from there. Of course, any access would be infinitely better than the current agony of legally-enforced estrangement, but a child belonged with his mother, and her life could not resume any semblance of normality until Ollie was again living with her.

'Ready for five minutes on the hearing?' Asvina had returned to the conference room, having momentarily left to escort Olivia Saddleworth to the elevator.

'So, we're on in about six weeks from now - just to remind you, it's Wednesday 19th at 2.00pm, so for goodness sake, make sure that's etched in stone in your calendar. As we agreed, we're going to ask for

Ollie to spend just an afternoon with you each month, and also to allow moderate contact via phone, e-mail and text during the month. We've talked about the basics before. You're going to have to show that your life is back on track after your breakdown, that you have a decent place to live and a steady job etc etc. Social services will also talk to Ollie to see how he feels about the situation. I know it seems crazy when he is only six but it's very likely that he is missing his mummy and that will have a great bearing on the case. Remember, the court's only concern is for the welfare of the child, they don't care at all about your feelings or your husband's either for that matter. Got all that so far? I mean, I know you're a lawyer Maggie, but family law is very different to criminal cases in the High Court.'

'Yes,' replied Maggie meekly. 'I understand.'

'Social services will also want to interview you before the hearing of course. They like to do it at home, and they also like to turn up unannounced to get the real picture of what home is like. So I need to ask you this Maggie so please don't take offence - but are you still drinking?'

What she meant was 'are you still drinking yourself into oblivion every night?' She thought about the last few months, where only the comfort of cheap Chardonnay had stopped her going insane. Eight, ten bottles a week, more if she was being honest with herself, but frankly, that's where you end up when you've screwed up big time. You have to drink to blot out the awful cost of that one stupid error of judgement, you wander around your dirty flat talking to yourself, crying, and hoping against hope that today is the day it will all turn out to have been a ghastly dream. But it isn't a dream, it's real, and no matter what you do, you can't erase the horror. *Who could?* All that pain, terror, loss. And all because of you and your stupid ego.

She realised that Asvina had repeated the question.

'No..., I mean yes,... well, I have been drinking too much, I know I have, but I've started to get a grip on it. I know how important it is that I do, really.'

And it was sort-of true, if only in the last forty-eight hours where at last there had been a tiny chink of light at the end of a dark, dark tunnel.

'Ok, Maggie, I believe you, but I can't say this other than bluntly. If social services find you drunk or hung over at home, or if they find your bins full of empty bottles -and believe me, they will look before they even knock on your door- then it's over - maybe for years. So I can't stress enough how important it is that you keep your nose clean in the next six weeks. Understand?'

'I understand.'

Asvina smiled. 'Good. Now, I've had a letter from Miranda Padgett your husband's solicitor, informing us that they intend to contest the case.'

'I knew that,' replied Maggie, remembering the events of the previous day.

'So just to set your mind at ease, there's no need for us to worry about that unduly. It's a pretty routine tactic where access is disputed and there's no likelihood of an amicable settlement. As I said before, the court is only interested in the welfare of the child, not the wishes or needs of either parent. Miranda knows that of course, so their approach will be to try and provide evidence that you are an unsuitable person to be responsible for the care of a six-year-old child. So please Maggie, don't give them any material to work with.' It was said with a smile but her tone was serious.

'I won't Asvina, and I can't thank you enough for all you've done for me.'

They hugged warmly before agreeing that they must meet for lunch in the near future. 'A dry one,' added Maggie with a wry smile.

But now there was just one more thing she had to do that afternoon. It would have been a similar scene on that terrible September day in Notting Hill, approaching two years ago. Specifically, the eleventh day of that month. *Nine-eleven.* Not a co-incidence either, but the date specifically chosen by Alzahrani for her first atrocity because of its symbolism amongst supporters of radical Islam. The greatest day in their history, according to their warped credo. And then almost one year later, and exactly one hundred days after Maggie had conspired to have her freed, she had repeated her ghastly crime at Ollie's school.

Today, just like then, at 3.15pm on a cool early spring day, mothers were beginning to gather around the school gates waiting for their children to come out. Three sturdy concrete bollards had now been erected in front of the school gates, and parents in the main were respecting the one hundred metre no-parking zone that had been established following the bombing, but in every other respect the scene was unchanged. Maggie had arrived a good half an hour earlier so that she could park her anonymous Golf at the first unrestricted spot just where the School Zone hatching began, the location being slightly elevated affording a clear view of the gate. In an attempt at disguise, she had thrown on a grey hooded sweatshirt and wore large designer sunglasses to conceal her features. It was a risk, but on previous occasions the swarms of mothers and child-minders streaming past on the pavement had paid her no attention, and today was no different.

Soon the children began to emerge from the school, at first a trickle and then a steady flow. She scanned the pavement looking for the comfortably rotund figure of Marta, Philip's new au pair - but she was nowhere to be seen. This was not in itself unusual, since Marta's time-keeping was not of the first order, and Maggie pictured her at that moment sprinting down North Street, terrified that she would miss the ten-minute deadline that the school imposed on pick-up time.

But then at last, there he was. Maggie's wonderful, beautiful, precious Ollie. He stopped at the gate, looking right, left and then right again, and then with a broad smile of recognition, ran excitedly to where Angelique Perez was waiting, throwing his arms round her in a loving embrace, before slipping his little hand into hers.

Chapter 11

It was well past eleven when Maggie finally made it into the office, after yet another sleepless night and another futile stupid attempt to drink herself into a pain-numbing stupor. For the first few hours, her brain had played over and over and over again the heartbreaking scene she had witnessed outside the school, only this time their hugs were more intense, their hands gripped tighter, their laughter louder. Later in the night, she became a fly on the wall of a dark depressing interview room, where Ollie was telling a nice social worker that he had a really nice new mummy now and he didn't want his old one back.

'No offence, but you look rough,' Jimmy said, raising an eyebrow. 'Big night, was it? Let me get you a coffee, you look like you could do with one. Elsa showed me how to work the machine, it was the first thing she did when I got here this morning.'

'Thanks Jimmy, I really could do with one.'

'And you can tell me what's wrong if you want to. After all, we've only known each other three days and already we know all of our deepest emotional traumas, so a few more won't hurt. And on that subject, take a look at this.' He passed her his phone.

It was the Facebook page of Astrid Sorenson. *Astrid Sorenson*. The beautiful star of country music, the genre-busting singer who was now famous all over the world. She had uploaded a photograph of herself striking a lascivious pose with her lips pressed against the sculpted cheek of an unidentified man who could easily be mistaken for a male supermodel. They looked like they were in an advert for an upmarket aftershave. The caption below read *New Man, New Band, New Life*, followed by ten smiley emojis.

'I didn't think you were a country music fan,' Maggie said, puzzled as to why he was showing it to her.

'So you've heard of her then? Astrid Sorenson is the woman who ruined my marriage. Correction, the woman who caused me to ruin my own bloody marriage.'

'What, *the* Astrid Sorenson? I'm sorry, I didn't even know you were married,' Maggie said, even more confused.

Jimmy shrugged. 'Aye, I was. Until Astrid bloody Sorenson came into my life. Maybe one day I'll tell you the story.'

That was going to be quite a story, she could tell that already. Captain Jimmy Stewart and the Swedish queen of country music. But she sensed now wasn't the time.

'Don't take this the wrong way,' she said gently, 'but if it hurts so much, why don't you just unfriend her?'

'Aye you're probably right.' It didn't sound as if he meant it. 'So, what about you, do you want to talk about what's eating you? No worries if you don't.'

She hesitated. 'No, not at the moment.' In fact there was nothing she wanted more than to share her agony with this strangely comforting man, a man she had known barely seventy-two hours, but instead she forced a smile. 'No, business first. Let's see if we can make anything of the Saddleworth case, shall we?'

She saw he had spread the meagre pile of documents that Asvina had given them across Maggie's desk. 'So where do we start?' she asked.

'Good question. I've been working on that for the last couple of hours, whilst you were having a lie-in.' He shot her a warm smile. 'Ha-ha, and to be honest we've got bugger all to go on. A fancy estate agent's brochure, a few receipts, an old letter from a Swiss bank. As I said, bugger all...'

'I thought as much.' She tried not to sound too despondent.

'...but,' Jimmy continued, 'so, I went on a cyber warfare course at Sandhurst a few years ago, and they taught me that data only comes alive when you draw a picture of it and attach it to a timeline. It was the only thing I remember from it actually, but it stuck in my mind. And I know it sounds like bullshit, but it actually works. Data visualisation, that's what they call it. Helps you see patterns and connections that you might not otherwise see. So that's what I've been doing. Here, take a look.'

On a sheet of A4 copier paper, he had drawn a table with four columns, headed *'Work', 'Relationships', 'Associates'* and *'Other Information'*. There was a row for each year going back about thirty years.

'So you see Maggie, although we don't have much hard data at the moment, we already can see some interesting connections. If for example we go back eight years or so to when that private deposit box letter was written, we can see under *'Work'* that he was at that time

MP for Sheffield South. And in opposition, not in government. We go back twenty years, and he was an official with the miner's union, and a local government councillor.'

'That's interesting,' Maggie said. 'And I see you've not got anything much earlier than that, but we know he was at Oxford with Philip and Hugo, and with Julian Priest too. A right little gang of pound-shop revolutionaries they were by all accounts. That's when Philip and his brother started up their *Action for Palestine* pressure group, with our much-loved Prime Minister Julian Priest.'

Jimmy smiled. 'I didn't know that, I'll stick that on the chart right now. And your husband is still heavily involved with the group, isn't he?'

'That's right,' Maggie said. 'He is. His brother Hugo too, at least he was before he got sent down. But Gerrard Saddleworth was never really into it all, as far as I know. He likes to cultivate the image of being solid working-class, warm beer and pigeon racing and all that. So he's always tried to distance himself from metropolitan liberals like Priest and his mates.'

'Mates like your Philip.'

'Exactly. Pretentious arseholes like my ex.'

Jimmy evidently decided against making a comment. Instead he said, 'Well, the web's stuffed with info about guys in the public eye like Saddleworth so it should be a doddle to get this chart fattened out.'

Maggie laughed. 'I'm not so sure about that, but at least it gives us something to go at. Anything else you've been doing this morning, or have you spent all the time chatting up Elsa?'

'Being chatted up more like. She's...'

They were interrupted by Elsa herself poking her head around the door.

'Do you want coffee Jimmy? I put fresh brew in machine just one minute ago. Just for you.'

Maggie was amused to see his face reddening. 'What?' he said distractedly. 'Oh, yes that would be great.'

'I go get it now. Oh, and your face, it is very strange colour,' she said, closing the door behind her.

'She's in love with you already,' Maggie teased, 'and such a pretty girl too.'

'I don't think so. I mean, the love bit, not that she's not pretty.'

Elsa returned a few minutes later with the coffee. Maggie was pleased to see she had brought her one too. 'Believe me, I need this Jimmy. My brain hurts.'

'Mine's ok actually. I suppose it's because it's so much younger than yours.'

'Cheek. I'm only thirty-nine I'll have you know.'

He raised an eyebrow but made no comment.

'Aye, well I'm going to do a bit of rooting around the net,' he said. 'See what I can dig out on Gerrard Saddleworth, then maybe we could have a wee bit of a brainstorm, see what else we can come up with.'

She gave him a thumbs-up. 'That's sounds like a plan, but if you don't mind, I'm going to have to pop out for ten minutes to get several packs of ibuprofen, because my brain is storming but not in a good way. So you carry on and I expect an answer when I get back. And no flirting with Elsa, ok?'

He snapped his heels together and made a smart salute. 'Yes ma'am.'

* * *

The problem was, where to start? You couldn't just Google *'Gerrard Saddleworth bank accounts'*, could you? Well actually, you could, and he did, with predictable results. Plenty of results about what Saddleworth's party politics would mean for your life savings, and on the administration's plans to create a national business investment bank, and a report about an obscure question he had asked in the House of Commons about foreign ownership of UK-registered financial institutions. But nothing about his personal financial affairs. That was no more than Jimmy expected.

So where to next? Maybe it would be worth looking to see if he could find out anything related to these fancy restaurant bills. At least they were something tangible. Some place called *The Bull* in Southwark, and another place up in Gloucester, they seemed to be amongst his favourites. Searches for *'Gerrard Saddleworth The Bull Southwark* 'and *'Gerrard Saddleworth Seven Cathedral Close Gloucester'* failed at first glance to bring up anything of significance, but as he scrolled further down the Google results, an item buried away on page eight caught his eye. The *Gloucester Journal* reported that the government minister Gerrard Saddleworth had visited GCHQ in nearby Cheltenham, meeting with the Director and several members of staff. The purpose of the visit was not disclosed. Jimmy checked the date - 14th October. Quickly, he looked down the list of receipts he had created earlier and yes, Saddleworth had dined at Seven Cathedral Close that evening. So that perhaps explained why he was in Gloucester, but would you really then entertain your colleagues - Jimmy was working on the initial presumption that the dinner was work-related- in such lavish fashion? Normal protocol would surely dictate a more modest venue, especially since it would be the Home Office expense budget that would be footing the bill.

Not bad for a first go, he thought, but it didn't help to identify who Saddleworth had dined with that evening. So he ran the searches again, but this time selected 'Images' instead of 'All' and included '14th October' in the search string. A micro second later, the screen was filled with a mosaic of photographs of the town's cathedral and its surroundings. Damn - too specific, maybe just try *'Gerrard Saddleworth Gloucester'*. Better - this time the mosaic was made up mainly of faces, pleasingly, some of the current Home Secretary, although surprisingly it appeared the world was not short of men with that name. Jimmy scrolled down, as the search engine relentlessly filled the screen with images, outpacing his gentle movement of the mouse, but there were none that captured that visit to the expensive restaurant on that evening.

It had been a long shot of course and he was disappointed but not really surprised by the outcome. But then something struck him, something he should have thought about from the start. The receipts showed that he had dined at the restaurant on four occasions. He obviously loved it, that was clear. But why should it be assumed that *he* always paid the bill?

Jimmy punched in *'Seven Cathedral Close October Saddleworth'*. No specific day this time, just the month.

Once again, the screen filled with images, but this time dominated by exterior and interior shots of the upmarket restaurant, many featuring diners appearing to enjoy themselves despite the extravagantly-priced menu.

And then, astonishingly, unexpectedly, there it was. Gerrard Saddleworth, looking serious with a glass of red wine raised to his lips. Beside him, a good-looking man of about fifty, formally dressed in an expensive-looking shirt and matching tie, holding up his glass for a young waiter to fill. Next to him, a younger man, south Asian, also well-dressed. From his expression it appeared that it was he who was leading the conversation at that moment. Opposite them, recognised from the photograph that accompanied her by-line, sat Penelope White of the *Chronicle*, engrossed in her mobile phone. Next to Penelope, a man with his back to the camera who Jimmy thought he vaguely recognised. He clicked on the image, revealing it had originally been uploaded to Facebook by someone called Amber Smith; the powerful Google web-crawlers linked to Facebook's clever automatic facial recognition technology had had no trouble linking Saddleworth's features to Jimmy's search. One more click, and he was on Amber's Facebook page and looking at her timeline. It always amazed him why people were so naive when it came to their social media privacy, but in this case he gave thanks. She was evidently a party girl, her timeline dominated by selfies of her having a good time. A pissed Amber with a gaggle of equally-pissed friends. A skimpily-dressed Amber snogging some man or other. A sunburnt Amber lifting her top to show off her small white breasts. Pure class.

It didn't take him long to find the picture he was looking for. Sure enough, it had been uploaded on 20th October, which turned out to be Amber's thirtieth birthday, explaining why she was at the upmarket establishment. The text with the picture read *'Out with ALL the girls for my 30th at this FAB place. A bit pissed, of course :-). This guy from the government is here, Samantha thinks he's called Julian Saddleworth and he's the chancellor or something, who knows xxxxxxxxx.'*

'Oh yes!' he bellowed to the empty office, 'oh yes, oh yes, oh yes!'

***

'So I've managed to make a wee bit of progress. Don't know how you're feeling but maybe you could come and take a look?'

Maggie had returned nursing a large Americano which she had strengthened with a double espresso shot. Simultaneously the ibuprofens were beginning to take effect and she was already thinking more clearly.

'Yes sure Jimmy. What have you got?'

'Well whilst you were out- for ages by the way, where did you get to?'

She raised her coffee cup and gave a sheepish grin. 'Got waylaid by Starbucks I'm afraid.'

'Aye right, well as I said, whilst you were out, I came up with what I can modestly describe as a mind-blowingly brilliant thought.'

He folded his arms, leaned back in his chair and said nothing.

She smiled. 'Well alright then, tell me.'

'Ok, so I took a look at a couple of these restaurant bills that Olivia discovered. So there were a couple of eight hundred quid- plus bills at Seven Cathedral Close - that's Paul Waterson's Michelin-starred joint in Gloucester, of all places. Then there's seven hundred quid at The Bull in Southwark - that's one of these pretentious bistros, claim they serve plain hearty food but it's fifteen quid for the soup and forty quid for a main course.'

'How do you know about these places? You move in these circles, do you?'

'Interweb. But the thing is, we're living in the social media age, worst luck, and no-one goes to a hundred-quid a head restaurant without posting at least a dozen photographs on their Facebook or Instagram. Not my generation at least,' he said, smiling.

'Shut up. I told you I'm only thirty-nine.'

'I thought you said thirty-eight. Anyway I rest my case, m'lady. But seriously, if you see someone in the public eye, like Saddleworth, it's ninety-nine percent certain you're going to try to get a selfie or at least a photo so you can say 'guess who's also here at the *very* expensive Seven Cathedral Close tonight'. So I reckoned with an hour or so online, there was a reasonable chance I might be able to find out who he was dining with at these restaurants.'

'And...?'

He pointed at the screen.

'And I found this. Look, these are some folks who were sharing a fancy dinner with Saddleworth in Gloucester. And the interesting thing was, it was the second night in a row he had eaten there, although it looks like someone else picked up the tab on this occasion. That looks like Penelope White on her phone, and if I'm not mistaken Maggie, that's your husband, isn't it, with his back to us? But I don't recognize any of the others, do you?'

Maggie stared at the photograph on the screen, struggling to make sense of it. For if Jimmy didn't recognise the other diners, Maggie did. *All of them.*

Adam Cameron, Queen's Counsel and superstar prosecutor.

Penelope White of the *Chronicle* and next to her, Philip Brooks.

But taking centre stage, clearly the star attraction judging by the way the others were apparently hanging on his every word, was Dr Tariq Khan, world expert in automatic facial recognition technology. The question was, why were they meeting only a few weeks before the start of the Alzahrani trial. Indeed, why were they meeting at all?

Chapter 12

For a moment she sat in stunned silence, rendered speechless by what Jimmy had just uncovered. Then finally she spoke.

'Cameron said he had never met Tariq Khan. He said he'd never met him. Christ, he lied to the judge. I was there, in that anti-room, and he lied. And Saddleworth and my husband, what the hell were they doing there? This is crazy, I just don't understand it.'

Jimmy voiced what she was already thinking. 'Do you think it might have something to do with your trial? '

'Khan, Cameron and Saddleworth in the same room? For goodness sake, what else could it be?'

She grabbed for her phone and swiped to her husband's number. It rang a few times before going through to voicemail. That didn't surprise her because now he never took her calls or answered her messages. It was as if for him she no longer existed.

'Philip, it's Maggie. You need to call me now'. Frustrated, she slammed the phone down on the desk.

'He's a pig. Look, I'm going to send him that photograph and ask for an explanation, that should make him call me back.' She could feel the anger rising up inside her like an erupting volcano.

Jimmy struck a cautious note. 'Perhaps we should just take a rain check on that. Don't you think we need to think this through a bit, try and figure out what it all means? Then we can decide what we should do. Cool heads and all that.'

Her brain was swirling as she tried desperately to make some sense of it all. What the hell was Philip doing there and why was Gerrard Saddleworth there, what did it all mean? It had to be something to do with the trial, didn't it? Perhaps Khan had made his concerns known to his GCHQ bosses and it had been escalated all the way up to the Home Secretary. Maybe they were trying to persuade him to just let it go, buttering him up with fancy meals and flattering him with a meeting with a top government minister. But that still didn't explain why Philip was there. None of it made sense.

'What?... sorry Jimmy, I was just thinking about the whole crazy thing. Yes, I suppose you're right, we should take a rain check. To be honest, I've no idea what...'

They were interrupted by the opening riff of Nirvana's *Smells Like Teen Spirit* blasting from his phone.

'Sorry, need to take this Maggie. It's my brother Frank.'

He didn't have to switch to speakerphone for Maggie to follow the conversation.

'*Well hello wee brother, how's it going?*' boomed the voice at the other end of the line. '*Long time no see. I hear you're not seeing the Swedish princess any more. Not surprised at that really, she was a right piece of work, best out of that one pal, if you want my opinion. Oh, and I heard about you getting a job, can't believe it. You, back on civvy street. Actually, I googled your new boss this morning. Now that Maggie Brooks, she looks one fit bird. Bit old for you maybe, but still in good nick, by the looks of it...*'

'Frank, Frank,' he shouted, desperately trying to stem the flow, his face turning crimson. 'Maggie is with me right now actually. And it's Miss Bainbridge now. Maggie Bainbridge.'

'*Aw great,*' replied the voice, seemingly unperturbed. '*Single is she? That's brilliant, I'm really looking forward to meeting her. So anyway I'm fine for tonight - about half-five in my Southwark office, and you're buying, right? See you later.*'

'That was my brother Frank,' Jimmy said, somewhat unnecessarily. 'Detective Inspector Frank Stewart. I'm really sorry about all that, he's a bugger.'

'Don't worry about it. Actually, he seems quite funny.' *One fit bird.* Less than poetic perhaps, but right now she would take that.

'A complete nutcase. But yeah, a good copper, so he tells me himself. Actually Maggie, that's why I texted him earlier. I hope you don't mind but I thought we might try and pick his brains about how you go about doing an investigation, you know, given that we... '

She finished his sentence for him.

'...given that we don't really know what we're doing?'

'We don't, do we? It's just that you... we, we are pretty new to this game...' He stopped abruptly, as if conscious of how easily he could cause offence. But he needn't have worried.

'No, to tell you the truth Jimmy, I *haven't* got any idea what I'm doing. I just kind of hoped if we followed our noses something would turn up. But it would be great if your brother was able to steer us in the right direction. And especially now that that photograph has turned up. So where is the meeting? His Southwark office did he say?'

'His little joke. He means the Old King's Head. It's a pub, just round the corner from The Bull actually. He's in there more than he's in the office. All strictly in the line of duty of course, that's what he'll tell you. I'm sure he'll be able to help us. I mean this thing with Cameron and Khan and the rest, it looks serious. It should be police business.'

***

It was only just past six o'clock, but the Old King's Head was packed to capacity, Thursday evidently being a popular night for after-office booze-ups. Jimmy had to shout to make himself heard above a cacophony of conversation and laughter as they threaded their way towards the bar.

'He'll be sitting on a bar stool and onto his second or third one now if it goes to form.'

'What?'

'Never mind,' he mouthed, shaking his head and taking her hand to drag her the last few steps to the bar.

She recognised him immediately, Jimmy's description of him as an older, shorter and fatter version of himself being broadly accurate, although he wasn't much shorter, she thought, five foot-ten at least, and she would have said strong and powerful rather than fat. Good looking too, like his brother, and probably around her own age. His pint stood on the bar, temporarily parked whilst he finished off a jumbo-sized sausage roll. Flakes of pastry were strewn on the floor beneath him and several surrounded his mouth. He wiped his face with his shirt sleeve as he saw them approach, then extended his hand. 'Hello wee brother. Looking good pal.'

'Wish I could say the same for you Frank. I see you've not gone vegan yet. This is Maggie Bainbridge, my new boss.'

'Good to meet you Maggie,' he roared, 'but c'mon, let's wander off to the pool room so we can hear ourselves think. There's a wee bar in there so we'll be fine.'

He swilled the last of his beer and indicated a door in the far corner of the bar. 'Be with you in a minute, just need a quick wee-wee. Get us another pint of Doom Bar Jimmy, there's a good boy.'

They settled in at a corner table in the dimly-lit room. 'He's a model of sophistication, my brother,' Jimmy said, then evidently remembering that morning's overheard conversation, 'but of course you know that already.'

'He's nice, I can tell that already.' More than nice, she thought. Just like you.

'My mate Pete Burnside from Paddington Green ran your attempted murder investigation,' Frank said on his return. 'Just as well for you it never went to trial because it would have been a damn lynch mob with all the publicity surrounding the case at the time. And for what it's worth, I never thought for a minute that you tried to kill your boy, and neither did DI Burnside for that matter. It was just our lily-livered arse-licking bosses bowing to the hysteria of the press, a bloody modern day witch-hunt.'

More than a year later, every second of that terrible terrible day was imprinted in her mind in vivid technicolor, as if it had only happened yesterday. And yet still she was unable to answer the critical question - had she or had she not, in her hopelessness and desolation, in her utter despair and in her blind hatred of Philip, really tried to kill herself and Ollie? Eventually the CPS had decided the evidence was inconclusive; they could not say for certain -and nor could she. But Camden Council Social Services did not need conclusive evidence. They could work on the balance of probability, and on the balance of probability they had concluded that Maggie Brooks was a danger to her son.

'Thank you,' she said quietly. 'It was a very difficult time.'

'Aye, sorry, I didn't mean to bring back bad memories. Shouldn't have said anything. Anyway, what was it you two wanted to talk to me about?'

'So Frank,' Jimmy began, 'what it is, is that Maggie and me need your help and advice on something that's come up on the big divorce case we're working on. The husband is Gerrard Saddleworth... '

'What, the Home Secretary?'

'The same. His wife Olivia is convinced that he hasn't been exactly truthful about his finances. She thinks he's got a wad of cash salted away somewhere, and we've been tasked by her solicitor Asvina Rani to see what we can find out.'

'Well this wife must be bloody sure about that wad of cash if she's using Rani, 'cos she doesn't come cheap, at least that's what I've read about her.'

Maggie laughed. 'You're right there, but she gets results.'

'Well I'm sure she does,' Frank said, 'but you know folks, I don't want to burst your bubble or anything, but the Met doesn't really do divorce cases, no matter who it is. But you might as well tell me what you've got, you know, like evidence and that.'

'We've not really got much bruv. A letter from about eight years ago suggesting he might have had a secret bank deposit box, a few mega bills from top restaurants, and an estate agent's brochure for a fancy pad in Wimbledon.'

'That's all?'

'I know it's not much, but it's all we've got. But actually, that's not really what we want to talk to you about. There's something else, not connected to our divorce case. Something we think might be a whole lot bigger than that.'

He passed his phone over to his brother. 'We came across this photograph on the net and we're not really sure where to go next.'

Frank took a moment to scrutinise it.

'I recognise Gerrard Saddleworth of course, the others I don't. Who are they?'

'The woman is Penelope White,' Maggie said. 'She's a columnist with the *Chronicle*...'

'Ah, well I'm strictly a *Sun* man myself, so I wouldn't know her,' Frank said.

'... and she also happens to be the woman Saddleworth is leaving his wife for. That man there is Adam Cameron. He's a barrister. He was my opponent in the Alzahrani trial. And the man with his back to the camera is my husband. He's quite well known as a human rights lawyer.'

Frank frowned. 'No, sorry, never heard of him.'

She laughed. 'That would really piss him off.'

'I don't like lawyers.' Too late, he remembered Maggie's profession. '...well, as a general rule, that is.'

He groped for a quick change of subject. 'Anyway, who's that other guy, the Asian bloke?'

'That's Dr Tariq Khan,' Maggie said. 'He's a government technology expert, and it was his unofficial intervention that caused the trial to collapse.'

Frank's eyes narrowed. 'Oh aye, I remember reading about that. In the Sun, as it happens. He wrote some report that said the facial recognition evidence was a pile of poo, didn't he? But forgive me for saying, but I don't really know where you're going with this.'

'Adam Cameron told the judge at the Alzahrani trial that he had never met this Dr Khan. This picture proves he was lying.'

He gave a low whistle. 'What, and you smell a conspiracy? This does sound a bit out of the ordinary, I must admit. So when exactly was this picture taken?'

'Just a couple of weeks before the start of the trial,' Maggie said.

'Whoa! And answer me this, what's your husband got to do with all of this?'

'We don't know yet, but he does know Saddleworth and Julian Priest from way back. They were all at Oxford together, involved in every fashionable cause. It was all typical student politics except some of them never grew out of it. But as for the reason for this dinner, I've asked him to explain, but we're not exactly on speaking terms at the moment. We're getting divorced you see.'

'Aye, well I'm sorry to hear that,' Frank said sympathetically. 'But you know, there's probably nothing in it. For a start, if you were going to be whipping up a big nasty plot of some kind, would you do it in full view of the public at some fancy restaurant? No, I don't think so. What makes you think this one is suspicious?'

Jimmy was the first to answer. 'As Maggie said, Adam Cameron told the judge at the trial that he had never met Dr Khan. This picture proves he was lying.'

'Aye, but come on. The prosecution getting together, getting their ducks all lined up, that's not so unusual, is it?'

'Cameron lied to the judge,' Jimmy said, spelling it out. 'In a terrorist trial. Or are you saying that's not unusual either? And what the hell is a bloody journalist doing there?'

'That's a fair point wee Jimmy. Well, we've probably kicked off investigations on a lot less, but this is the Home Secretary. That's potential dynamite, and we'd need a lot more than you've got to persuade my gaffers to take this one up, if that's what you are asking me to do.'

'We didn't really have a plan,' Maggie said uncertainly. 'We were really only looking for some advice. So have you any suggestions what else we could do?'

'Just let me get another round in first and I'll think about it on the way to the bar. Large Chardonnay again Maggie and another Doom Bar for you, wee brother? And three sausage rolls?'

'I shouldn't,' she replied, then, 'oh why not, yes to both please Frank. I'm actually starving.'

'He's buying you dinner already,' Jimmy said, grinning. 'I think you're in there.'

'Shut up, will you.' But just for a moment she thought how nice it would be to go out on a proper dinner date again. She was still thinking about it when Frank returned with a tray and set the drinks and napkin-wrapped sausage rolls on the table.

'Right, where were we.' He picked up the nearest sausage roll and took a large bite. 'Excuse me talking with my mouth full. Yeah, so it's stating the bleeding obvious that the meeting was either innocent or it wasn't.'

Jimmy laughed. 'Aye, bleeding obvious.'

Frank spoke through a mouthful of pastry. 'So what you will find in my experience is that if it was innocent, if you talk to any of the participants, they're ninety percent certain to tell you quite straightforwardly what it was about. Nothing to hide so might as well tell the truth.'

'Makes sense,' Maggie agreed.

'But if there was something dodgy going on, then it's very different. Generally they won't answer or they'll tell you some crap, but it's what happens afterwards that's often the most interesting. Because no matter how cool they think they are, they always get spooked when people start questioning what it was all about. There'll be panic phone calls, attempts to get stories straight, you might find that someone breaks ranks and won't go along with the collective plan, all sorts of shit hitting the fan. That's when all the good stuff starts to come out. Then when you get the mobile phone records it all starts to unravel.'

Maggie nodded. 'Yes, I get that.'

'So, of course you guys could do this in your role, as what is it...?

'Investigation services,' Jimmy said. 'Investigation services to the legal profession.'

'Aye, whatever. However, no offence, but it would be a lot more effective if they got a wee call from the police.'

'What, are you saying you could help us with this Frank?' Maggie asked, surprised.

'It would be a lot more successful if you did,' Jimmy said. 'I know you can be very scary when you want to be.'

'Thanks, I'll take that as a compliment, but we can't have coppers harassing innocent citizens willy-nilly, especially if they are government ministers, *Chronicle* journalists and big-time QCs. But look, I'm intrigued with all of this so I'll have a word with my gaffer, see what she thinks. I'm not promising anything mind you, but she's not that keen on lawyers and politicians and things are a bit quiet at the moment, so you never know.'

Frank picked up his pint and drained the last dregs.

'Oh, and one other thing I just thought about. Have you got a copy of that report you were talking about, you know, the Khan one?'

'Yes, I've got one,' Maggie replied.

'Well you see, one of the wee jobs I'm working on at the moment is connected to AFR, you know the facial recognition stuff. It's a big thing at the moment, with all the worries about civil liberties and everything, and I've got a wee lassie working with me who's a bit of an expert on the subject. Obviously not to the level of your Dr Khan, but I think she does know her business. Actually, she's a bit of an expert on just about everything technical.'

Jimmy looked puzzled. 'Where are you going with this Frank?'

'Not sure at the moment Jimmy, not sure. There's just a wee thought going around in the back of my head and well, I'd just like the lassie Eleanor to take a look, that's all.'

'We'd be so grateful for your help Frank,' Maggie said. 'You know, anything you can do would be fantastic.'

'Aye, no bother. Anyway, must get on now, loads of bad guys to catch. I just hope I was some help to you. Oh, and Maggie, I better have your phone number, in case anything comes up.'

It was an innocent request, but she was still surprised by the unexpected flutter in her stomach. But then it had been a long time since anyone had asked for it.

Chapter 13

Department 12B of the Metropolitan Police occupied a dank and musty room stuck at the end of a dank and musty corridor of Atlee House, a scruffy sixties office block that had started life as an outpost of the Department of Health and Social Security. Eventually deemed too decrepit for even the careworn job-centre automatons, it had passed through a succession of ever more obscure government departments before being reluctantly adopted by the Met. This was the office that DI Frank Stewart now called home.

'Morning ma'am.' He slouched in, crumbs from a recently-despatched cheese croissant still visible on his chin, 'big day ahead, eh?'

This was his habitual greeting to his boss. Generally speaking, there were no big days to look forward to in Department 12B, although today, to be fair, was looking a bit more promising than most.

'Morning Frank,' she said brightly, 'Yes, big day ahead indeed. Get yourself a coffee and we'll go through what you've got on at the moment. Joy of joys, I've got my monthly meeting with the Chief Super to look forward to this afternoon and I need to get up to speed with what's occurring.'

DCI Jill Smart just about managed to suppress the groan. It had never been on her career plan to end up in this godforsaken department, in fact it would never be on anyone's career plan, but for Jill, it had been a convenient fast-track to the DCI rank that she had long coveted and deserved, and so she had gritted her teeth and accepted the post when Chief Superintendant Wilkes had offered it. Not that she had much choice, but she was determined to make the best of it. Give it a year or so, make a reasonable fist of it, move swiftly on, that was the master plan.

The role of the department was fuzzy at best, but in essence it was the dumping ground for cases that couldn't quite find a home with more conventional investigating teams - cold cases, internal corruption enquiries, the early stages of suspected fraud and suchlike. It was also the dumping ground for detectives who had been chucked out of more conventional investigating teams, which is why Frank Stewart had ended up on the team.

He returned to her desk clutching a tepid white coffee from the ancient vending machine and a Mars Bar from the same source.

She grinned at him. 'Breakfast?'

'No, done that one already. Call this elevenses. I love a Mars Bar, you know that, can't beat them. You should try one sometime yourself. You're too skinny ma'am, no offence.'

'None taken.' He was always teasing her about her fanatical dedication to her daily gym sessions, she responding with interest about his terrible diet. She liked Frank, considering him one of the only jewels amongst the motley collection of losers, loners and has-beens that she had inherited with Department 12B. 'And by the way, it's nowhere near eleven o'clock by my watch. Anyway, can you just give me an update on what you've been working on.'

'Aye, well it's only really been that corruption enquiry down in Brixton, but it's going well, 'cos I'm pretty sure now that DS is on the take. You remember I said that I got some CCTV footage of him associating with known drug-dealers on his patch? So that caused me to mount a wee one-man surveillance operation, and a couple of days ago I got him on my iPhone just as a wee brown envelope was being handed over. He was wearing a hoodie and shades but my new best pal Eleanor says that's not going to be a problem because some new facial recognition software she's got a hold of will still nail him. A good capture, that's what she said my photograph is. Better than DNA, that's what wee Eleanor says.'

'Sorry Frank, who is this Eleanor of whom you speak so highly?'

'Haven't I mentioned her before ma'am?' He knew he hadn't. Frank had learnt to keep these things quiet, otherwise the other disreputable rejects who clogged up Department 12B would be muscling in, getting her to take a look at their half-arsed cases too. He wanted to keep this highly-valuable resource all to himself.

'Eleanor Campbell, she's fairly new to the Forensic lot. An automatic facial recognition specialist amongst other things. She's telling me that the technology around automatic facial recognition is just advancing so quickly, and soon every force in the country will need to have an expert on their team. The Met were one of the first to get one.'

'That's great Frank, and great timing for my meeting with the Chief Super.'

'Aye, well boss, I'm glad it's all worked out quite well. We can probably hand it over to the regular anti-corruption squad next week.'

Since that had gone quite well, he decided to strike whilst the iron was hot.

'So boss, there's a new one come to my attention that might be worth a look. I need to declare an interest, it's come to me from my wee brother Jimmy, but nonetheless I think it might be our sort of case. And before you say anything, I know our investigations are supposed to come by referral from other departments, but well, this one's a wee bit different... anyway, see what you think.'

He showed her the photograph on his phone and explained who was present at the dinner. Jill seemed intrigued.

'And you think this might be connected to the Alzahrani case? But that's still a live enquiry, isn't it? The suspect is still at large.'

'Aye, more than a year now and still not a sniff of her ma'am. I expect she's fled the country by now. But this is actually to do with the trial itself, because that picture was taken just before it started and of course it might be nothing except *that* guy...' He pointed at the photograph. '...Adam Cameron, said in front of the judge, that he'd never met *that* guy, Dr Tariq Khan.'

Smart furled her brow. 'Ok I can see what you're getting at, but shouldn't this go straight to our Alzahrani team?'

He adopted his favoured sarcastic tone. 'What, you mean to the fat-arsed detecting genius that is DCI Colin Barker? Oh aye, I think that would work.'

She laughed. 'Oh yes, I'd forgotten, he was the DCI that you punched, wasn't he?'

'All in the line of duty ma'am. He was and still is a complete moron and had it coming to him. The way I look at it, it was sorely needed to raise the morale of the rank-and-file. I took one for the team, that's all.'

And there was quite a few of his peers and senior officers too that rejoiced in the obnoxious Barker getting his face smashed in. In actual fact, it was only that unspoken support amongst the senior ranks that had prevented Frank Stewart being sacked on the spot. Instead, he was ordered to take three months' sick leave due to 'stress', his HR file was quietly marked as 'unsuitable for a leadership role', and then he was shunted off to Atlee House.

'And he got his reward by being given the Hampstead bombing investigation. Completely typical of the Met, promoted to your level of incompetence. Present company excepted ma'am,' he added hurriedly. 'So I know it obviously will have to go to Barker eventually, but I'd like to do a few hours on it first, follow up a couple of hunches, and see where they lead. I think this might be a good one for the department ma'am.' *And for you and your career too, might even hasten your escape.* He knew how to push her buttons.

She smiled. 'Well ok Frank, you can give it a few hours but I don't want to open up a new case at this point.'

'Too much paperwork, eh ma'am?'

'Exactly Frank, the bane of my life. So just try and lose the hours somewhere, will you?'

'Yes ma'am, will do.'

He found Eleanor Campbell skulking in the semi-dark just behind the coffee machine, her phone wedged between ear and shoulder, a flimsy plastic cup of indeterminate pale brown liquid in each hand.

'Lloyd, frig's sake Lloyd...Lloyd, look I've told you about a thousand times...No Lloyd, you must be frigging joking...Look Lloyd, you know I can't discuss this now...'? The conversation had evidently ended abruptly, as she let out a loud four-letter explicative before placing the cups on the ground to enable her to retrieve her phone.

'Problems?' He hoped he had succeeded in making it sound diplomatic.

She held up her hands in an apologetic gesture.

'That was Lloyd. He's my sort-of boyfriend.'

Frank decided to take the matter no further, although there was a tinge of disappointment about the discovery of this sort-of man in her life. He didn't know why that should be, other than the fact that he had of late developed a soft spot for the kooky forensic scientist. Not in any sort of romantic way, definitely not, but then to his dismay he realised what it was. *Fatherly concern.* Not good, since he doubted if he was much more than ten years her elder.

'Lloyd eh? Aye well, I hope it all works out,' was the best he could come up with. 'Anyway Eleanor, I've got this report that's come into my possession which is right in your field. Guy called Dr Tariq Khan wrote it, you might have heard of him?'

'Yes, I have. He like spoke at a symposium I was at a few months ago. Smart dude.'

'Oh good. So I was wondering, could you take a look at the report, and let me know what you think about it? Just a general opinion will do, I don't need too much detail at this stage. I'll email it to you when I get back to my desk.'

'Sure Frank. Do you have a case number I can book my time to?'

He laughed. 'Bloody bureaucracy. I forgot you guys can't even wipe your backsides without a case number.'

'Not allowed Frank, the boss goes like mental.'

'All right I'll get you it, it's on my phone. It shouldn't need more than a few hours of your time I wouldn't think.'

Lose the hours somewhere, that's what Jill Smart had said. That wasn't going to be a problem.

'Here it is Eleanor, M-P-4-7-3-9-4'. He figured the Alzahrani case could absorb a few more hours, after all they had already spent over a million quid and still not a sniff of her since she vanished into thin air. Not that it was a great surprise with an idiot like Colin Barker in charge.

'Ok thanks Frank, I should be able to take a look at it later today,' she replied, as they wandered back to the office.

It wasn't just the back room teams who were under the thumb of the bureaucrats and bean-counters. It had extended to the front-line officers too, under the catch-all banner of 'safeguarding.' So as he booted up the ancient mainframe user interface of the Police National Computer system, Frank too was obliged to enter a case number before beginning his search. No problem, it would be a pleasure to stick a few more hours on Barker's budget. This was one thing Maggie and Jimmy couldn't do, looking into citizens' criminal records. And there was another thing they couldn't do either. More recently, and unbeknown to most of the population, the police had gained access to certain MI5 databases, so that intelligence on 'persons of interest' could be shared between the police and the spooks. Most of the persons on these databases had committed no crime, and their very existence occupied a murky legal no-man's-land between protecting the public from harm and protecting their civil liberties. Especially now since version two-point-naught of that software included facial recognition search. It wasn't just the *Guardian* that would go mental if that ever got out into the open.

But unfortunately, Frank couldn't get access either, not at this point in time at least. It was good that Britain still paid some regard to civil liberties and human rights and all that stuff, of course he agreed that, but it could really slow things down when you were working on an investigation. To get access to the MI5 databases, you needed the say-so of a senior officer, DCI rank as a minimum, and they had to get an official form signed by their boss too. Fair enough, but it really was a pain in the bum. Especially in this case, since it was public knowledge that Gerrard Saddleworth had a history of student activism. It was odds-on therefore that he would have come to the attention of MI5 at some point in the past, so that would be worth looking at. And senior GCHQ staff like Khan were given an MI5 file as a matter of routine, even if there was nothing of interest to put in it. But no matter, he would ask Jill later and maybe she would take a quick look for him, off the record.

The PNC was a reasonable place to start in the meantime. After eighteen years in the force, Frank knew that success in a case came from putting in the hours, slogging through reams of forensic data, trying to make sense of conflicting witness statements, looking for that little overlooked nugget of information that tied it all together. That was his experience, and he had no reason to expect this one to be any different. Which is why it was all the more surprising that just twenty minutes after he had sat down in front of his computer, he was feeling like he'd just bagged a hole-in-one at St Andrews in the Open.

He had started with Gerrard Saddleworth and Penelope White, but had drawn a blank. Squeaky-clean records as far as the police were concerned. He wasn't too worried about that, because the juicy stuff on Saddleworth, if there was any, would most likely turn up on the wee MI5 database.

But then five minutes into his search came the remarkable discovery that Dr Tariq Khan had a criminal record, and one serious enough that he would surely go to extraordinary lengths to keep it buried deep in the past. This was a hell of a lot more serious than a parking ticket. No, it was absolute dynamite.

Then just a few minutes later, bang, another one. Unbelievably, Adam Cameron had a drugs bust. Thirty-odd years ago, when he was up at Oxford. Just a caution for possession, but he had been damn lucky it hadn't derailed his career. Not something to boast about in his profession.

And then he had got the call from Eleanor, with her initial verdict on the Khan report. She sounded hesitant.

'Frank, I've had like a couple of read-throughs and I have to admit I don't quite know what to make of it.'

'What do you mean?'

'Well, I need to qualify this you'll understand, because he's one experienced dude and I've not got half the knowledge that he's got, but well, it's like a bit weird. What I mean is the conclusion and summary is black and white, he says that there's an eighty-six percent chance that the identification by that dashcam is wrong. That's as close to a hundred percent certain as you can be in scientific terms.'

'So what's the problem?'

'It's the workings. I mean the scientific evidence he uses earlier in the report to reach his conclusion. You see, to me, and as I said, I'm nowheres-ville compared to him, but to me, it doesn't stack up. Without getting technical or anything...'

'Aye, please don't,' he grimaced, 'or I'll get lost.'

'Don't worry, I'll keep it simple - well simple-ish. So facial recognition systems work by recording the geometry of the face, how far apart your eyes are, the distance between the tip of your nose and your mouth, that sort of thing. These are called facial landmarks, and the technology uses around seventy of them. These are unique to each face and once you have them it's actually simples-ville to do matching searches on a database. Too simple, some might say, but that's another story. The other thing is, and this is either like really scary or really powerful depending on which way you look at it, you don't need all the seventy landmarks to be able to do an accurate match. And Frank, it's this feature that your case depends on, isn't it? The terrorist's face was partially covered by sunglasses and a headscarf, but the photograph captured enough of these landmarks to allow a match. That's how she was caught, I think.'

'Ok.' He spoke slowly. 'I think I understand this. Carry on.'

'Right, so what the Khan dude is saying in simple terms is that the plumber's dashcam photograph didn't capture enough facial landmarks to allow a reliable match. He dresses it up in some highly technical words that I don't understand, but that's the essence of it.'

'But I'm getting the sense that you don't agree.'

'Correct, I don't. I haven't seen the actual photograph, but I would have thought that there would definitely have been enough landmarks recorded for a positive identification. In fact I'm sure of it.'

'So you're saying that Dr Khan's conclusions might not be correct?'

'Just my opinion as I say, but yes. And remember, he's probably forgotten more about the subject than I'll ever learn, so you know, I might be like way off the mark here.'

'Yeah point taken Eleanor,' Frank said, 'and I'm obviously not going to hold you to it or anything, don't you worry about that. But it's very interesting, although I'm not sure if I have a clue right now what it means. But yes, thanks again for your efforts.'

'Any time Frank, and I hope it helps.'

So not a bad morning's work, all in all. Two of the persons of interest with something to hide, and a technical report that might not be all it seemed. What it all meant, he had no idea at the moment, but this was the way you worked the early stages of an investigation like this. Dig out some interesting facts and gradually start piecing them all together until a pattern emerges. Do the leg work, put in the hard graft and you'll get results. Time now to smooth-talk Jill Smart in to opening up that MI5 database.

Chapter 14

It was over twelve hours since Maggie had received the irritating phone call from Frank. Some extremely interesting facts had emerged that warranted further investigation, that was the tantalising message. *Extremely* interesting, he had said, not *quite* interesting or just merely interesting. She had pressed him for more, but he said it was too complicated to discuss on the phone. So for further details, she would have to wait until she and Jimmy met up with him later that evening. The truth was, she had been in turmoil since that photograph had turned up, and the wait was only going to add to the agony. Because now there was something tangible, something that might help her answer the question that had haunted her every moment, waking or sleeping, since the end of the trial. Who was it that had lied about the point in time when she had received Khan's report?

Further contemplation of the situation would have to wait however, because today was an important day. The most important in her life for over a year. Because today was Ollie's seventh birthday, and Philip had grudgingly agreed that she could see him for one hour. Just one hour. It wasn't nearly enough, nothing like it, but right now her ex-husband held all the cards and she had no option but to go along with it. Her mum was coming too, and would soon be arriving at King's Cross. *Damn*. She glanced at her watch and realised that she was already too late to meet her at the station. The news from Frank and the gut-wrenching anticipation of the day ahead had knocked her for six and she had already lost all sense of time. But maybe Jimmy could help. Was it a bit cheeky to ask?

He answered his phone after just one ring.

'Hi Jimmy, it's me.'

'Aye, I know, it says 'mad woman' on my phone.' He seemed to have detected the agitation in her voice. *'Are you ok?'*

'Where are you at the moment?'

'I'm just walking down from St Pancras now. About half way down Judd Street.'

'Jimmy, I don't really like to ask, but I've really screwed up my timings this morning. Would you mind awfully going back to King's Cross and meeting my mum off the Leeds train and directing her to the Victoria Line? We're seeing Ollie at the McDonalds in Oxford Circus at twelve and there's no way I can get to the station to pick up mum without making us all horrendously late. What if I tell her to stand outside WH Smiths and wait for you to call her? I'll tell her to look out for a tall dark stranger that some people might call handsome.'

He laughed. '*Ha ha, visually challenged people do you mean? Consider it done.*'

'I can't thank you enough Jimmy, you've saved my life.' *Again*, she thought. She changed the subject. 'So what do you think about all that stuff that Frank found out yesterday? I assume he called you too?'

'*Aye, I spoke to him last night. It is crazy, right enough, I don't really know what to make of it. We're meeting up at his pub tonight aren't we? Anyway, I'll drop you a message once I've chucked your mother onto the tube.*'

Maggie reached Oxford Circus with fifteen minutes to spare and made her way to McDonalds where she was pleased to see her mother was already waiting. They hugged warmly, drawing strength for the momentous hour that lay ahead.

'Mum, I'm so sorry I didn't make it to the station,' Maggie said. 'I just lost all track of time.'

'Darling, I'm only sixty-six years old and perfectly capable of navigating my way across London. But it was very nice to meet your Jimmy, he's lovely and ridiculously good-looking, I must say. Yes, I'm not too old to notice.'

'He's not my Jimmy mum,' Maggie laughed.

'Well, he should be, if I'm any judge.'

'And how's dad?'

'About the same. He gets very confused still but he is perfectly happy as far as I can tell. And he asked me to take plenty of pictures of Ollie, so he does remember some things, thank goodness.'

'That's nice.'

They fell into silence, nerves jangling with excitement but some apprehension too. It was over two months since Maggie had last been with her son. Social services had quite rationally ruled that she couldn't be trusted, so it was entirely down to Philip when she could see him if at all. He used it like a nuclear weapon, inflicting unimaginable agony that with every second of separation burned a searing pain into her heart. Her recurring nightmare was that Ollie had already forgotten her, warm and secure in the care of the dazzling Angelique Perez. She knew that her mum was suffering too, the grandparents as so often being the forgotten collateral damage in a marriage breakdown. It was completely understandable therefore that despite Asvina's strict advice to the contrary, she was still driving to Ollie's school once or twice a week to catch a fleeting glimpse of her son, however brief, but that only succeeded in making the pain so much harder to bear. Today she just wanted to hold him in her arms and never let him go, ever, but she knew that could not be. But it wasn't long now until the custody hearing, when surely no court would decide that a child should be separated from his mother. That was the only thing that mattered and she had to stay strong.

At ten past one they still had not arrived, her mum fussing that they had got the arrangements wrong and should have been at another restaurant. But Maggie knew differently. This was just another of Philip's little power games, designed to cause maximum suffering. Right from the start, she knew that she had made a mistake in marrying him, but she had been nearly thirty-five and single and obsessively conscious of her biological clock ticking ever faster. Like a fool, she had gone ahead with the marriage, believing that she could grow to love him, like some ill-fated heroine of a Victorian novel. But she had grown to hate him instead. And now she found herself inextricably linked to him through her adored son.

Her mum was pointing to the door. 'Here they are at last.' There was Philip, with Ollie. And with them, unexpected and uninvited, Angelique Perez, holding Ollie's hand. They were laughing, sharing some private joke, a scene no doubt orchestrated by her ex-husband to maximise the pain. *Pig*. And now Maggie was struggling to hold it together.

Her eyes welled up. 'What is she doing here mum? What the hell is she doing here?'

Her mother gripped her arm. 'Let it go dear, just go to Ollie.' He had caught sight of her and was snatching his hand free from Angelique's and running towards her.

'Mummy, mummy. My mummy.'

Maggie scooped him up in her arms and hugged him tight to her breast, as tight as she dared. It was going to be alright.

'My darling, my darling.'

A muffled voice came from the folds of her arms. 'Ugh, you're squeezing me mummy.'

She released him, planting a gentle kiss on his head. They started to laugh, quietly at first, then a bit louder, and soon so uproariously that everyone in the restaurant suspended their refuelling to look. It was going to be alright.

'You've got one hour,' Philip said coldly. 'We'll be back then and don't try anything stupid. Come on Angelique.'

It was awkward at first, of course, because so much of the easy babble of family conversation depends on the quiet routine of normal life, a life which cruelly they no longer shared. But the laughter had helped, and there was 'happy birthday' to be sung, candles to be blown out and piles of presents to be opened, brought in four garishly-decorated gift bags. 'Star Wars Lego!' Ollie shouted as he tore the wrapper off a particularly large package, 'and a new football! Thank you mummy, thank you nana!'

They laughed when he squeezed his Big Mac too tightly and a jet of ketchup shot out and splattered down his new clean t-shirt, they laughed when he let out a huge burp, and of course they laughed at his terrible seven-year old's jokes, fresh to him but fondly remembered from Maggie's own schooldays. For an hour, it was as if the last eighteen months had been a sick dream from which they had now thankfully awoken, but then all too soon it was over. Philip was back, alone this time, tapping his watch theatrically. Just fifty-four minutes had elapsed, exactly what Maggie had expected.

'Right, that's it, time's up. Ollie, come to me please.'

Ollie began to cry. 'No, I don't want to. I want to stay with my mummy.'

Maggie cuddled him close. 'Darling, we've had a lovely time but you know what we said. You need to go with daddy just now. It won't be long until I see you again and we will have another lovely time, won't we? Now go and give your nana a big kiss and a hug. I love you darling.'

He struggled to dry his eyes on the sleeve of his sweatshirt. 'I love you too mummy.'

He kissed his grandmother on the cheek then shuffled over to where his father stood. However, it seemed that Philip was not yet ready to leave. 'Ollie, go back and sit over there with your nana and play with your new toys,' he said sharply. 'I need to talk to mummy for a few minutes.'

Maggie noticed he was carrying a buff A4 envelope.

'You need to see these I think.'

He extracted a sheaf of large photographs and spread them across the table. The scene they depicted was unmistakeable.

'You pig, you complete pig.' And then, comprehension. 'You've had someone following me. I can't believe that.'

'Your own fault Maggie, nobody else's. Skulking around outside a primary school with a camera and binoculars, that's just pathetic. Anyway, I just want you to know that this morning I've raised an injunction at the High Court to prevent you going anywhere near Ollie's school again, or anywhere else where Ollie might go. I've taken advice, not that I need it, and I fully expect it to be granted tomorrow. Of course, that's you up shit creek as far as access is concerned. I mean you can still go ahead with the hearing if you want, but you've got two-thirds of bugger-all chance of it being granted now.'

She struggled to make sense of what he was telling her. 'You can't do that Philip. It's too cruel, even for you.'

He looked at her with contempt.

'I can do what the hell I like and you can't do anything to stop it.'

A fierce anger swelled up inside her, fired by the utter injustice of her situation. It wasn't fair that he could keep her from seeing her own son, and she wasn't going to just lie down and let him walk all over her. Not now that she knew all about that Cathedral Close dinner. She didn't know what that was all about but she was bloody well going to get to the bottom of it if it was the last thing she did. Red-faced, she walked over and violently pushed him in the chest with her outstretched palms. Taken by surprise, he was toppled over by the force of it, ending up prostrate on the floor, face upwards. An instant later, she was straddling him, her face inches away from his, her forearm locked across his throat.

'You listen to me you pig. Don't you ever threaten me again, do you understand?' Reaching in her back pocket, she took out her phone and pushed the photograph into his face.

'You see Philip, I know all about your scheming. I don't know what it's all about but believe me I'm going to find out and when I do, you'll be sorry. I'll make damn sure of it.'

An excited crowd had gathered round, led by the manager of the restaurant in his striped green shirt and 'here to help' badge. Maggie bounded to her feet, running her hands through her hair and smoothing down her t-shirt.

'Nothing to get worried about here.' She shot a sweet smile in the direction of the manager. 'My husband and I were just having a bit of a domestic. We do this all the time. Very therapeutic. Come on darling, get up.'

The manager looked at her uncertainly. The last thing he wanted was to have to call the police, with all the hassle and disruption that would bring. 'Well, if you are sure...'

'Yes, we're quite sure, aren't we darling? Come on, up you get.'

It took several seconds for him to struggle back to his feet, like a boxer trying to beat the count. He looked rattled but his voice spat defiance.

'I don't know where you got that photograph, but you really are a stupid woman Maggie, imagining all sorts of drama and conspiracy when there's really nothing there at all. It was just an innocent dinner between friends and colleagues, nothing more.'

'I don't believe you.'

'Well that's up to you. But what really puzzles me is the obvious thing that you and your genius Scotsman haven't worked out yet.'

She looked him straight in the eye. 'What thing?'

'You mean you don't know?'

'What thing?'

She could feel the anger and loathing burning her up. How could she have ever loved this man? All through their relationship he had revelled in his ability to wound her, exploiting her weak spots like a mediaeval swordsman finding gaps in the armour, and now she could spot the signs of another attack.

'How a useless barrister like you got to defend Alzahrani in the first place. Forty-two years old, still not a Queens Counsel, and a variable record at trial to put it mildly. Just saying.'

He snatched his son's hand and with a terse 'Come on Ollie, we're going now,' swept out of the restaurant.

What did he mean by that? Nigel Redmond, the Clerk at Drake Chambers, had been straight with her when the brief came her way. Normally one for a QC, this one, that was what he said. She remembered how her initial reaction was utter astonishment and disbelief, that it must be a mistake and that he had meant it to go to one of the more illustrious members of their chambers. But no, he had confirmed that the CPS were happy for her to defend the case. He offered no further explanation and she did not ask for any, accepting it as a gift of fate, a wonderful gift that she meant to take full advantage of. But now the nagging doubts she had at the time began to resurface. Did Philip know something that she didn't? But forget all of that for now. Because there was no doubt about the look on his face when she had showed him the photograph. He had been scared shitless, not to put too fine a point on it.

She shouldn't have shown him it, she knew that the second she had done it, but it was done now and shortly, she assumed, a huge dollop of dung was going to hit a bloody great spinning fan.

Chapter 15

The phone calls and messages started within seconds of him leaving the fast-food restaurant, setting off a wave of panic, anger, recrimination and fear. For the first time for many of them came the stomach-churning realisation that because of that damn dinner, careers might be ruined and lives trashed. But who would succumb meekly to the inevitability of being unmasked, and who was prepared to fight to the death, that was the question. And who could be trusted to keep their mouth shut?

Meanwhile, in an exclusive gentlemen's club on Pall Mall, the distinguished member relaxed in a comfortable leather armchair, sipping on a fine malt and coolly contemplating how to react to this interesting news. There had always been a risk of it getting out and it was as well he had made plans to deal with the eventuality. A bit of a shame of course, much better if they could have kept it under wraps, but he had no doubt his associates would do a tidy job and nothing would connect it back to him.

It needed only a simple encrypted text and the operation was up and running. *Plan B*. Signalling the waiter to fetch him another whisky, he gave a wry smile and returned to his copy of the Guardian.

Chapter 16

'What are you drinking Maggie?' They were back in Frank's surrogate office at the Old King's Head, quieter on an early Wednesday evening than on their last visit but still buzzing.

'I'll just have a lime and soda please,' Maggie shouted over the hubbub, 'it's my new regime, I mean, have you seen the size of my bum right now?'

Just in time, Frank remembered the two-day 'ethics at work' training course he had been recently forced to attend. Generally, he had thought it was a load of bollocks, but even he could see that the first response that had come into his head - 'actually Maggie, you've got a lovely arse' - was probably inappropriate, if unarguably true. This evening he was in high spirits because the sainted DCI Jill Smart had quietly and efficiently worked the system to gain permission to access the precious MI5 database, and what she had discovered from no more than a cursory search was absolute pure gold.

'And I'm going to start running again. Jimmy said he would be my personal trainer. He said I should start with just half a mile but I'm aiming to do a 5k.'

'Aye, well rather you than me.'

'You should try it,' Jimmy said. 'You look like you're carrying a bit of timber at the moment.'

'Bugger off.'

'Boys, boys,' Maggie said, smiling. 'Anyway, I bet your days weren't as interesting as mine. Wait to you hear this.' And then she launched into a colourful dramatisation of the earlier events in the fast-food restaurant.

'...so in the end I just lost it you see. Went completely mental. You should have seen his face afterwards though. It was priceless.'

'Interesting day right enough,' Frank said, draining his pint.

'Good for you,' Jimmy laughed. 'That arse had it coming to him. I wish I'd been there.'

'Aye, but I wish you hadn't shown him the photo,' Frank said, more seriously. 'I did say not to, didn't I?'

'Yes, I know Frank, I'm sorry, but I was just so bloody angry.'

'Aye, well I can understand that. It's done now.'

'Yes, look I knew you might not be too pleased, but it just sort of happened.'

'I'm not really angry Maggie, it just makes things a bit more difficult, that's all. Anyway, let me bring you up to speed with what I found out yesterday. You're going to love this, believe you me. But before that, I think another drink is called for. You still on the orange juice?'

Her resolve to go easy on the alcohol had lasted all of five minutes.

'Chardonnay please Frank. Large one if you don't mind.'

'Aye, no bother. Jimmy, your round I think.'

'What a cheek,' Jimmy protested, but he set off in the direction of the crowded bar nonetheless. It was nearly ten minutes before he returned.

Frank took his drink and raised the glass in silent appreciation. 'So, here's what happened. It's about three years ago, Cheltenham Spa railway station. It's about eight o' clock in the evening and one of the ticket office staff is just about to knock off for the night. Then he realises he's pretty desperate for a crap so heads along to the gents at the end of platform one. Pushes open the door of the first stall, which he assumes to be empty, and is surprised to find a bloke sitting on the bog with his pants around his ankles whilst a young lad kneels in front of him giving him a nice wee blow job. Taken by surprise, the lad jumps up, barges past the railway guy and disappears off into the night. The ticket officer is of upstanding morals and so calls the police, who arrive five minutes later and arrest Dr Tariq Khan under the Sexual Offence Act 2003, which has a lot to say specifically about acts of indecency in a public convenience. Under questioning the ticket guy, who's a racist bastard, says he's pretty sure that the lad pleasuring the good doctor couldn't have been more than thirteen or fourteen. Suddenly it's all got a lot more serious, and Khan is in deep shit. Sex with a minor, I mean, that's a life sentence potentially. Not to mention the shame in his community.'

'Bloody hell,' Maggie said.

'Aye, exactly, bloody hell. But it turns out that Dr Khan is working on some very important stuff for the government, top security, very hush-hush and it's not really the kind of work he could do from a cell in Belmarsh Prison. Furthermore, the police aren't able to find the youth, and the station's CCTV footage which caught both his arrival and his escape, is inconclusive with regard to his age. Naturally he's wearing a hoodie, so he could be fourteen, he could be twenty-four, it's impossible to tell. What's more, Khan says it had been purely a commercial transaction, arranged over some dodgy gay encounters website. Cost him fifty quid apparently.'

'Rent boys in leafy Cheltenham?' Maggie smiled. 'Who would have thought it?'

'Yes I know. But anyway, it's not long until there are a few discreet phone calls, quiet words in the ears of some of the CPS bigwigs, a rubber-stamp from the Home Office and suddenly it's all conveniently swept under the carpet. Khan gets away with a caution and two weeks later he's back at work as if nothing's happened.'

'He must be pretty good at his job then,' Jimmy said.

'Yeah, I think we can assume that's the case. He manages to avoid an entry on the Sex Offenders Register too. Of course, he's now got an MI5 file as thick as a telephone directory but only a wee caution on the criminal records system.'

He took a large swig of his pint then emitted a loud burp.

'Ah, that's better.'

'Pure class,' laughed his brother.

'Anyway, this brings us neatly on to that report of his. I think I might have told you about Eleanor Campbell, that wee girl that's been helping us with my bent copper enquiry? She knows a bit about facial recognition herself and not surprisingly, she also knows all about Dr Khan and his reputation too. I ask her to take a look at the report, and about an hour later she's on the phone, bamboozling me with techno-speak about how this AFR works - that's what we experts call it, by the way, automatic facial recognition to you lesser mortals. You probably don't know this, but it's all about facial landmarks and geometry and stuff like that.'

'Stuff like that,' Jimmy said, grinning. 'Stuff like what, exactly?'

'Eh, how big your eyes are, the size of your nose, that kind of stuff.'

'Oh yes, that's very clear.'

'Shut up will you? Anyroads the thing is, whilst the report undoubtedly dishes the dirt on the evidence that Professor Walker produced in court, Eleanor thinks the actual science behind Khan's conclusion is a bit suspect. As if he was trying to make the facts fit the conclusion that he wanted. Which is damned annoying, because it's all the wrong way round if it's going to fit in with a half-arsed theory I've got spinning around my head.'

Jimmy frowned. 'So?...I don't think I get this at all.'

'I don't get it either,' Maggie said. 'It's just.. well, weird.'

'No I didn't at first either,' Frank said, 'but just an hour ago I learned something from my boss Jill Smart that perhaps made some sense of it. Well I think so at least. Or maybe not, I'm not sure.'

'Come on then, tell us,' Jimmy said.

'Patience Jimmy, patience. Before we start, I sense we are in need of further refreshment. Toddle off to the bar will you, and refresh our glasses, there's a good lad.'

'I got the last one, you cheeky bugger.'

Frank looked at him deadpan. 'Aye but this information I'm about to share with you is worth it. At least two drinks' worth, if not three.'

Maggie laughed. 'Now then boys, don't make me tell you again. Actually, I think it's my shout. Same again?' They nodded in unison as she left for the bar.

Frank glanced over his shoulder to make sure she was out of earshot. 'She's nice Jimmy, is she not?'

'What, fancy her do you?'

'Who wouldn't brother, who wouldn't? But do you fancy her, that's what I want to know'

'Think I'd tell you if I did pal? No chance. But what's this all about then? You suddenly fallen in love or something?'

Before he could answer, Maggie returned with the tray of drinks. They fell into an awkward silence.

'What's going on here?' She laid the tray down on the table.

'Nothing, nothing.' It wasn't exactly convincing.

Frank raised his glass. 'Cheers Maggie. So, let me tell you what I found out from my boss just a wee while ago. She's brilliant Jill Smart, so she is.'

'Fancy her too, do you?' Jimmy said.

Frank glared at him. Jill was nice but he wasn't going to give his bloody brother any more ammunition to work with. 'No, being serious for once. As I said, Jill's brilliant and it only took her about an hour to get the green light from her boss to look at the MI5 database...'

'Which database is that?' Jimmy said.

'You don't want to know brother, believe me. You don't even want to know that it exists at all. Which in fact it doesn't, officially, if you know what I'm saying. Anyway, if you don't mind me continuing...'

'Please do.'

'So Jill's rooting around the database looking for anything on our persons of interest. Naturally, she starts with our excellent Home Secretary, the Right Honourable Gerrard Saddleworth MP, and low and behold comes across a heavily-redacted MI5 file marked 'Top Secret'...'

Jimmy was unable to help himself. 'Ooh, top secret, so that means she couldn't look at it. That's a shame.'

'Will you shut the bleep up please, if you'll pardon my bleeping French. So it turns out that just six weeks before the start of the Alzahrani trial, Gerrard Saddleworth is in Moscow in a seemingly unofficial capacity, purpose unknown. Naturally, an MI6 agent on the ground over there is given a surveillance brief, that's standard procedure for something like this apparently.'

Maggie raised an eyebrow. 'You mean our security services are spying on our own government? And that's standard procedure?'

'As Frank said, standard procedure,' Jimmy said, 'I know this from my army days. These MI5 and MI6 guys are still mainly public school, Eton and Oxbridge all that, and they're still expecting to uncover reds under the beds, even thirty years after the fall of the iron curtain.'

'Exactly as Jimmy says. Anyway, for the first day or two, there's nothing much of interest, just a few meetings with some low-level government officials and the like. But then on the day that Saddleworth's due to return to London, he's whisked off early doors in a government limo to a dacha about thirty miles from the city. Naturally, he's tailed by our agent who on reaching the dacha, parks his car out of sight and settles himself down behind a convenient tree with a pair of high-powered binoculars and a camera fitted with a telescopic lens. Fifteen minutes later another black Mercedes turns up, and who should emerge but Miss Fadwa Ziadeh, who had not long before been anointed as leader of Hamas following the retirement or resignation, call it what you want, of her father Yasser.'

'Ziadeh?' Jimmy said. 'She's the woman who's coming here soon for that peace conference, isn't she?'

'Exactly. So Saddleworth and Ziadeh are in there for about an hour or so, topic of conversation unknown, then our agent snaps them leaving, exchanging a polite handshake on the porch. Saddleworth is then whisked off straight to the airport and returns to London that evening, where he attends the House of Commons to support some big three-line whip.'

'The thing I don't get is that Saddleworth's never been a big supporter of the Palestinian cause,' Maggie said. 'In fact, he's been pretty scathing about the Party's fixation on it over the years. Says it doesn't play well on the doorsteps in his constituency. So how come he suddenly becomes all matey-matey with Miss Ziadeh?'

'Well I don't know,' Jimmy said. 'Maybe it's not such big news that he's meeting with her. I guess it could be something to do with the peace conference that's coming up.'

'Well yes possibly, but why a secret meeting in Moscow? No, I don't think so. You see, I've got a theory - a crazy theory - which I think might explain why they were meeting and also might explain what was going on at that Cathedral Close dinner.'

Frank knew his idea was a bit left-field, but no matter how hard he tried, he just couldn't think what else it could be. With a bit more time and a bit more information, he might be able to come up with something better, but for now, this was the best he could do. But probably better to run it pass Maggie and Jimmy before making himself look a pure idiot in front of the professional cynic that was DCI Jill Smart. There was only one problem, a big problem that he would have to face up to in the next minute or so. It was absolutely certain that Maggie Bainbridge was not going to like what he had to say.

'All right then, tell us,' Jimmy asked for the second time that evening.

Frank inhaled deeply. 'Ok, what I think is... and I emphasize, it's only a half-cocked idea at this moment ...what I think is that this was all about making sure Dena Alzahrani definitely was found guilty. An insurance policy if you will.'

'Explain,' Maggie said, looking puzzled. 'I'm struggling a bit at the moment.'

'So, we've read a lot about how Fadwa Ziadeh seems to be wanting to take Hamas in a new direction. No more rockets being fired into the West Bank, no more suicide bombers on Jerusalem buses. She seems to be offering an olive branch to the Israelis in return for financial investment and greater self-determination for her people. But after decades of murder, or freedom fighting, depending on your viewpoint, the organisation is not trusted in the West and certainly not in Israel. Given this background, the last thing she needs is a notorious terrorist like Alzahrani getting off. No, she wants her found guilty and locked away for life so she can condemn her barbarous act publicly in the world's media and give full support for the punishment that's been dished out.'

'I think I see where you're going with this,' Jimmy said.

'Yeah, so what if Ziadeh arranges to meet with her old friend Saddleworth, and says Gerrard, what can you do to make sure the case is as tight as it can be? Saddleworth's not a fanatic but he's broadly sympathetic to the cause, so he agrees to help. When he gets back, he talks to Lady Rooke, big boss at the CPS, he talks to his old mate Philip Brooks. He says, guys, have you any ideas what we could do to make this happen?'

And now it was time to bring the elephant into the room.

'So perhaps somebody asks, who's in line to prosecute, and Rooke tells them that Adam Cameron's the favourite for the job. Who, by the way, also has a wee secret that he might want to keep well-buried. But anyway, he's a top man they say, with a brilliant track-record, never loses a case and everyone's happy with that. Thank god he's not defending then, someone laughs. And that puts an idea into their head.'

Frank paused for a moment, conscious that he had better choose his words carefully. But there was no way to sweeten the pill.

'It would be better, someone says, if we can steer the defence to someone well, a bit more plodding, a bit more average...'

He looked at her, seeing the anger in her expression as she began to understand.

'So they picked me. Because they thought I was rubbish.'

'Sorry Maggie, but I think that's maybe what happened.' His tone was sympathetic.

'It's not your fault Frank,' Maggie said. 'I've been a bit of a fool, haven't I?'

Jimmy placed his arm around her shoulders and held her close. 'No you haven't been a fool, not at all. And anyway, it didn't exactly work out well for them, did it? Backfired big time.'

Frank, unsure if he had done the right thing, swilled down his beer and stared into the distance, lost in thought. His theory made sense of course, except for two glaring facts that shot it out of the skies. Firstly, why would a government minister go all the way to Moscow just to say 'we're doing what we can to get her put away.' Why not just send a bloody text? And secondly, surely the smart thing would have been to get the world-renowned Dr Khan to shore up the facial recognition evidence, to make it absolutely bullet-proof in the eyes of the court. With his little past indiscretion he's not in any position to say no, so you would think he would write anything he was damn well told. But instead, his report blasted the expert witness's testimony out of the water. Why?

Yes, it was all the wrong way round, but he consoled himself by reflecting that you often found that in the early stages of a case. Two persons of interest with something to hide, government ministers attending secret meetings in Moscow and an expert's report that wasn't quite what it seemed. That was a decent haul so far. And not to forget a nice-but-average barrister cynically parachuted into a high-profile trial.

A barrister who shouldn't have shown her ex-husband that bloody photograph.

Chapter 17

Penelope skimmed through the opening paragraph one more time then gave a faint smile of satisfaction. Yep, that read just right, powerful but succinct and to the point. It had to be of course otherwise Clark would ask for a rewrite or even do it himself and she hated when he did that, not that he dared do it very often.

It was a relief to be able to bury herself in work after the unsettling events of the last couple of days. She had never trusted Philip Brooks, a slimy snake of a guy if there ever was one. God, she couldn't stand the man. She had only gone to the bloody dinner because Gerrard had arranged for them to have a yummy overnight stay in a nice Cotswolds country house hotel nearby. A little bit of business, and then it's all pleasure, that's how he had described it. She was happy to go along with it on that basis, and it couldn't be denied that it had been an interesting evening. It was meant to be a celebration of some deal or other that Brooks and Gerrard had concocted, although that guy Khan hadn't seemed in a joyful mood. Which wasn't a surprise once she found out what it had been all about.

Now Brooks was in a funk, on the phone about a dozen times urging her to keep quiet about everything that was said, wittering that if it got out it would ruin everything and there would be what he called 'consequences'. Ruin everything? What was there to ruin? Stupid little man.

Forget that, it was time to get on with her work. The first few lines read pretty well, she thought. *Barely eighteen months ago, on a cold and wet night in Belfast, Captain James Stewart sent twenty-two-year-old Sergeant Naomi Harris to her certain death. Despite an army cover-up, this paper exposed the truth, and now her parents are demanding justice. They deserve no less.*

She uploaded the document to her email and clicked 'send'. Now the paper's lawyers would review the article and if it passed muster, Clark would concoct a suitably lurid headline and they would be ready to go. Barring the emergence of any particularly big stories in the next day or two, it would make the front page of Saturday's edition, with a two or three-page spread across the inner pages too. Just how she liked it.

It was her high public profile that had caused the grieving Dawn and

Peter Harris to contact the paper in the first place, and she had met with them a few times over the last few weeks as she pieced together the story. Nice enough couple she thought, but a bit stupid. It was tragic what had happened to their daughter of course, but what had they expected when she had decided to join the bloody army? That was besides the point because White knew a blockbuster story when she saw it. Dawn Harris was good-looking like her daughter, sexy even, appearing much younger than her forty-four years, and her husband Peter was dark, brooding and rugged like the hero of a Victorian novel. The photogenic couple were sure to capture the public's imagination, and leaving nothing to chance, the paper had already spent a small fortune on stylists and photographers to help them look their best. The Chronicle just loved a big campaign and what a campaign this was going to be. Rod Clark had already composed the launch headline and for once it met with Penelope's approval. Simple but powerful.

Today, the Chronicle calls for Captain James Stewart to face court-martial.

It had everything, this story. The beautiful victim, the distraught relatives, the flawed hero and his link to Maggie Brooks. Then there was Stewart's wronged wife Flora, a classically pretty Scottish redhead, and the stunning temptress Astrid Sorenson, the woman he had left her for. Sorenson's image alone on the front page was enough to sell another fifty thousand copies. Of course, she knew the army wasn't going to court-martial Captain Jimmy Stewart, not in a month of Sundays, but that didn't matter to Penelope. What was important was the story. This was one that would run and run, with endless angles and viewpoints. First, there would be the strident calls for the court martial. *Justice must be done and be seen to be done.* After a few weeks when it was clear that was not going to happen, there would be the attacks on the government and military establishment, with accusations of cover-ups and of ministers and the military brass closing ranks. Then, when the public was losing interest in all of that, they could focus back on the tragic but attractive parents, crestfallen, defeated and crushed. Yes, this was going to be some story, no doubt about it.

She heard the faint click of the key in the front door and then the quiet thud as it was closed.

'Gerrard? I wasn't expecting you this evening my darling.'

Darling Gerrard. Yes, he was her darling, but strictly in a part-time basis for her, if not for him. He was fun, good company and she very much enjoyed their love-making, but that was it. In truth, relations had been strained since she made it clear she had no intention of marrying him, for it was then he told her he was breaking it off and going back to his dull wife. Such a drama queen. But she didn't believe him, he didn't have the balls, and anyway he knew he couldn't resist her. And just to prove it here he was again, slinking back to her like a love-sick puppy.

'Gerrard?'

Still there was no answer from the hallway. Strange that.

'Gerrard darling, stop mucking about and come through. I want a kiss.'

Turning round, she caught only a passing glimpse of her assailant framed in the doorway. The figure, wearing the white protective suit, mask and gloves normally reserved for scene-of-crime officers, wordlessly raised the silencer-equipped handgun and with deadly efficiency despatched three rounds from close range. Blowing her head apart and splattering a torrent of blood all over the designer wallpaper of the stylish flat. Satisfied with his work, he retraced his steps back into the hallway and called the elevator. On the way in he had disabled the CCTV system through the simple expedient of taping over the lens, so was able to remove his protective garments unobserved, placing them in the small backpack which he had conveniently left just outside her door. A few seconds later, a subtle 'ping' announced the arrival of the lift, descending from an upper floor. He had factored into his thinking the possibility that the lift might be occupied, which would present an irritating but easily-resolved complication, but fortunately it was empty. Soon the lift glided to a halt on the ground floor and the assassin slipped out into the dark evening.

Back in Pall Mall, the distinguished member relaxed in his armchair with the Guardian, insouciantly awaiting the encrypted text that would confirm that the first task had been completed satisfactorily. Plan B, up and running.

Chapter 18

It hadn't been Maggie's overt intention to pry into Jimmy's private life, but once again she had been unable to sleep, consumed with anger about what Philip had done to her. She couldn't be sure, but it now seemed pretty likely that he was involved in some way in her getting the Alzahrani defence brief. We need a crap barrister, that's what they had said, and bloody Philip had suggested her. Such love and loyalty.

Giving up the struggle, she had risen at 5.30am, arriving in the office well before seven. As she sat at her desk drinking the customary mega-strong first coffee of the day, she found herself idly googling 'Astrid Sorenson'.

She was beautiful, there was no doubt about it. Tall and slim with a huge mane of blonde curls, piercing blue eyes and a look that radiated an intoxicating sexuality. She was older than Maggie had imagined she would be, going on thirty-five, which might be considered ancient for an up-and-coming pop star, but Astrid's genre was modern country, where a predominately adult audience lapped up syrupy tales of kids and family and home. It was a massive business, and though she had had some hits in Scandinavia before moving to London, it was only since relocating to Nashville that her career had gone stratospheric.

What's more, Frank Stewart's description of her as the Swedish princess, rather than being the mild insult she imagined it to be, actually turned out to be true. A minor royal admittedly, but nonetheless she seemed to be a favourite of the Swedish tabloids, her every move arousing intense interest and documented in graphic detail. And yes, there she was about four or five years ago dressed in army desert fatigues, in Iraq or Afghanistan on a morale-boosting visit to Swedish troops attached to the UN force. Was it then she had met up with the rugged and handsome Captain James Stewart, kicking off an unlikely and doomed relationship, a relationship that he seemed to now bitterly regret?

And then Maggie noticed the photograph. It was from The *Sun* showbiz pages about a year ago and had caught Astrid with Jimmy at some minor awards ceremony, she dazzling in a minimal gold lamé mini-dress and six-inch stilettos, he looking uncomfortable and self-conscious stuffed into formal evening wear. But it was the headline that stopped her in her tracks.

Astrid boyfriend is Hampstead Hero.

He had managed to keep that quiet. The army had never revealed the identity of the bomb squad officer involved in the incident for obvious reasons of security, but here it was for all to see in the Sun of all places. *Brave Captain saves six-year old Amelia.* The veracity of the revelation had neither been confirmed or denied by the army, who stuck to the usual bland statement that they did not publicly comment on operational matters for reasons of security. Whatever the truth of it, there must have been some intense hush-up activity behind the scenes, because as far as she could tell the paper nor any other media outlet for that matter hadn't mentioned it again.

She was interrupted by the soft vibration of her phone on the desk. Glancing at the screen, she saw it was Asvina again, calling for the fourth or fifth time since yesterday evening, no doubt to talk about Philip's injunction. She had a good idea what her friend was going to say, that it was really serious, and that Maggie would blow even the slim chance she had of having Ollie back in her life if she broke its terms. She knew all that, but really, what could they do to her that was worse than what she had already suffered? Better answer it this time, she thought.

'Hi Asvina,' she said, sighing, 'yes, I know, it's very serious and I promise to be a good girl.'

'*What? Oh, yes the injunction. Well I'm very glad to hear you're intending to behave for once, but that's not why I called.*'

'Oh? I'm sorry Asvina, I just assumed...'

'*No, what it was is there's been a development in the Saddleworth case. A big one, in fact. Olivia has just phoned to tell me.*'

'And...?'

'*According to her, Gerrard and Penelope White have split.*'

'What?'

'*Yes. Apparently it's all over and he wants to go back to Olivia and try again.*'

Maggie was shocked. 'So does that mean she's calling off the divorce?' Putting her and Jimmy out of work at the same time.

Asvina had read her mind. '*Don't worry, she's not having him back under any circumstances. She actually sounded quite upbeat when she told me about it. Gerrard told her he was in big trouble and was almost pleading for her help. She said it had been a great pleasure to tell him to sod off. Her words, not mine.'*

Big trouble. So the pressure was getting to them, just as Frank said it would.

'Well this is unexpected Asvina, but as far as Saddleworth verses Saddleworth is concerned, I guess we still need to track down that money. We'll keep trying as hard as we can, obviously.'

'Glad to hear it,' she laughed. *'Well best of luck with your investigations, and above all, please, please, please, don't break that injunction. I mean it, I really do. Bye now.'*

It was nearly nine before Jimmy arrived at the office. It had become his routine to enjoy several minutes of flirtation with Elsa in the reception area before settling in behind his desk, but today he walked straight past her without a word, and his mood seemed sombre and downbeat.

'Morning Maggie, you ok?'

She was bursting to tell him the news. 'Yes, not bad. Well actually, I'm pretty good in fact. But you'll never guess what Asvina has just told me. Gerrard Saddleworth has chucked Penelope White.'

'What? You're kidding.'

'No, it's true.'

'That's bloody interesting, isn't it? You don't think this could this have anything to do with the Cathedral Close dinner?'

'More likely the Cathedral Close photograph. I'm thinking Saddleworth must be really spooked by it. But look, I've been awful, I didn't ask how you are.'

'Aye, well to be honest, I've been better. Actually, I wanted to talk to you about something, you being a proper lawyer and all that. I got this letter yesterday morning. From the bloody *Chronicle* of all people.'

He took the sheet from his pocket and handed it to her. 'Here, take a look.'

She unfolded it and began to read, growing more uneasy with each word. The letter, phrased in formal legalise, was forewarning him that the newspaper was about to run a story questioning his role in the Belfast bombing, that the paper was satisfied that everything it was about to publish was truthful and factual, but suggested that nonetheless he might wish to appoint a legal adviser to 'protect his interests,' as they put it.

'Jimmy, this is awful, it's nothing more than a witch-hunt. Obviously I can help with the legal side but... I don't think it will be possible to stop them printing this. It's ridiculous that they can do this, it really is. And I see this is one of Penelope White's. She really is a bitch.'

'I know it's not going to be good, Maggie. You know, I understand the pain that Naomi's parents must be feeling. And it was my fault, I should have stopped her.'

'It wasn't Jimmy,' she said. 'I'm sure it wasn't.'

'She was scared. It was her first operation, and I played down the danger when I should have scared her shitless. But she just opened the bloody door before I had a chance to stop her. I've asked myself a million times if I could have done anything different but I couldn't. She just opened that bloody door and stepped out.'

'She was young and inexperienced,' Maggie said. 'It was her mistake, not yours. You can't keep blaming yourself, it won't do anyone any good and it won't bring her back.'

He gave her a look steeped in regret. 'Aye maybe, but it doesn't make it any better.'

'You never told me it was you who was there on that awful day, at Ollie's school,' Maggie said, anxious to change the subject. 'When I read about what you did, it was just so unbelievably brave. You saved that little girl's life, it was incredible.'

He shook his head, a tight-lipped expression on his face. 'You found that bloody Sun story I suppose. It's not something I like to talk about, to be honest, not good memories. Because if you want to know the truth Maggie, I screwed up that day, good and proper, but it was an impossible situation... I mean, you always try for the best possible outcome, work out probabilities, but sometimes...' His voice tailed off, aware of how inadequate it all sounded.

'I don't expect you know this,' said Maggie quietly, 'but it was my niece that was trapped under that van.'

'I didn't know that. I'm really sorry. I heard she died...'

'She did, but what you did gave her a chance. Her father was with her when she passed, and that wouldn't have been possible if it hadn't been for you. It was important. For all of us.'

To her surprise she saw his eyes moistening. 'I'm sorry. I'm so sorry...'

In a moment she was standing behind his chair, wrapping her arms around him, her head nestling on his shoulder. Now it was her turn to be the comforter.

'Just let it all out,' she whispered, 'remember, that's what you told me. Just let it all out.' And there they remained, locked together in silent grief, united by tragedy and a deep pain that now seemed impossible to bear. Until unexpectedly, he turned and kissed her, softly, gently, his lips barely touching hers.

'Thank you. Thank you Maggie.'

And then the moment had passed, evaporating into the atmosphere as if it had never happened. But it had happened, and could not be easily undone.

Chapter 19

'I'm just going to go and talk to him, that's all. I've got to do something or I'll go crazy.'

It was early afternoon and Maggie and Jimmy had been forced to repair to the local Starbucks, the office's in-house machine having suffered a catastrophic failure on account of Elsa omitting to re-order sufficient, or indeed any, coffee beans. The incident of the previous afternoon had not been mentioned, but it was there, evidenced by an uncharacteristic awkwardness between them.

'Mad woman, that's what comes up on my phone when you call me.' Jimmy Stewart was smiling but his tone was serious, 'and believe me Maggie, that would be bloody mad, total madness. That's just my opinion of course.'

'But the pig set me up. Have you any idea how that feels, to be set up to be so humiliated by your own husband?'

She was beginning to realise that it wasn't the action itself that hurt the most, but the fact that his professional opinion of her advocacy skills had been so low. *We need a rubbish barrister so we thought of you.* That hurt.

'Ok Jimmy, so you think it's mad, and I'm sorry, but I'm going round there to have it out with him. The damn injunction only applies to Ollie, not to him, doesn't it?'

He gave a wry smile. 'I don't suppose anything I can say will make you change your mind?'

'No.'

He sighed. 'Ok then Maggie, if we must.'

'We? What's this we?'

'Aye well, there's no way I'm letting you do this on your own. Goodness knows what you might do. I seem to remember you punched him last time you met, if I'm not mistaken. In bloody McDonalds of all places.'

She smiled broadly. 'Pushed, not punched I think you'll find. I might smash his face in this time though.'

He shook his head. 'Yeah exactly, that's why I'm coming with you. But I still don't know what you are hoping to achieve.'

The offices of Philip Brooks LLP were located halfway up Gray's Inn Road, just ten minutes' walk from Starbucks' Fleet Street branch. Until the breakdown of her marriage she was a frequent visitor to the chambers, and she was pleased if a little surprised to see that Samantha Foster was still on reception duties. Philip was not the easiest man to work with and so his admin staff rarely stayed long, but Samantha was the exception. Maybe that was because until two years ago Samantha had been Samuel, and it wouldn't be a good look for the human rights champions to be on the end of a trans discrimination suit.

'Mrs Brooks, it's nice to see you again.' The greeting was spontaneous and genuine, although Maggie couldn't help notice the hint of surprise in her voice.

'Nice to see you too Samantha. This is my colleague Mr Stewart. We're here to see Philip. Is he in?'

'Yes, he is in, but you don't seem to have an appointment.' She narrowed her eyes as she scrutinising her computer screen, her manner suddenly guarded and suspicious, the initial bonhomie evaporating.

'We don't need one, we're family,' Jimmy said bluntly. 'C'mon Maggie.' He walked over to the glass-panelled double doors that led through to the main office, and pushed. They were locked.

'You need a pass for our access control system.' The tone was officious. 'You won't be able to get in without one.'

Jimmy walked slowly back to the reception area, placing his hands on the desk and leaning forwarded until his face was just six inches from Samantha's. It was meant to be intimidating and it succeeded in being so. 'So you'd better give us one then, hadn't you, my love?'

'I don't know, I'll need to check...'

'Give us one.' Now his voice was gangster-movie menacing, causing Maggie to let out an involuntary giggle.

Samantha's voice dropped an octave, betraying her provenance. 'All right, just give me a second.' She took a credit-card sized pass from a drawer and slotted it into the reader on her desk. 'There you go. All set.'

Maggie smiled sweetly. 'Thank you ever so much Samantha.' She touched the card against the proximity sensor mounted on the door frame, triggering a loud click as the lock was released and then a quiet whirring as the automatic doors slowly opened inwards. 'Follow me Jimmy, I know where I'm going.' Behind them, the receptionist was already on the phone, ringing ahead a warning.

'His office is just here on the left.' They entered a generously-proportioned wood-panelled office furnished somewhat incongruously with upscale chrome and glass furniture. It was empty, but only temporarily vacated if the piles of papers and half-empty coffee-cups, two of them, were any guide.

'Looking for me darling?' Philip's voice was cold and menacing as he stood in the doorway, 'and I see you've brought your trained gorilla with you. How quaint.'

Jimmy smirked and stared him straight in the eyes. 'Aye, and you best not forget that either. Gorillas can be dangerous.'

He gave a dismissive look. 'My god, you are the complete neanderthal, aren't you? Anyway, what do you want Maggie? I'm a busy man.'

'Philip, is that us finished...' Brooks had been joined at the door by a smartly dressed man of about his own age.

Maggie's eyes widened with surprise. 'Well well, if it's not Adam Cameron. Now fancy meeting you here.'

'Hello Maggie.' His expression was cold and suspicious.

'You look well Adam.' He didn't actually, but it was the kind of thing you said to someone you hadn't met in a while. His hair was greasy and unkempt and his nose red and bulbous from over-indulgence on the fine Merlot she knew was his penchant. 'Everything ok with you?'

'As if you would care, after what you did to me.' Evidently it was still irking him after nearly two years.

'What I did to you? I didn't do anything. And to be honest, I think you got off rather lightly. No deliberate attempt to mislead? Don't make me laugh.' She couldn't contain her bitterness.

'Look, can we cut the psychodrama,' Philip said coldly. 'What is it you want Maggie, I haven't got time for all of this.'

Cameron interrupted before she could reply, struggling to conceal his obvious anger. But it wasn't with her he was angry. It was with Philip.

'I'm going now, and you heard what I said. I need you to fix this, do you understand? It's frigging important. Fix it.' He picked up his coat and swept out without another word.

'Shitting himself about the photograph is he?' Jimmy said. 'I would be if I was in his position right enough.'

Brooks shook his head slowly, disdain written all over his face. 'Really, you are so out of your depth. Both of you.'

'Aye, you've said that before. Quaking in my boots mate.'

Brooks ignored him. 'Come on Maggie, I'm waiting. What is it you want?'

It was a perfectly reasonable question. But as she stood here in front of this man, her nemesis, the truth was plain to see. Because she didn't know what she wanted other than for some stupid fairy godmother to suddenly appear and wipe away the last two years with a swish of her magic wand. And that wasn't going to happen, was it? But she had to say something.

'Did you set me up for the Alzahrani trial? You did, didn't you?'

'I don't know what you're talking about.'

'The government. They wanted to make sure Alzahrani was convicted, so they thought they would get a rubbish barrister to defend her. It was all your idea, wasn't it? Push the brief out to Drake Chambers and let Nigel Redmond do the rest. That's what you meant that time in McDonald's.'

He gave a withering look. 'I've said it before, but you really are a stupid bitch, aren't you? I mean, what makes you think I've got that sort of influence? It was perfectly natural that the case should go to Drake. They have an excellent reputation, which makes it all the more puzzling that they would give it to a second-rate barrister like you. Why the hell that weasel Redmond did that is simply inexplicable. I assumed you must have been sleeping with him.'

Maggie struggled to keep her cool. 'I don't believe you for one minute. I know you were involved and I'm going to find out how. And then I'm going to make you pay for it. I don't know how and I don't know when, but I will.' It sounded like a bad line from a bad movie, she knew that, but it was all she could think of. Pitiable.

'Heard all of that before Maggie.' She could almost reach out and touch the malevolence in his voice. 'You really are so pathetic. Now if you're quite finished, I suggest you both leave.'

With a sudden lunge, Jimmy grabbed Brooks by the lapels and pushed him against the wall, his voice spitting anger. 'Oh no pal, we're not finished, far from it.' Brooks staggered back, stunned, before steadying himself against the tall book case. The look of fear on his face was unmistakeable, any thought of retaliation rapidly extinguished by the realisation that he stood no chance against the six-foot-two former soldier.

'What are you doing Jimmy?' Maggie's voice betrayed alarm.

'I came here to stop you doing anything stupid to this bastard. I didn't say I wasn't going to do something myself.'

Now he turned his attention to her cowering ex-husband. 'You think you are so bloody smart, don't you mate, but you don't frighten us, not one bit. We're on your case, and it's you that had better feel the fear. We're going to make sure all of this comes crashing down around you. And don't you bloody forget it. Come on Maggie, we're done with this arse.'

***

'That was bloody amazing, but bloody stupid too. You realise you could get me struck off.'

They were making their way back down Gray's Inn Road towards the office, Maggie a few paces behind, straining to keep up with Jimmy's adrenalin-fuelled stride.

'I thought you were already struck off?'

'Black-balled, actually, it's not quite the same thing.'

'Got it. But anyway, do you really think he's going to report us to the police? I don't think so. I looked him right in the eye in there, and behind all that bravado he looks scared out of his wits. No, he's not going to call the police.'

Maggie reached out and grabbed his arm, struggling to catch her breath. 'Will you slow down please? I've got something to show you.'

She began rummaging in her handbag. 'Here we go, take a look at this.'

He looked at her with an amused expression.

'You stole Philip's phone?'

'Just borrowed. It fell out of his pocket when you and him were having that little heated discussion. Anyway, what's so funny?'

Jimmy plunged his hand into his jacket pocket. 'Great minds think alike. Sneaked Cameron's out his coat when he was having that wee conversation with you.'

Chapter 20

The delegation had landed at Stanstead just after midnight aboard an elderly British Airways 757, generously paid for by the British taxpayer, although whether they would have approved of this use of their hard-earned money had they been asked was open to question. The Essex airport had been chosen because it was felt to be marginally easier to secure compared with Heathrow or Gatwick, but it still required a huge operation from the army and the police, involving more than three hundred personnel. The terminal had been cleared of all passengers at 6pm, operations being diverted to Luton, not exactly convenient for the thousands of travellers affected. The flight itself had been escorted all the way from Beirut-Rafic Hariri International Airport by a brace of RAF Typhoons, causing further outrage in the press about the considerable expense of the operation.

Now the fleet of armoured limousines was speeding through the deserted early morning streets, the flashing blue lights of the police escorts reflecting back from darkened bedroom windows, their occupants' sleep disturbed by the howls of the sirens as the motorcade raced past. Fadwa Ziadeh shared an affectionate smile with her teenage son who sat opposite, momentarily distracted from his game of *Call of Duty*. After all was said and done, it was all about family, and at last her family, her poor oppressed Palestinian people, ignored and marginalised for seventy years or more, despised even in the Arab world, were to be given a voice. A new era dawned, more outward-looking, more conciliatory, more civilised. What did she care about the hard-liners in her party who were trying their best to undermine her every move? They had tried it their way for the last seventy years, and where had it got them? Nowhere. Now it was time for a new approach. Not before time.

In two days' time, the peace conference would begin. Sure, Israel had declined to officially attend, but they too were under pressure in their own country from a new younger generation, tired of the old conflicts and eager for a different future. So they had sent an observer instead, unofficial maybe, but an important step in the long and winding road to reconciliation. *The peace conference*. The British Prime Minister Julian Priest, her old dear darling friend Julian, had made all of this possible and she meant to take every advantage of the opportunity in front of the world's press. This was the new Hamas under her dynamic leadership, terrorism and violence to be replaced by diplomacy, exploiting the glamour and sexual power she knew she still possessed, captivating the dull grey men who still by and large held the power in western democracies. Fools, all of them.

In the car behind travelled her personal security detail, shadowy assassins armed to the teeth and trained by her Iranian allies. Hopefully they wouldn't be needed, especially since it seemed the team on the ground were already doing a good job, but it was always wise to have insurance just in case the diplomacy failed. Now it would be like an old eighties band getting back together. Julian and Philip and herself, the classic line-up. No Hugo of course, but he was always the crazy hothead, didn't every band need one? All these sweet entitled upper middle-class boys, Oxbridge-educated and safely wrapped in the comfort blanket of mummy and daddy's money, furiously trying to deny their privileged upbringing through their devotion to the cause. The smart ones grew out of it, becoming barristers or something big in the city, embracing their privilege, every one of them. Luckily, there were enough like Julian and Hugo and Philip, useful idiots keeping the conflict in the public eye, recruiting febrile support from young left-leaning idealists. And most importantly, keeping the cash rolling in. It had been her life for nearly thirty years now and it had been a good life. Excitement, international travel, lovers - everybody in the band had been her lover at some time - recognition, she had it all and she wanted it to continue forever. She feared that Julian's well-meaning conference was doomed before it started, that was a pity, but it was a significant step in the process, and it did give her another chance to get on CNN and deliver her message of conciliation to America and Israel and the West.

But more importantly, there was the other matter to be dealt with. Julian had said he would fix it, and so far he had been true to his word. She had never liked Gerrard Saddleworth, a pathetic little man with an inflated opinion of himself, but the British Prime Minister could hardly have come to Moscow himself, and to be fair, it looked like for once Julian's poodle had actually delivered. Now there was just a few minor details to be sorted out, that's what he had said, and then her living nightmare would finally be over.

They were on the last leg of their journey, the sirens and lights switched off as they glided silently down Pall Mall. Had she chanced to look out the window of the Mercedes, Fadwa might have caught a glance of the elegantly dressed middle-aged man slumped in the doorway of the Oxford & Cambridge club, his expensive navy wool overcoat already stained with blood seeping through from the deep stab wound which was draining the life from him.

Eight miles away in Hounslow, Olga Svoboda rubbed her eyes then stretched out an arm to put her phone alarm on snooze. Four forty-five, too damn early for most people, but she was used to it now. Thank god her sex-mad boyfriend was still asleep, and she had a chance of getting out the door on time. Not that she minded too much of course, it was rather lovely and it was nice to be desired, but work was work and the agency had made it plain that they would sack her if she turned up late at a client's again. Five more minutes and she would need to be up and about and then just ten more to get showered and dressed then hurry down to the station for the journey to St Katherine's Dock. As she prepared to leave, she double-checked that she had Miss White's key, slung the back-pack containing her cleaning materials over her shoulder and closed the door behind her.

Chapter 21

Journalist Penelope White murdered at home.

The news was of course all over the papers, not least the *Chronicle*, where she had been the undoubted star attraction. She wouldn't have liked that headline, so dull and unimaginative, but she had been much too young to have already written her own obituary. Alongside the rather too-fulsome eulogies, the paper was furiously speculating on the motive. The police had already admitted to being puzzled, given the obvious professional nature of the killing. Campaigning journalists like White made plenty of enemies, but they didn't usually get murdered, not in this country at least. So who could have wanted her dead?

The same thought was occupying Maggie's mind as she hurried along Clapham High Street towards what she now was forced to call home, her collar turned up against the biting April wind. But unlike the police, she knew that White had been at that Cathedral Close dinner.

Flat 4A, number 98 was beautifully situated above Kalib's Kebabs, a bargain at fourteen hundred and fifty pounds a month. The takeaway was destined never to receive a Michelin star, but was popular with its loyal and frequently inebriated client base and this evening was no exception, with ten or more customers packed into the tiny shop and one or two more waiting outside, puffing cigarettes and slurping from cans of strong lager. She wasn't a food snob, but the smell from Kalib's turned her stomach, and so she was glad she had managed to grab a Pret A Manger at Waterloo.

Access to the flat was through a narrow passageway on the left side of the takeaway and then up a rickety staircase. She pushed open the rot-infested wooden gate and made her way down the unlit path.

'Maggie.' The man's voice came out of the darkness, literally making her jump. She recognised it immediately.

'Christ Adam, you scared the shit out of me. What the hell are you doing here?'

'I need to speak to you. About everything. Everything that's going on.' He sounded frightened.

'Sure, come on up. And watch these steps, they're lethal in the wet.' As she fumbled in her handbag for her key, she remembered the mobile phones. Two days since she and Jimmy had stupidly stolen them, but yet they had heard nothing from either of them about it. Neither Philip nor Adam. Not a word.

'Would you like a drink? I've got tea and coffee, just instant I'm afraid, and I might have some Chardonnay in the fridge if you would prefer.' No might about it, she always had some Chardonnay in the fridge.

'A glass of wine would be nice. Thank you.'

They sat at either ends of the cheap but comfortable flat-pack-store sofa, glasses resting on the cheap flat-pack coffee table. They weren't stylish by any means, but Maggie was inordinately proud of her achievement in assembling them single-handedly. For nearly two months after moving in, she had sat on an uncarpeted floor in the echoey room, paralysed by the trauma of her breakdown. Buying and building the sofa and table had been a critical step in her slow rehabilitation into something like a normal life, and now she would not part with them for anything.

Cameron took a large gulp from his glass then cradled it in his hands. Maggie saw that they were shaking.

'We took your phones. Yours and Philip's. It was a mistake. The police have them at the moment, but you and I both know that nothing that is found on them can be used in evidence, given the circumstances in which they were acquired.'

It was a little white lie, because the police didn't have them yet, but they would pretty soon. When she plucked up enough courage to tell Frank what they had done.

'The police have them?' His eyes betrayed his anxiety.

'Well, *a* policeman, to be accurate. He's attached to a special department of the Met and he is trying to figure out at the moment what to do with them. They're a bit of a hot potato to be honest.'

He did not appear to be listening.

'What do you know? I mean, about that meeting. The dinner. I know you have the photograph of it. What do you know?'

Maggie's eyes narrowed. 'We don't know anything. We weren't there, were we? I was hoping you would tell me what it was all about.'

He didn't answer.

'Come on Adam, you can tell me. What was it all about?'

'It was just an innocent get-together. Just a dinner with friends and colleagues.'

Maggie recognised these words immediately. So that was why he was here, sent by her ex-husband to find out what they knew. Too cowardly to do his own dirty work, that was just *so* Philip.

'One of the people at your cosy little dinner has just been murdered Adam, for god's sake. And in case you've forgotten, you told Judge Henderson that you had never met Tariq Khan, who I don't think you could describe as either a friend or a colleague. So it wasn't a bloody innocent little dinner, was it?' Maggie's voice was steady, her manner crisp. Just like the old days in the courtroom, cross-examining the witness, exposing the inconsistencies in the testimony. As if she had ever been any good at that.

Cameron hesitated before answering. Maggie could see he had prepared like a witness in the dock, pre-programmed with pat answers to the questions that were expected to be thrown at him. The difference was hardened criminals were good liars, distinguished QCs less so.

'The murder is awful of course, quite awful, but it doesn't have anything to do with the dinner. Penelope White had made many enemies in her career. She was always getting death threats.' It wasn't convincing.

'So why are you here then Adam, behaving like a frightened little rabbit?'

'I'm not frightened.'

'Of course you're not. Why would you be when all you've done is attend a dinner where the topic of conversation was so innocent that someone got murdered to keep it quiet? Believe me Adam, I would be frightened if I had been there. So don't give me that crap.'

'It was an innocent dinner. I don't know why Penelope has been killed.' That was his story and he was going to stick with it.

'Well that's good for you,' Maggie said, 'so it's safe to assume the police won't find anything interesting on your phones when they examine them.' She knew from the other's reaction that she had struck a raw nerve.

'Ok you're right,' Cameron said. 'There was a reason why we held that dinner. The truth is, we had lost some confidence in the authority of our expert witness Professor Walker. We heard about Dr Khan's reputation and wondered if he might not be a better bet. That was all.'

'So why meet in such a public place?' Maggie said. 'And why did it have to be kept so secret that you were prepared to lie to the judge about meeting him at all?' This evidently was a question he had not rehearsed.

'He...well, it was simply the fact he worked in GCHQ in Cheltenham and it made sense to meet locally. We thought if we entertained him and made him feel important, then it might persuade him to help us.'

'What, so you and a cabinet minister and a journalist and my shitface ex-husband traipsed up the M5 to a one-hundred quid a head eating place just to smooth-talk some geeky boffin? A geeky boffin, by the way, who works for the government and could just have been ordered to co-operate. And then, someone dies. Coincidence? No, I don't think so, you'll have to do better than that.'

'Well that's what happened. If you don't believe me, that's your prerogative.' He had regained some of his composure, buoyed no doubt by Maggie's admission of how little they knew.

Without asking, she topped up his wine glass.

'I do know something, as it happens. I know there was a move to make sure someone rubbish was appointed to defend Alzahrani. Whose idea was it to get me appointed as defence barrister? Oh yes, you don't need to look so surprised, because that's one thing we have worked out. The crap barrister plot, let's call it that.'

To Maggie's surprise, Cameron gave an audible sigh of relief, the words blurting out before he could stop himself.

'So that's all you think it was?'

So that's all you think it was. Condemned by the words from his own mouth. Of course, it had to be much much more than that, something big enough to cause someone to be assassinated and to scare the life out of Adam Cameron QC. Something very big indeed. But she was pretty certain he wasn't going to tell her what it was.

She picked up his almost-full glass and stood up.

'I think you'd better go now Adam. Tell Philip whatever you like, but believe me, we will get to the bottom of all this. Oh, and I'll get you your phone back as soon as I can.'

He gave her a distracted look, his mind obviously on more important matters. 'What, that? You can keep it, I've already got a new one.'

Afterwards, Maggie reflected that perhaps she hadn't played the meeting as well as she could have. Perhaps she shouldn't had given away how little they knew. That was a mistake, but still, a lesson learned. Cameron had come to find out what they had, and had gone away with the knowledge that they had nothing. Mission accomplished as far as she was concerned. So far.

***

Pall Mall was all but deserted when Cameron's taxi dropped him off at his club. Hell, how he deserved a drink this evening. In fact maybe he would spend the night there, get a good sleep, with a nice cooked breakfast to look forward to. Right now, there was plenty of time for a shower and to enjoy some of the excellent steak and ale pie, washed down with a nice bottle of Merlot.

The evening passed pleasantly enough and he was feeling much better as bed-time approached. He checked his watch. A quarter past twelve, he hadn't realised how late it was. Just time to slip out for a quick smoke and then he would retire.

The entrance was well-lit and covered by a barrage of close-circuit cameras, although they hadn't really helped the police in the subsequent investigation of his killing. The best they could say was it was a slim tall figure, almost certainly young and male based on his lithe movements, face indistinguishable behind the balaclava and dark glasses. They had got a capture, but unfortunately nothing for the facial recognition software to work with. A single stab wound, driven upwards with force into his heart.

A neat professional job.

Chapter 22

It took nearly four days for the second victim's identity to be released to the press, but only one day for the Met to put DCI Colin Barker in charge of the investigations.

'What's the bloody place coming to ma'am?' Frank was on the phone to his boss as he drove through the morning traffic towards Paddington Green police station, where the incident rooms had been established. 'Crappy Colin running a double murder. I mean, come on.'

'Are you hands-free?'

'Yes boss,' he lied.

'Good. Well if you look on the bright side, it's a big boost for the Alzahrani investigation now they've taken him off it. Maxine Wood has taken that one over, and she's a good cop. Now listen Frank, just tell him what we know and then leave and please, don't get into any more trouble. That's an order.'

'Me ma'am, trouble? When do I ever cause trouble? Not getting into trouble in any way whatsoever is my middle name.'

'Very funny. You know what I mean. Just do your job in a nice professional manner.'

'I promise ma'am, I'll be a very good boy indeed. All I'm going to do is see what the knobhead has to say and then I'll report straight back to you. See you later.'

It turned out the police station car park was full, but then he spotted a gleaming silver BMW bearing the registration number 'CB 3' in a reserved slot next to the main entrance. It said everything about the tiny-dick syndrome of the man that he had gone to all the trouble of getting a private plate on his police motor. It would have taken hours of form-filling and a tower of bureaucracy to get that one signed off. Crazy. And what did the '3' signify? Probably the number of cases he had ever solved. Or the length of his dick. In centimetres. He pulled his battered Mondeo up behind the BMW, blocking him in, and blocking up the rest of the car park too. Not to worry, this was only going to take five minutes at the most.

There were mutters of surprise and anticipation from the investigation team as Frank wandered insouciantly through the huge open-plan office towards Barker's glass-walled enclave. He had worked with many of them in the past, and was pleased to see that his old mate Pete Burnside, veteran DI and witness to that punch that had sent cheers reverberating across the Met, occupied one of the untidy paper-strewn desks. He gave a friendly 'Hey Frank, good to see you mate,' which was acknowledged with a thumbs-up.

A pretty uniformed WPC sat at a desk alongside the door to Barker's office. Down the pub, he probably called her his personal assistant. What an arse.

'Morning constable,' said Frank cheerily, flashing his badge, 'I need a wee word with the DCI. Important stuff about these murder cases. I'll just go in now, ok?'

The WPC looked up in alarm. 'Well sir, I think he's in a meeting...'

Frank spread his arms, gesticulating through the glass at the empty office.

'What, a meeting with himself? You know what they call guys who play with themselves.'

She blushed faintly and tried to suppress a smile.

'What I mean sir, is I think one's about to start...'

'Aye, well, I'll tell you what constable, I'll have a wee meeting with him now. I'll only be five minutes, won't take up much of his time.' Smiling, he strolled past her into Barker's office.

The DCI was on the phone, pacing the office with his back to the door and from the obsequious tone, Frank gathered that he was speaking to his boss.

'Yes sir, we'll have them wrapped up pretty quickly I hope. The reason I called actually was to let you know we've already got someone in custody for the Cameron stabbing... yes, that's right...we're pretty confident we'll be charging him before the end of the day...yes sir, it is quick work on my part...thank you sir... yes, you know we always get results when I'm in charge...yes... ok sir, I'll give you an update later today.'

He was evidently surprised and not terribly pleased to see Frank in his office.

'What the hell do you want Stewart? I thought they'd made you a traffic warden, or was it a lavatory attendant, I can't remember.'

'Morning sir. No, not been promoted to those jobs yet, I think they're still keeping them open for you. Oh, and did I really just hear you say we always get results when I'm in charge? You mean like the Alzahrani job they've just had to take you off to save further public embarrassment? Aye, you always get results right enough.'

Too late, he remembered his promise to Jill Smart. *Don't get into any trouble.* But this time it seemed he had got away with it, as Barker either ignored or was oblivious to the insults. He shouted out to the young WPC.

'Ellie, will you get DI Burnside in here right away. So what is it you want Stewart, I'm a busy man.'

'I've got some information on the Cameron and White murders from another case I've been working on sir. My boss DCI Smart felt it was our duty to share it with your investigation and sent me over. It's up to you what you do with it'.

DI Pete Burnside entered the office, winking at Frank and ignoring his superior officer.

'Great to see you Frank mate. How's tricks?'

'Good Pete, really good. It's a laugh a minute down in Department 12B, I can tell you. You should apply for a transfer, DCI Smart's always looking for smart guys like you, ha ha.'

'I might just do that mate.'

'Aye, it's good. We don't get the free coffee to be fair, but there's a well-stocked vending machine. Twixes and Mars Bars usually.'

'Look, can we just get on with this,' said Barker impatiently. 'So what crap is it you've got for me?'

'Aye, all right then sir. So we've just started on something in the Department, it's connected to the Alzahrani case as a matter of fact.'

He took his phone from his pocket and scrolled to the Seven Cathedral Close photograph.

'Look, you can see here. That's Adam Cameron and that's Penelope White, your murder victims. This was taken about two years ago, just before the Alzahrani trial kicked off. Doesn't mean their murders are connected of course, but it is something of interest I think. The reason I'm saying that is because, you see this other guy in the picture? That's Dr Tariq Kahn, you know he was the guy who wrote that report that the CPS suppressed, causing the mistrial and all that.'

He wasn't surprised by Barker's reaction. It was no more than he had expected from the useless halfwit.

'So you've wasted my time with a picture of some guys having dinner together? What does that prove? Bugger all Stewart, bugger all. I've already established that there's no connection between these two murders. One was a shooting and the other one was a knifing for a start, or maybe you didn't figure that out.'

'But sir,' Frank said, persisting, 'the other thing is, Adam Cameron said to the judge that he had never met Khan. This picture proves that for a reason we don't yet know, he was lying. Do you see what I'm saying? Why would he lie if he didn't have something to hide? And if he had something to hide, maybe that's would be a motive to shut him up permanently.'

'Frank, do these guys know of the existence of this picture?' Burnside asked.

'You're a very clever guy Pete,' Frank said with pointed admiration. 'Aye, I think there's every chance that they do. One of them does certainly, that's this guy Philip Brooks, and I would bet my pension that he's gone and told everyone else by now. That was the other thing I came here for. We need to bring Brooks in for questioning pronto, see what he knows.'

'Brooks, who the hell's he?' Barker said. 'Not on my radar'.

Not surprising thought Frank bitterly, you wouldn't recognise a suspect if he was wearing a t-shirt with 'suspect' printed on the back in capital letters.

'Sir, don't you think Frank might have something here?' asked Burnside cautiously. 'What I mean is, if someone wanted to keep the purpose of this meeting a secret, as he says, that might be a motive for the murders. And if this guy Brooks knows that the meeting is all out in the open now, maybe we should bring him in, find out what he knows...'

'That's total bollocks,' Barker replied shortly. 'What, you start murdering people just because of a dinner conversation? Complete shite. No, I told you, there's nothing connecting these murders in my very expert opinion, and I'm a man who knows what he's talking about. And anyway we've already got someone bang to rights for the Cameron stabbing.'

'Aye, I heard you saying that to your boss,' Frank said suspiciously. 'There's no way that can be true.'

'Well, we have and it is true,' smirked Barker. 'The result of superior police work, but of course you wouldn't know anything about that, would you?'

'Superior police work from you? Yes, I must bow to your superiority, no doubt about that sir.'

Petulance was evidently Barker's default mode. 'You just remember Stewart that you are talking to a senior officer and it's none of your business frankly, but we just happened to stop and search a youth the next day and low and behold, wasn't he found in possession of Mr Cameron's phone.'

This was a turn of events that hadn't occurred to Frank. It was beyond bad luck that some opportunist thief had taken Cameron's phone as he lay dying.

Barker gave a sickly smile. 'Stop and search. I've always believed in it. Gets results you see. And now we've got it all wrapped up. Neat and tidy, just the way we like it.'

'Aye, fitted up more like,' said Frank bitterly, 'and don't tell me, you've not been able to find any DNA or fingerprint evidence connecting this poor lad to the murder, but you're working on it. And that's because you haven't found the knife yet but you're working on that too.'

'We don't need to worry about these little technicalities, do we Burnside? They're all the same, dangerous thieving little toe-rags, every one of them. But this one wasn't so smart, was he? He was found with the phone in his possession, he hasn't got an alibi for his whereabouts at the time of the murder, and it turns out he's got a string of previous convictions as long as his arm. CPS lawyers are happy with it, they agree it's all we need to charge him, all neat and tidy. Nice speedy clear-up, just the way the Super likes it. DCI Colin Barker strikes again. Yes!'

He pumped his fists in a grotesque gesture of triumph. Frank could feel the anger swelling up to bursting point.

'You're an arse-licking bent bastard,' he said quietly, 'and a bloody disgrace to this force and every other. Well, I'm going to see you get exposed for the lying fuckwit you are if it's the last thing I do.'

Burnside looked alarmed. 'Calm down Frank, just calm down mate. Don't do anything stupid.'

Now Barker was hitting his stride, arrogant and confident in equal measure. He evidently knew how easy it was to wind up Frank Stewart.

'Well, you'll no doubt be pleased to know that we've got a suspect for the Penelope White case too. We found out from her paper that she was working on a big story to expose the army officer that was responsible for the death of that young soldier in Belfast. A right bloody coward, letting that young girl die while he sat all safe and sound in the armoured vehicle. And now that's she's dead, that coward is off the hook. Very convenient, don't you think Frank? You see, that's what I call a real motive for murder, not some stupid dinner party.'

Burnside tried to stop him, but he wasn't quick enough. Frank leaped forward, grabbing Barker by the lapels and smashing him against the wall.

'You go near my brother, and you're dead Barker, understand that? I mean it.'

Taken by surprise, Barker struggled for breath as Frank wrestled him to the floor. Burnside tried again to restrain him, grabbing him by both arms and pulling him back.

'C'mon Frank, he's not worth it. Just leave it. Please mate, leave it.'

Frank shrugged him off, directing a final withering glance at Barker as he lay prone and dazed.

'Aye, you're probably right mate. But make no mistake Barker, I'm coming for you. There's nothing worse than a bent copper, so you'd better start browsing the job sites. Because you're finished here.'

With that, Frank turned on his heels and with a pleasant, 'it was nice to meet you' in the direction of the young WPC, strode purposefully through the incident room towards the exit. To his delight he was accompanied by a discreet ripple of applause, causing him to smile and tip an imaginary cap in the manner of a major-winning golfer striding towards the eighteenth green.

Driving back to the office, he reflected that maybe he could have handled it a tad better, but what was certain was that the case was going be a bloody disaster under that fool Barker. The black lad had been stupid to nick Cameron's phone as he lay dying, but there was no way he could have carried out what was an obviously professional killing. And now valuable police time was to be wasted on a stupid investigation of his brother Jimmy, whilst the real killers were still on the loose.

Because if as he strongly suspected the murders were as a direct result of the Seven Cathedral Close dinner, then there were people clearly anxious to make sure nobody talked, meaning there was every chance they would strike again. Now he desperately needed to get Jill Smart's backing to make the investigation official. Department 12B wasn't supposed to run parallel cases, but he felt confident that when he gave Jill the feedback from his meeting with Barker, she would be supportive. They needed access to phone records, they needed to be able to bring the participants in for interview, and they needed clearance from the spooks to talk to the elusive Dr Khan, and for all that to happen, the investigation had to be official.

Above all, they needed to find out what the hell was going on before the killer or killers struck again.

Chapter 23

'Means, motive, opportunity, that's what we have to think about isn't it? For every suspect.'

Maggie and Jimmy had been joined at their Fleet Street Starbucks by Frank, who was in dire need of a caffeine infusion after a gruelling and uncomfortable morning with his boss. He shook his head in mock disgust. 'The good Lord save us from the amateur detective. Anyway, is this your new office or something? You're always here.'

'No, it's just that Elsa's ran out of beans again and we were desperate. But don't you change the subject Frank Stewart. I am right, aren't I? About means motive and opportunity? I've seen it on that whiteboard on Midsummer Murders.'

He struggled to suppress a smile. 'Aye, so it must be true Maggie, that's an authoritative source, so it is.'

She could sense they were all trying hard to remain upbeat, but the truth was that for different reasons it was all getting a bit difficult. She had suffered a rapid crash in her mood when she realised that it might have been her impetuous decision to show Philip that photograph which had triggered the murders of Penelope White and Adam Cameron. Frank had expressly told her not to, but in the heat of the moment, she had lost control, with terrible consequences. It was increasingly her opinion that everything she touched turned to disaster, an opinion strongly backed up by facts that could not easily be ignored. And if that wasn't bad enough, she was now beginning to realise the practical implications of Philip's court injunction. Not being able to see Ollie, even at a distance, was unbearable agony, made even worse by the loveliness of the fleeting hour she had spent with her son on his birthday. But she knew that her chances at the upcoming custody hearing were already slim, and that incident at his office the other day had hardly helped matters. Any further transgressions would surely ruin them for good. Now her determination to get revenge on Philip was dissipating as she faced up to the hopelessness of her situation.

Jimmy smiled, judging the mood. 'We're a right bunch of miseries, aren't we? Anybody would think the end of the world was nigh. C'mon, it's not that bad, is it?'

Frank did not seem to share the sentiment. 'Speak for yourself pal.'

'I'm sure I would feel a lot better if we could actually do something,' Maggie said. 'I don't mind admitting I'm really struggling at the moment. Look at this.'

She showed them a Facebook post with a photo of a laughing Ollie playing catch with Angelique Perez on Hampstead Heath.

'Maggie, why are you following Angelique's social media, for goodness sake?' Jimmy said. 'Do you really think that's going to help?'

Frank gave him a withering look. 'Says the man who checks out the Swedish princess ten times an hour.'

Jimmy ignored him. 'Take it from me, it doesn't help at all.'

'But you still look, don't you?' Maggie said kindly.

'No, not now. Never.' She could tell he was lying.

'Social media, I've always said it's a curse.' This from Frank, the man who did not even own a smartphone.

'Aye, and you know all about Facegram, being mister techno man and all that,' Jimmy said, 'You've still got a flip-up phone for god's sake.'

'My star trek communicator, do you mean? It works fine for me. And yes, I do have a Facegram account. I get lots of likes, me.'

Jimmy caught Maggie's eye. She was trying very hard not to laugh.

'Ah well Frank, we'll look forward to looking up your Facegram page later,' she said, 'although I can't say I've heard of that app before. Anyway, how did you get on this morning with your boss? Did you manage to get the case up and running?'

'Well, the answer is yes and no. To tell the truth, Jill and I had a wee bit of argy-bargy when I told her about my run-in with DCI Barker...'

Jimmy eyed him with suspicion. 'What run-in?'

'Nothing for you to worry about son, we just had a little disagreement, that's all. So as I said, yes and no. Jill thought there wasn't enough solid evidence of conspiracy at this point for her to open up a full enquiry and devote all the resources that would demand, which is fair enough. But the good news is she's cleared the decks so that I can work on it full time for the next two or three weeks. Then, if *I* - I mean *we* - uncover anything of significance, she'll look at it again. Can't really complain about her decision, it's what I kind of expected to be honest.'

Maggie suspected the decision suited Frank very well. She guessed he preferred to work on his own whenever possible. From his point of view, it probably saved a lot of tedious cocking-about time which could be used more profitably on the case.

'That sounds good,' she said, 'so what's the plan?'

'Well, I know I laughed at you earlier, but we do actually need to look at means, motive and opportunity for each suspect.'

'See, told you.'

'No, this is serious. For a start, we have got to face the possibility - no, stronger than that, the likelihood - that one or more of that dining group could actually be responsible for the murders. Looking at motive, then it's got to be that someone or some group did not want the subject of that meeting to get out. That would be my initial thought.'

Jimmy nodded his assent. 'Yep, agreed, but it would be good if we actually knew what was said at that dinner, wouldn't it?'

'I think we can probably make a guess at that, can't we?' Maggie said. 'If it's all about how to make the case watertight, maybe they are trying to put pressure on Khan to write a report that does that, or maybe even trying to get him to appear as an expert witness.'

'It might be that, right enough,' Jimmy agreed, 'but what we don't know is, what were the dynamics around that table? What I mean is, who was driving the agenda? For example, was it the Government as represented by Saddleworth putting pressure on the CPS and their barrister.'

Maggie had been thinking about that. 'That's all plausible, but what's been puzzling me is why they held that meeting in a public place.'

'You can't kick up a fuss in a public place, can you?' Jimmy said. 'I'd imagine that was the main reason.'

'Yes. I hadn't thought of that,' Maggie said, unconvinced. 'That's probably what it was. But what was Penelope White doing there? Perhaps it was to put more pressure on Khan. He must have this constant terror that he is going to be exposed, so whoever is behind all this brings a journalist along so that he is reminded what will happen if he suddenly decides not to cooperate with whatever plan they have cooked up.'

Frank broke his silence. 'Aye, but it's all wrong, this case. I've said it before but it's all the wrong way round.'

Jimmy looked puzzled. 'I don't understand what you're saying brother.'

'Look, is it credible to think that this wee dinner can lead to two murders if all they were trying to do was beef up the case against Alzahrani? No, it isn't, there must be more to it than that. Remember, our mastermind DCI Barker hasn't figured this out yet, but these killings were professional jobs. Penelope White was shot cleanly through the head three times, and not a single neighbour heard a thing, which points to a silencer being used. And I've been told by my mate Pete Burnside that the SOCOs have not found any DNA or fingerprints in her flat that shouldn't be there. Not a trace. And then we have Adam Cameron, killed by a single upward stab through the heart, clean and accurate. That wasn't done by some scumbag mugger, I can assure you of that. No, as I said, this whole thing has got to be about something way more serious. Something deadly serious.'

Maggie was mulling over whether this was now maybe a good time to bring up what was likely to be a slightly delicate subject. Uncertainly, she decided to go for it.

'Frank, is it right that you said it was normal procedure after something like this to check the phone records of the suspects? You said there would be panic calls and attempts to get stories straight and stuff like that. I'm sure that's what you said.'

Frank looked at her suspiciously. 'Aye, I did, but Jill Smart hasn't given me the go-ahead to do that yet.'

'Well maybe we could help you with that. It's rather unofficial, but well...'

She rummaged in her bag, emerging with the two smartphones and laying them on the table. 'These are Philip Brooks' and Adam Cameron's. We thought they might come in handy.'

Frank's expression registered utter disbelief. 'You stole their bloody phones? And one of them a murder victim? This is crazy, I shouldn't even be looking at these, never mind being anywhere near them. I should arrest you two, so I should.'

Maggie shot him a weak smile and pointed at Jimmy. 'Arrest him you mean, nothing to do with me. I'm just a lawyer.'

'You lying toad,' Jimmy laughed, and then wished he hadn't.

She could tell that Frank was struggling to suppress his anger. 'This isn't something to joke about guys. Christ, if Jill finds out about this, I'm a dead man.'

'I don't know about that,' Maggie said, raising a quizzical eyebrow, 'but I'll tell you what's strange about this. Neither Philip or Adam Cameron ever tried to contact us to get them back.'

Frank was shaking his head with obvious disgust.

'Bloody amateurs, that's what you are. And bloody dangerous amateurs at that. Of course they haven't asked for their phones back. Because when they realised they were gone, then their panic and fear would have been off the scale. The bloody dial was always going to be jacked up to eleven. God knows what you two have set off. It doesn't bear thinking about, it really doesn't.'

He picked up Brooks' iPhone and punched the home button. It was locked of course, as he expected, but a notification box showed it had received more than thirty missed calls in the last twenty-four hours. Adam Cameron's, the same.

'You'll have seen that I expect, he said, shoving the phone in her face. 'The shit's really hit the fan.'

Maggie looked sheepish. 'Yes, we know. We thought it would be good if we could find out what these calls were about.' Her tone was contrite. She knew they had screwed up and was anxious to get back on the right side of Frank.

But only because she knew he had access to Eleanor Campbell. And she would know how to crack a phone password.

Chapter 24

Naturally the distinguished member had made contingency plans, but now it seemed there was a definite risk of this matter spiralling out of control. Careless and stupid in equal measure. So now they had to assume the police would be all over the phone records, and goodness knows where that would lead. And it's not as if they hadn't been warned. *Careless talk cost lives.* Keep your bloody mouths shut, whatever happens. That's what they had been told.

So be it. Now the decision had been made for them. Regrettable of course, it would have been better if this little messiness could have been avoided, but now there was no other option. Plan B, robust thus far, would need to be seen through to its logical conclusion. There were a few new obstacles to be overcome, but that was to be expected, and it was built into the programme.

He placed his empty glass on the walnut coffee table and signalled for the attendant to bring his coat. Another one would have been nice, but he was expected back at the House for another tedious division bell. Plan B. The Ayes have it.

Chapter 25

Frank stood outside Atlee House puffing on a cigarette and reflecting on the day's events. When he got back to the office, Jill had reminded him that the evidence pack for the pre-hearing on his drugs corruption case needed to be with the CPS the next day. Being forced to work late, he was not in the best of humours. On top of that, the stolen phones had been handed over to Eleanor but that hadn't gone as smoothly as he had hoped. It was his own fault really for letting slip how he had come by them, and she was insistent that she would not touch them with a bargepole. He'd forgotten her fondness for form-filling, and it was only when he promised, lying, that he would get her an authorising e-mail from DCI Smart did she take them off his hands, and that was with great reluctance. 'Don't you trust me Eleanor?' he had asked guilelessly. 'No,' she had answered bluntly. So not a great day overall and he still had the big issue weighing on his mind. He knew there was something very wrong in their analysis of the Cathedral Close case.

Maggie had been set up, that was *probably* true. Dr Tariq Khan had been coerced into writing that report, that was *definitely* true. But whilst he could understand why the Home Secretary wanted Alzahrani locked up -after all, keeping the country safe was in his job-spec and he was no friend of Palestine - why the secret trip to Moscow to meet Ziadeh?

He was just about to head back inside when his phone rang. It was DI Burnside, sounding ebullient as ever.

'Hey Frank, how's things mate?'

'Aye, good Pete, good.' It was always nice to catch up with his pal and he cheered up a little.

'Well that's funny, 'cos a little bird told me there was some trouble about a couple of nicked phones, top of the range ones from what I hear. You running a little business on the side or something? I'm looking for a new Galaxy myself.'

'How the hell did you find out about that Burnside?'

The man was incredible, with an uncanny knack of finding out just about everything that was going on in the Met. Except it wasn't really a knack, more the result of running a small army of inside informants across the organisation.

'Ear to the ground pal, ear to the ground. And on that topic, you will definitely want to hear what a little bird told me the other day.' When you heard his signature phrase 'a little bird told me', you knew you were in for a gem.

'This is a different little bird, I assume? Well, all right then, lay it on me.'

'Yeah, well you know we're working on the Penelope White murder?'

'The one that Barker thinks has got nothing to do with the Cameron case.'

'I think even he's now beginning to acknowledge that there might be a connection. Anyway, getting back to the White case, as part of our investigation we talked to her paper to find out what else she had been working on. Routine and all that.'

'You know she was doing something about my wee brother Jimmy, don't you? Bloody outrageous.' And it had been White too who had christened Maggie the most hated woman in Britain. If that wasn't a motive for murder, what was? Luckily Barker was too stupid to ever work out *that* connection.

'Yeah, we know that but I was able to get it into the gaffer's thick head that your brother didn't know about the Chronicle's campaign at the time of her murder. He's off the hook.'

'Cheers for that mate, he'll be bloody relieved.'

'No problem, all part of the service. What we did find out though, was that she was investigating something else, what was it called...wait a minute, I've got it written down somewhere...oh yeah, the Miner's Emphysema Trust. It was some big scandal a long time ago, nearly fifteen years ago in fact. 2004. This trust thing was meant to look after sick miners, but it turned out the chairman was running a massive scam and creaming off some of the cash for himself. When it all came out, the guy killed himself. Len Pringle, that was his name. He was an ex-miner.'

'I don't remember anything about that.'

'Well as I said, it was a long time ago. Pre-internet era and also I think the government of the time tried very hard to hush it all up. Point is, there was a lot of money went missing that was never accounted for. Two million quid in fact. That was the story that Penelope White was working on. Where did the money go, and who took it, all that sort of stuff.'

'That's a big story right enough. But Pete, why are you telling me all this?'

'Patience boy, patience. The reason I'm telling you this is because amongst the trustees at the time was one Gerrard Saddleworth MP.'

'Christ, that *is* interesting. You know that they're lovers, don't you? Gerrard and White. I mean, they *were* lovers, before she died.'

'Of course I knew that mate. That's the whole point. It seemed she was quite prepared to shaft her lover in pursuit of a story, if you'll pardon the expression. Nice girl.'

'Yeah exactly. So did White think that it was Saddleworth who took the money then?'

'I don't know, she was obviously just at the early stages of her investigation. But she had been in touch with the accountants that were brought in afterwards to clear up the mess. Reed Prentice & Partners they're called. They're still going, quite a big firm based up in Leeds. Anyway, her editor thought that that was the angle she was most excited about. I've got a contact name, Lily Hart, she's a partner or something. No idea what it's all about but it could be one for Department 12B to follow up on whilst us grown-ups work on the proper crimes.'

'Frig off Pete. But thanks, I'm grateful for this.'

'No problem mate. I'll text you what I have, and by the way, you owe me a pint. And let me know how it goes. Over and out.'

One for Department 12B? Frank wasn't so sure that Jill would sanction him swanning round the country on what might turn out to be a wild goose chase. But there was nothing to stop his hopeless amateur assistants filling the gap, and he figured their Saddleworth divorce case could easily stand the cost of a return rail ticket to Leeds. He picked up his phone and dialled his brother.

'Hey Jimmy, how do you fancy a wee trip to Yorkshire?'

Chapter 26

To say that events began to move fast following the brutal murder of nineteen-year-old Jack Wyatt would be the understatement of the millennium. Within hours, the new case had been wrestled from the grasp of the Gloucestershire Constabulary and allocated to the dead hand that was DCI Colin Barker. Not much later, DCI Jill Smart had learned from Eleanor Campbell that Frank Stewart was in possession of two stolen mobile phones, one belonging to a recent murder victim, and thus had no option but to grass him up, as he might have expressed it. All of this being why Barker and Smart and Frank and Maggie Brooks *nee* Bainbridge had been gathered together in the faceless Number Two conference room at Paddington Green police station on the orders of an apoplectic Chief Superintendant Brian Wilkes. Just down the corridor in two separate interview rooms languished the hot-shot international lawyer Philip Brooks and, sensationally, Her Majesty's Secretary of State for the Home Department, The Right Honourable Gerrard Saddleworth. Over in Cheltenham, the same Gloucestershire force was trying to track down Dr Tariq Khan, who seemed to have gone AWOL. It was all kicking off big time.

'I really don't know where to begin.'

Wilkes paced up and down at the front of the room, the sleeves of his crisp white shirt rolled up above the elbows. The atmosphere was tense. With only a year or two until retirement he didn't want his pristine reputation sullied by a momentous screw-up on a high-profile murder case like this.

'I'm grateful to you Jill for bringing it to my attention.' DCI Smart smiled back sweetly, ignoring Barker's drawn daggers. 'So who's going to bring me up to speed with where the hell we are with this bloody car crash of a case?'

'I will sir.'

Jill Smart did the introductions. 'DI Frank Stewart sir. He's one of the best DIs in my 12B team.'

Wilkes peered down his nose at him. 'One of the best, eh?' He knew the competition wasn't exactly stiff in that department. 'I know all about you Stewart. You've got history, haven't you?' Barker shuffled uncomfortably and stared at the floor.

'Yes sir.' The answer shot out like an arrow from a crossbow. 'Proud of it sir.'

'Well proceed DI Stewart, and keep it short and to the point.'

'I will do that sir. So you know the sort of stuff we do in the department, early investigations of things that might turn out interesting and that...'

'I know what you do in 12B,' Wilkes said impatiently, 'please get on with it.'

'Aye, sorry sir. So the latest victim is Jack Wyatt. He's only nineteen and he worked as a waiter at the Seven Cathedral Close restaurant in Gloucester. The lad was killed last Friday evening whilst on a night out with some mates in Cheltenham. A single stab wound through the heart.'

'So what's this got to do with the other two murders then?' Wilkes asked.

Maggie stood up. 'He was in our photograph.'

'Who are you again?' Wilkes barked.

'Maggie Bainbridge. I was the defence barrister on the Alzahrani case and now I'm an investigator working on a divorce case. Saddleworth verses Saddleworth. That's the Home Secretary and his wife Olivia.'

'I've heard of you. You're the most hated woman in Britain, are you not?' She wasn't sure, but it sounded like a compliment.

'Not any more I hope,' Maggie grinned. 'So I'll spare you the details, but as part of the investigation into Mr Saddleworth's financial status, we came across this photograph.' She had loaded the picture onto her phone earlier, in anticipation of the direction the meeting would take.

Wilkes took the phone and peered at it closely. 'So, what am I looking at here?'

'We were interested in this because in the trial -the Alzahrani trial I mean -Adam Cameron - he was the prosecuting barrister - told the judge that he had never met this guy - Dr Tariq Khan. The photograph proves he was lying and we wanted to know why. And then two of the diners were murdered and it all got serious and scary. And now poor Jack Wyatt is dead too. That's him pouring the wine.'

'More than a coincidence, eh sir?' Frank said. 'One dinner, three murders. And wee Jack could only have been killed for one thing, and that was to make sure he couldn't tell anything he might have overheard. '

'That's why I took the initiative and brought Mr Brooks and Mr Saddleworth in for questioning.' Jill Smart knew that she had acted way outside of her brief, trampling all over Barker's investigation, but she was ready with a semi-plausible justification. 'As you heard, there was suspicion of conspiracy in our case sir, and therefore we had plans to interview all the diners. That was before Jack Wyatt was murdered, of course.'

'Sir, what she did was completely out of order.' Barker face was slowly turning purple. 'She could have ruined my investigation.'

Frank stepped in.

'You knew as much as we did Colin and could have acted. After the first two murders, I told you all about the photograph and the big lie we'd uncovered, but you're obviously so much cleverer than me and you decided that my theory was bollocks. Total bollocks in fact, I think was your exact words. Am I right sir?'

To Frank, it looked as if DSI Wilkes was ruing his decision to move Barker off the Alzahrani case onto this one. The guy was a liability and he of all people should have known that. Now he slammed the table in frustration.

'Barker, is what the DI says true? You were aware of this possible connection and you decided to ignore it?'

'Yes, but we had other promising lines of enquiry...'

And now Frank went in for the kill.

'What DSI Barker is trying to say is that he already had someone in the frame for the Cameron murder sir. For what it's worth, I thought his evidence looked a bit flimsy but of course I'm just a lowly DI.'

Wilkes shook his head in disbelief.

'Christ's sake. And now we have a third murder. An innocent boy, barely more than a child. This really is a total arse-in-the-air shit-fest.' Frank knew Wilkes would be thinking how the press would play it when it got out that Jack Wyatt's murder was linked to a case they were already working on. Already there was revulsion across the nation about the death of the kid and it wasn't going to look good for the force.

'We're running the operation on very tight resources sir. It's easy to miss things when you're several heads light.'

Wilkes gave Barker a look of contempt. 'I don't want to hear any more from you DCI Barker.'

'But sir...'

'Shut up Colin.' The brutality of the put-down momentarily silenced the room. He turned to Jill Smart.

'You did good work bringing in those other two Jill. How did you manage to get Mr Saddleworth here, that couldn't have been easy?'

She hesitated for a moment. 'That photograph... we believe the group of diners had got to know of its existence. I emailed his office telling them that we wanted to talk about a dinner that he had attended several months ago. When we told him we had a photograph, he didn't even ask which dinner. Just agreed to come in.'

'So he had seen it.' Maggie said. 'Philip must have shown it to him, or at least told him about it.'

'Aye, well hopefully Pete Burnside is asking them just that question as we speak,' Frank said.

'So you've got DI Burnside on your team?' Wilkes mood seemed to lighten a notch. 'He's a very sound officer in my experience. A good man. Thank god we still have some of them on the force.' It was obvious to whom the last remark was directed.

'Aye, he's a top guy right enough. Just a pity guys like that have to put up with piss-poor leadership.' Frank was enjoying Barker's discomfort. 'Not in my case, of course sir.' He aimed an exaggerated smile at Jill Smart.

There was a quiet knock on the door. A few seconds later, it was pushed open and the head of Burnside peered round.

'Come in Burnside,' Wilkes said warmly. 'Come and tell us all you know.'

'Thank you sir.' He sat down at the head of the table and nervously flicked to the top page of his notebook.

'So obviously we went through the routine stuff you would do on a murder enquiry. Principally, establishing where they each were at the times of the murders. The funny thing was, their reactions were quite different but also a bit odd. So Mr Saddleworth, he seemed relieved when I told him my questions were about the three murders.' Burnside paused to check his notes. 'That was so strange, considering that he had allegedly been in a relationship with one of the victims, and so would obviously be a prime suspect. But what he said was 'so it's not about the money then' and when I asked him what he meant by that, he clammed up. I found that interesting, particularly in the light of another line of enquiry that is proceeding at the moment.' He gave Maggie a knowing glance, hoping he could brush over the unofficial nature of that investigation. Wilkes' eyes narrowed.

'What money?' he asked sharply.

'We don't know right now sir,' Burnside replied, 'but as I said, we have a lead on that one.'

'Who's working that?' It was getting a bit awkward and Maggie decided to help out.

'My colleague James Stewart is following up something on that one. Saddleworth's estranged wife believes he has hidden some money away, cash that he has not declared in the divorce financial statement.'

'Your colleague? So we've got some bloody amateur working on a triple murder case? God save me.' It wasn't clear to whom the remark was directed, but Jill stepped in to smooth the waters.

'Sir, I think it's just a coincidence that this came up on Miss Bainbridge's divorce case. That's a civil case, but I will of course get an officer allocated to it right away now that it's clear it's a police matter.'

That seemed to satisfy him. 'Well, just make sure you do Jill. Carry on Burnside.'

'Ok sir. Well anyway, as far as Mr Saddleworth goes, we will be following up his alibis of course, but with his reaction I'd say it's odds-on that they will stack up. I mean, it seems highly unlikely that a cabinet minister can sneak out of parliament unnoticed to shoot his lover then dive out again to expertly stab a QC. Every hour of his life is arranged by his advisers and civil servants, isn't it? Not to mention the fact that he's shadowed by security officers twenty-four-by-seven.'

'There's sense in that,' Wilkes said. 'So, tell us what this Brooks guy had to say for himself.'

'He's a smart-arsed bastard sir, that's one thing I can tell you. I had to restrain myself from shoving his teeth down his throat.'

'You're not allowed to do that nowadays,' Frank said, 'more's the pity.'

Burnside laughed. 'Yeah, exactly Frank. Anyway, I think he's another one with alibis that are going to stack up. When I said I was questioning him in connection with the murders, he just lounged back in his chair and laughed at me. Arrogant little shit. Then I asked him about the dinner, what it was all about and everything. He said it was just an innocent dinner with a few colleagues.'

'That's the party line,' Maggie said. 'We've heard that one before.'

'Sure, but anyway I told him I didn't believe that for a minute, and that I was quite happy to let him stew until he came up with something better. So finally, he spins a line that they were just trying to shore up the case against Alzahrani. He said that he had been invited along to give advice because they were worried she might try and pull some human rights stunt, and he's an expert in that field. Khan was there to offer his opinion on the recognition evidence, to see if it would stack up.'

'Did he say anything about me?' Maggie asked quietly. 'That the CPS had steered the case towards a less experience barrister?'

'No, he didn't. Neither of them did.'

'And did you believe their accounts?' Wilkes asked.

'Well, I don't know sir. It's all a bit irregular perhaps, but I can't see anything illegal about it at first glance. Although it's probably not something they would want to widely advertise, you know, trying to manipulate the outcome of a trial and all that.'

'The CPS are doing that every other day of the week,' Wilkes said bitterly. 'You know what, this is all nonsense. The whole thing.' His outburst was as unexpected as it was definitive. 'Pure unadulterated nonsense.'

'Sir?' Jill Smart could not hide her surprise.

'I've been a copper thirty years and believe me, I recognise a heap of dung when I see it. Whatever was being plotted at that dinner was serious enough for three people to be killed. Three people, for god's sake. This story that Brooks and Saddleworth are spinning just doesn't stack up. No way. There's something massive buried in here, I can feel it.'

He drummed his fingers on the table, his lips pursed in thought. Finally he spoke.

'Look, this is in danger of getting out of control and making us look mugs. Jill, I want you to take charge of the case with immediate effect. I assume you'll want DI Stewart and DI Burnside on the team, and you've got a free hand to draft in any officers you need. I want a result on this and I want it fast, do you understand?'

Maggie could see Jill struggling to conceal her pleasure at this turn of events. 'Yes sir, I'll get on to it right away.' DCI Colin Barker didn't look quite so delighted. He tried to mount a rearguard action.

'Sir, I assuming that DCI Smart will be under my command?'

The response was brutal. 'You assume incorrectly Colin. Come and see me at my office tomorrow and we'll have a chat about your future.' Code for *you're finished*.

Frank didn't try to hide his triumph. 'You'd better learn how to use that parking ticket machine Colin. Nice wee steady job that, gets you out in the fresh air. Good for the complexion.'

Maggie sat quietly at the far end of the table, her body surging with adrenalin, her mind racing. It was the words that DCI Wilkes had used that had triggered the thought. He was right, the story didn't stack up. Whatever was being plotted at that dinner was serious enough for three people to be killed. *Three people*. And as the fog blew away, she could see it all too clearly. She didn't know why and she didn't know how, but she had never been more certain about anything in her life.

Because that dinner hadn't been about making sure Dena Alzahrani got convicted. *No way*. It was about making sure she got freed. And *that* was a secret you would kill for.

Chapter 27

It had taken all Jimmy's considerable powers of persuasion to set up the meeting with Reed Prentice. Whilst it was relatively straightforward to sweet-talk the receptionist into putting him through to the senior partner, using a combination of charm and what he imagined was his commanding voice, Lily Hart proved a tougher nut to crack. The mention of the Miner's Emphysema Trust caused an instant transformation in her demeanour, and she became at once both guarded and taciturn. Only when Jimmy mentioned, in desperation, that he was working as an agent of the Metropolitan Police did her mood soften and after some hesitation she agreed to a meeting - 'but only twenty minutes, and I can't fit you in until four-thirty.' That was good enough.

The journey to Leeds passed without incident, and two hours later Jimmy was leaving behind the bustling and impressively restored art-deco station. On the phone, she had assured him that their office was only ten minutes from the station, but Lily Hart's estimate had been optimistic to say the least, and it took nearly half an hour at a brisk pace to reach the offices of the accountants. Reed Prentice & Partners occupied a tastefully converted former rectory located on a leafy street on the edge of the university campus. On arrival, an efficient elderly receptionist ushered him through to a small meeting room, took his order for coffee, and with a brisk 'Mrs Hart will be with you in a few minutes,' retreated.

Hart was not at all what he had imagined. From her voice, he had pictured her as short, plump and dowdy, dressed in an old-fashioned knitted two-piece. In fact she was tall, slim and rather attractive. She looked around forty, wearing a crisp white tailored blouse and navy pencil skirt which accentuated a nice figure. Her hair was blond, probably natural he thought, with just a hint of grey beginning to show through. She exuded the cool and confident aura of a woman at the top of her game.

'Look I'm sorry Mr Stewart...' she began.

'Jimmy, please...'

'Jimmy, and I'm Lily... yes, so I'm really short of time so I hope you don't think I'm rude but I can only spare twenty minutes or so.'

Jimmy gave her his maximum-charm smile. 'I totally understand and it's great that you could see me and so quickly. As I mentioned on the phone, we're interested in what Penelope White was investigating around the Miners Trust affair. We wanted to ask you what you know. I believe you've found out something about it.'

She looked at him warily. 'You said on the phone you were with the Metropolitan Police.' This could be awkward, he thought.

'So Lily, I'm not exactly with the Met, but we - that's my firm, Bainbridge Associates - are working on a divorce case that's kind of transformed itself into a murder case, which is how the police got involved. Saddleworth verses Saddleworth, that's the divorce case. Gerrard Saddleworth, the Home Secretary. It's the wife Olivia who's seeking the divorce.'

'But you're not from the police then?' To his surprise, she sounded relieved.

'No, but they are aware of my visit. You can check with them if you'd feel more comfortable about it. I have the name and phone number of the Detective Inspector who's in charge of the case, I'm sure he would be happy to reassure you.'

'No no, it's just that.. well, what has come to light, I've thought about it, and to be honest, I don't really know whether I should go to the police or not.'

'Well without knowing, I'm not really in a position to advise you. Why not just start at the beginning, if that would be ok?'

His answer appeared to mollify her. 'Ok Jimmy, thank you. So how much do you know about the Trust?'

'Assume nothing.' That was pretty much the truth.

'It was reported in the media at the time so it's no secret, but it was more than fifteen years ago. Emphysema has always been a massive health problem in the mining industry. It's a terrible disease. It badly damages the lungs through breathing in all that coal dust.'

Jimmy nodded. 'Yeah, I sort of knew that much.'

'So, it had been known about for over a hundred years but it was just seen as collateral damage. But after the industry contracted in the eighties, the government had a sudden outbreak of guilt and decided to do something about it. They established a compensation scheme, and the sums involved were very substantial. More than fifty thousand pounds for each living miner. The initial fund from the government was nearly four hundred million pounds of taxpayer's money.'

'Bloody hell, that *is* huge,' Jimmy said.

'Exactly. A massive sum. Of course it was all very politically charged, and that's why they agreed to put a chap from the miner's union in charge of the organisation.'

'That was Len Pringle? '

'That's right. There was a lot of scepticism amongst ordinary miners at the time as to whether the trust was a government stitch-up, and so it seemed a good idea to put one of their own in charge. Pringle was the perfect candidate. He'd been a big hero during the miners' strike and so they trusted him.'

'And how did that work out?'

'Not good,' she replied. 'He scammed the fund out of millions in the end.'

Jimmy gave a low whistle. 'Goodness, nice work if you can get it. So how did the scam work?'

'It was ridiculously simple really. The trust was a rather shoestring operation. They only had about thirty staff administering the whole thing from a scruffy office in Barnsley. They kept a database of miners on a spreadsheet, running to about thirty thousand names, and twice a year they sent out an information pack which explained what a former miner had to do to claim their compensation. They just had to fill in a simple form accompanied by a doctor's letter confirming they were suffering from the disease and that was it. Nothing else. Then all it needed was Pringle's signature on the form and the cash was paid out.'

'And no other authorisation was needed?' Jimmy asked. 'That sounds like a gift to a fraudster.'

Lily nodded. 'It was. So of course in the natural way of things the list was being reduced by deaths, nearly a thousand a year. These guys didn't exactly have a great life expectancy, and in its wisdom, the rules of the trust were that eligibility for compensation ceased on death, which was cruel on the families who hadn't yet had the benefit of a payout.'

'So how did they get to find out when a miner had died?'

'Again, that was quite straightforward,' she replied. 'They got a note through from the miners' pension scheme and then they updated their spreadsheet accordingly. And that's the loophole that Pringle spotted and exploited. Not long after the trust was set up, he began to take personal responsibility for updating the records when a miner died. Or not, as was actually the case. It was then a simple job for him to fill in a benefits form in the name of a deceased miner, forge a doctor's certificate and divert the funds to a bank account he had set up for that specific purpose.'

'Goodness, was it as simple as that?' Jimmy said. 'But surely there was at least some scrutiny, an annual audit or something like that, with all that public money washing about?'

'Yes, of course. That was in the hands of Morton Waterside the London firm, but frankly they did a rather poor job. But you have to remember that the political pressure was to show that the former miners were getting their compensation, and frankly no one cared too much if a few rogue claims slipped through the net. Success was judged by how much was paid out, not how much was saved.'

She stole a glance at her watch. 'Look, I'm sorry Jimmy, I've only got ten minutes or so...' She sounded genuinely apologetic.

'No no, that's fine Lily, I really appreciate the time you've given me already. So how much did he get away with?'

'A lot. Nearly seven million pounds was siphoned off over four years.'

'As much as that? Crikey.'

'Yes, but remember that Pringle only had to make around a hundred false claims out of about five thousand legitimate ones that were processed each year. So you can see why it was so easy for him to conceal what he was doing.'

'Very clever,' he agreed. 'So how did he get found out in the end?'

Lisa smiled. 'There was a keen new girl joined the trust's admin team, Carrie Jackson I think her name was. She had a customer services background, worked in a big car dealership before, and she thought it would be a great idea to do a satisfaction survey. You know, to find out what the miners thought about how they had been dealt with throughout the application process. So one day, completely off her own bat, she sent a little survey form out to everyone who had been awarded compensation that year.'

'I see,' Jimmy said, smiling. 'I guess some letters would have gone to miners that were actually dead, causing their relatives to kick up a stink.'

'Exactly. Within days Miss Jackson had received seven or eight replies from indignant loved ones castigating the trust for its insensitivity. Naturally she was somewhat surprised by this, and decided to do a bit of digging and was shocked to discover that all the money supposedly awarded to these miners had in fact been paid into a single bank account. A smart girl, she went straight to the police and that's when it all started to unravel for Pringle.'

'And that's when you guys got involved?'

'That's right. I wasn't a partner at that time, just one of the young associates doing the legwork. To be honest it wasn't that difficult to uncover the money trail. It wasn't a sophisticated operation by any stretch of the imagination.'

'What do you mean?' Jimmy asked.

'Well, Pringle had set up a company selling garden sheds...'

'Garden sheds?' He couldn't explain why he found that so funny.

'I thought that would make you laugh,' she replied, smiling. A very nice smile, he noticed. 'Yes, garden sheds. Expensive ones costing a few grand each, and all sold online so he never had to hold much stock. He laundered all the embezzled money through the shed company and again its auditors never once smelled a rat.'

He was conscious that time was running short, but Lily Hart now seemed happy to ignore her own deadline.

'Carry on please,' he said, 'only if you have time of course. This is fascinating.'

'Sure, no worries, I can spare a few more minutes. So anyway we uncovered that over four years he had processed one hundred and thirty-seven fraudulent claims, worth a total of six-point-eight million pounds.'

'That's unbelievable. And what did he do with it all?'

'Well, not very much at all, that's the odd thing. He took his wife on a couple of exotic cruises and that was about it. No fancy cars or big houses or anything like that. In fact we found nearly four and a half million sitting in the deposit account of the shed company earning a miserable one point five percent.'

'But wait a minute,' Jimmy said, 'by my rough calculation he still managed to get through nearly two million quid, or am I missing something?

'Yes, very perceptive Jimmy. In fact when we checked his bank statements, we found he had been withdrawing large amounts of cash, which we assumed he then squirreled away in a safety deposit box somewhere as a kind of rainy day fund. A sort of under-the-mattress stash if you like.'

'But I'm guessing you never managed to track that down?'

'Well, at the time, that was true,' Lisa said. 'He obviously knew where it was going, but even when questioned by the police he wouldn't say anything. In the end, the authorities were happy to be able to recover a fair chunk of the money and sweep the whole thing under the carpet.'

'And then Penelope White got involved. How did that happen, do you know?'

'Well, yes I do. Did you know that Len Pringle committed suicide soon after the affair was exposed?'

'Yes, I did know that,' Jimmy said. 'The police told me.'

She smiled and for a second, their eyes met, exchanging a look that suggested the meeting might not end at five o'clock sharp as scheduled. Or was he just imagining that? He was too out of practice to be sure.

'So, he was found dead in his office, slumped over his desk with his wrist slashed. A knife was found lying on the floor beside him. The obvious conclusion was that he'd killed himself because of the shame of it all. It made perfect sense of course. But then a few weeks later, allegations appear in the press that the police had fouled up the crime-scene investigations. A police whistleblower told the Yorkshire Post that some idiot Detective Sergeant had picked up the knife, meaning that any chance of getting fingerprint evidence was lost. At the inquest, the coroner was highly critical of the officer in charge, but the political pressure was to tidy the whole thing up and so a suicide verdict was returned.'

'But from how you describe it, I'm guessing there were doubts,' said Jimmy.

'Oh yes. The family never accepted the verdict but they couldn't get anyone in authority to pay attention.'

'What, they think he was murdered?'

'They always have maintained he was, even after all these years. But earlier this year, they decide to take a different approach. They contacted Penelope White at the Chronicle and she started to take an interest in the story.'

'She's a damn terrier that woman. Was, I should say.'

'I met her you know. She came here just a few weeks ago. I quite liked her, she was funny. I couldn't believe it when I heard she had been murdered.' Lily gave a frown as if the consequences of that visit had entered her mind for the first time. 'You don't think her death could be connected to this, do you?'

Suddenly she looked frightened.

Jimmy did his best to reassure her. 'The police are still trying to establish a motive. She made a lot of enemies in her line of work. But no, I don't think they are suggesting it was connected to this.' For now at least.

'You see the thing was Jimmy, at the time I always thought our firm was anxious to wrap the whole thing up as quickly as possible. Too quickly I thought. There was a lot more digging that myself and the team wanted to do, but Neville Prentice wouldn't approve the work.'

'Neville Prentice?'

'He was the managing partner here and took personal charge of the project. The only grandson of one of the founders, you know, the guy with his name above the door. He was the last of the line.'

'Is he still around?' Jimmy asked.

'Physically yes, mentally no. He's in his eighties and now stuck in a retirement home in Harrogate with dementia. He was already pushing seventy at the time of the affair and retired soon afterwards.'

'So did you take over from him?'

'Goodness no, I was only twenty-eight at the time. We've gone through three managing partners before I took over earlier this year.'

Jimmy laughed. 'Yeah sorry, dumb of me.'

'No,' she smiled, 'it's very flattering.' She reached across her desk and picked up a buff folder. 'But remember I told you that something had come to light? Partly as a result of the Penelope White investigation? It's very delicate.'

'I'm intrigued,' Jimmy said.' Please tell me more.'

'Well, a couple of months ago we were having a clear-out of our archives. We pay a lot of money to store them securely off-site and it doesn't take long to fill up our allocated space. So we operate a fifteen-year rule, anything older we review and then dispose of. It's a lot of work as you can imagine, but unfortunately rather necessary.'

'Glad I don't have to do it,' Jimmy smiled.

'It *is* a pain, and particularly for me, because I have to make the final decision as to whether a file can be shredded or not. Not surprisingly, the staff err on the side of caution, so much of it gets dumped on me. Which is why this particular file ended up on my desk.'

The front of the folder bore a printed label with the legend *MET-Private & Confidential*. She opened it and took out a letter bearing the Reed Prentice letterhead.

'Obviously I was interested in this in the light of Penelope White's visit. Needless to say I was badly shocked by what I found.' Jimmy took it from her and began to read.

'As advised, I have set up a security deposit account with Geneva Swiss Bank, Lombard Street, London EC3. A welcome pack with full instructions will be sent to you within the next working week. Naturally, privacy is assured since as you will know under Swiss law the bank is prevented from divulging the identities of its account holders.

As agreed, my fee for this service is one hundred and fifty thousand pounds, payable please in cash. I enclose the signed non-disclosure agreement as drawn up by your legal advisors, and assure you of my utmost discretion on this matter at all times.

Yours faithfully,

Neville Prentice

Jimmy gave her a look of astonishment. 'Lily, this is unbelievable. Who was this addressed to?' Of course, he already knew the answer.

'There were two copies. One was sent to Gerrard Saddleworth. As you know, he was a trustee at the time. The other was to the solicitor who drew up the non-disclosure agreement.'

So Olivia Saddleworth was right all along. Sneaky little Gerrard did have a mountain of cash stashed away. A bloody humongous pile in fact. Asvina Rani was going to be very pleased indeed.

'And your senior partner was in on it too? I can't believe that. A hundred and fifty grand quid to keep his mouth shut. And he covered his arse with an NDA. A very smart guy.'

'Yes, it seems bizarre there should be an NDA involved in what is a very shady affair, but in fact when I thought about it, old Neville probably didn't actually do anything illegal himself. He may have known how Saddleworth came by the cash, but he wasn't involved in procuring it in any way so he could turn a blind eye. As you said, a smart guy.'

'And how *did* he come by the cash, do you think?'

'I don't know for certain, but I'd speculate blackmail. It's my guess that Saddleworth found out what Pringle was up to, and made him pay up to keep quiet.'

Jimmy nodded. 'Yeah, that stacks up. And as long as he kept the cash hidden out of sight then even if Pringle grassed him up to the authorities, there would be no evidence. He could just deny everything.'

Lily gave him a wry smile. 'Exactly. So you can see my dilemma Jimmy. This looks bad for the firm, but I don't think I can keep this under wraps. I need to tell the police.' It was half-question, half-statement of fact.

Suddenly a chilling thought came to him. 'Do you think Saddleworth might have murdered Pringle? Perhaps he'd decided to confess what he had done, and take Saddleworth down with him. So he was killed to shut him up.'

She looked surprised. 'That I think is a step too far, isn't it? Government ministers don't go around murdering people.'

'Except he wasn't a minister back then. But you know Lily,' Jimmy said, his mind racing, 'what if that's what Penelope White had found out? It would be the story of her life, wouldn't it? *I was in love with killer minister.*'

And then perhaps her lover had decided that she had to be killed too. Because Jimmy knew from his brother's long experience that the crime-novel cliché was actually true. That when you had killed once, it was much easier to do it again.

'Look, I'll make sure the police are informed about all of this,' Jimmy said, 'and of course let them know that it wasn't your fault in any way. That you didn't know anything about Neville's NDA.'

He noticed her stealing another glance at her watch.

'I'm sorry Lily, I know I've overstayed my welcome, I'm really grateful for your time...'

'No no Jimmy, I was just checking if it was five o'clock yet. I wonder, are you rushing back to London this evening? I could really do with a drink and something to eat.'

The offer was tempting. *Very tempting.* A drink, a quick dinner and then back to London on a late train. He looked again at her lovely face.

A face that said there wasn't much chance that the evening would simply end with coffee. And for just a moment he wavered. Until he thought of Flora. If he wanted his wife back, and he did, and desperately, then sleeping with beautiful accountants would not help the cause.

'I need to get back to London.' He could see the disappointment in her eyes. 'It would be lovely, but really, I have to get back.' He wasn't sure who he was trying to convince.

As he walked back to the station he was able to console himself by reflecting on the success of the mission. Now they had proof that Saddleworth had squirreled away two million pounds in a safety deposit box, the transaction conveniently arranged by his financial advisor. A financial advisor who had covered his own backside with a non-disclosure agreement, drawn up by a lawyer mate of Saddleworth's. And though it was only a guess, he'd put money on that mate being Philip Brooks. A web of deceit, and a web he was convinced had its sticky silk wrapped all around that Cathedral Course dinner.

He was just about to go through the ticket barrier when he felt his phone vibrate in his pocket. It was a text. From Lily Hart.

Still time to change your mind xx.

Chapter 28

It was nearly two o'clock before Jimmy made it back to Kings Cross. Maggie had no idea what had made it necessary for him to stay overnight in Leeds, but no doubt he would tell them when they met up in a few minutes' time. A few days earlier he had added her to his *Find a Friend* list, which meant she was now able to track him as he crawled down Grays Inns Road at a pace normally reserved for old ladies pushing wheeled walking frames. Normal duration, twelve minutes. Time expended so far, twenty-three minutes. He was obviously in no hurry to get back to the office, which wasn't at all like him. She jabbed the call button and flicked it on to speakerphone.

'Hi Jimmy, are you anywhere near our Starbucks?' She knew he was, and he would know that she would know too. 'Elsa's run out of bloody beans again and I was desperate. I think Frank's going to pop round in a bit too.'

'*Funnily enough, I'm just a couple of minutes away,*' he said, his voice feigning surprise. '*Quite a coincidence that you should call when I'm only a skip and a jump from the front door.*'

'So, how did you get on?' Maggie asked as he pulled up a stool alongside her. 'Must have been a worthwhile visit given how long it took.'

'Yeah sorry about that. I took the opportunity to look up an old army pal afterwards. From the Helmand days. Had a few beers and grabbed something to eat and then crashed out on his sofa.'

She didn't like to tell him that she already knew some of that, having tracked his about-turn at the station and all his movements thereafter. Except of course, she didn't know who he had been with. Although she'd found it interesting that he had walked back to Lily Hart's office just twenty minutes after he'd left.

'That's nice.'

'Yeah, it was,' he said hesitantly. 'It was a great evening. He's a good lad, old Lawrence. One of the best.'

Maggie gave him a wry smile. 'And Lily Hart? What was she like?'

He shrugged. 'Lily? Yeah, good, very helpful. And smart. She reminded me a bit of you actually.'

She assumed it was meant as a compliment, but if he had spent the night with her, she wasn't sure she welcomed the comparison. And she didn't really want to find out either, so she steered the conversation onto business.

'But did you find out anything interesting from her?'

He too seemed keen to move on. 'You could say that,' he said, grinning. 'Aye, you could say that.'

And then he told her. About the Trust, and the safety deposit box stuffed with two million in cash, and the non-disclosure agreement. The non-disclosure agreement that had been drawn up and witnessed by Philip Brooks.

She wasn't at all surprised by the revelation. Philip hadn't told her anything during their marriage, let alone what he'd done before they met, and this would be just one more in a long list of skeletons in his cupboard.

'Did you know he was involved?' Jimmy asked. 'I guess it was quite a few years before you married him.'

She shrugged. 'No. One of many things he kept from me.'

'But don't you think the whole thing is bloody unbelievable?'

'What's unbelievable?' Frank had strolled in, taking a final drag on his cigarette before extinguishing it between his fingertips, ignoring the reprimanding stare of a tattooed barista.

'All of it.' Her mind was racing, trying to process this new information that Jimmy had mined up in Yorkshire. Even with a cursory review, she could see that it supported her crazy theory. One hundred percent. She *had* to be right, there was no doubt about it now, and it couldn't be kept to herself any longer. The words rushed out in a torrent.

'Guys, I want to run something past you. Something that came into my head yesterday when we were with Chief Superintendent Wilkes. Something mental.'

'Aye ok,' Frank said calmly. 'We're all ears.'

'I like mental,' Jimmy said.

And then she told them. *It was all about freeing Alzahrani.* Yes, they hadn't misheard her, that's what she had said. There had been a conspiracy to ensure that Alzahrani walked free. She didn't know why, and she had no idea who was behind it all, but she couldn't be more sure she was right. There was a long silence as each of them tested the sense of Maggie's premise, trying to force the facts of the case into place, like pieces in a particularly complex jigsaw. Frank was the first to speak.

'There's a lot of stuff going on in this case, stuff that's way, way out of the ordinary. Five people have dinner and now two of them have been murdered, along with the waiter who served them. Professionally murdered too, don't forget. And now we know that at least three of them have big secrets that they really wouldn't want to come out into the open. Dr Khan with his fondness for rent-boys, and now we find out Brooks and Saddleworth are all implicated in a multi-million fraud. That's all serious shit.'

'And what about Saddleworth's visit to Moscow?' Jimmy said, 'and Cameron's drugs bust and the fact we think there's something suspicious about Maggie getting the defence brief.'

'Yes, there's all of that,' Frank agreed. 'As I said, a lot of stuff going on.'

'It's got to be Saddleworth, hasn't it?' Jimmy said. 'Behind all of this, I mean. He's got the most to lose.'

'Or Philip,' Maggie said. 'Remember, he's a long-time supporter of the cause.'

But then she thought about it again. Yes, he was a supporter, but not a believer. Philip wouldn't give a sod whether Alzahrani got freed or not, because Philip didn't believe in anything other than himself. The rights of the Palestinian people were no more than a lucrative market niche, a niche that paid big bucks. Money, that was all that Philip believed in.

Frank did not answer directly. 'You know, it's not exactly rocket science but people with big secrets are vulnerable to coercion. And I think that's what is in play here. Maybe all of these guys are being forced to do something they really don't want to do.'

'*Were* being forced,' Maggie corrected. 'Penelope White and Adam Cameron are both dead.'

'Aye, and that's the next step when coercion stops working,' Frank said, looking serious. 'I laughed at you two when you brought up the means, motive, opportunity thing, but guys, I'm not laughing now. We're still struggling with the motive, but it's the other two I'm worried about right now.'

'What do you mean?' Maggie asked.

'What I mean is we've got professional killers on the loose here and they've always got multiple options when it comes to both. We've had a clinical shooting and two expertly-executed stabbings. So as I said, professionals.'

'So where does that get us?' Maggie asked.

'Nowhere,' Frank said flatly, 'because until we know why someone wanted Alzahrani freed, we're buggered. Totally buggered.'

***

It was Yash Patel at the Chronicle who had originally broken the 'Saddleworth and his murdered lover' story. Poignant too, given that the lover in question was his former boss Penelope White. Not that he had shed many tears for her himself. She was a bitch, and a racist bitch too, although she had tried hard to keep that under the radar. Keen too to take all the credit for everything, when often as not it was him who had put in all the legwork. But what the hell, now he was the columnist with the photoshopped mug-shot alongside his by-line, so you could say that whoever had murdered her had done him a big favour. That's the way he saw it and the paper was secretly pleased with the outcome too, having previously been a bit light on diversity amongst its columnists. He wasn't too modest to admit it had been a stonking article, with just enough innuendo for the readers to go away thinking, you know what, maybe he did kill her. Perhaps he had, Yash wasn't ruling it out. What a story that would be.

And now Gerrard Saddleworth was doing what all politicians did after being caught with their pants down. Round up the wife, children and pets, stick them on a platform in a nice conference room in a nice hotel convenient for the media and turn on the tears. Except Saddleworth's estranged wife Olivia had told him to bugger off, so he was left only with his beautiful nineteen-year-old daughter Patience by his side, and judging by her expression, she didn't look too pleased to be there either. The room was packed with hacks and TV crews from all around the world, so much so that it was standing room only. Yash had anticipated this and had arrived nice and early, being rewarded for his diligence by a seat in the front row, close enough for a bit of subtle upskirting, and Patience had unintentionally obliged by wearing a micro-skirt and no tights. An innocent pastime in his eyes and ridiculous that it had been made illegal, but on balance, probably not the subject for one of his campaigning articles.

The party's press officer stood up, cleared her throat, gave a weak smile then began reading from a prompt card. 'Ladies and gentlemen, thank you for coming. May I introduce Gerrard Saddleworth, Minister of State for the Home Department. Gerrard.' She hadn't had to bust a gut to come up with that introduction, but maybe he was being a bit harsh on her. It was odds-on she had written what was to follow too, but even that wouldn't have been too difficult given the number of times she'd had to do it. A simple cut and paste job, no more than that.

Saddleworth was wearing the standard man-of the-people uniform of navy suit with blue open-necked shirt. On the outside at least he appeared relaxed. Having stood in for PM's questions on many occasions, he was hardly going to be fazed by this lot. He smiled fondly at his daughter and she scowled back at him with a look that so clearly said 'wanker.' Yash assumed it was only the threat of her allowance being withdrawn that had brought her here.

'Ladies and gentlemen, thank you for coming,' he parroted. 'I've come here to apologise publicly to my constituents, my party and above all to my wonderful family for letting them all down...'

Yep, pretty much the same words that his colleague the Right Honourable James Haggerty had used just over six months ago when his pregnant Russian lover had spilled the beans to the *Sun*. Now there would be some crap about the pressures of office and no man being immune to temptation, and how much he deeply regretted his actions blah, blah, blah. The assembled press guys were listening politely and some were even taking notes, but this was only the starter for the main course to come. Because as soon as Saddleworth had finished, a hundred hacks were going to blurt out the only question everyone in the room wanted answered. 'Minister, did you kill Penelope White?' Already, the TV correspondents were making sure their camera crews and sound guys were properly lined up to make sure that it was nicely captured for the millions back home.

The risk assessment for the event had come back as only a Level 2, so they had decided to keep the security pretty-low key. They would go with just his regular undercover team, stationing one at the door and the other to the side of the stage. Adequate, and besides, he didn't want the press bitching about the cost of policing what was essentially a private matter. Both of them would be armed of course, but with no guns on display. More than enough to deal with anything that might arise that afternoon. Except that it wasn't.

The policeman watched on warily as the smiling young woman

approached the closed doors of the meeting room. There was something familiar about her, he thought, but he couldn't quite put a finger on where he'd seen her before. She was holding out a press pass in front of her for inspection. He took the pass from her and smiled back.

'You're a bit late love. I think he's already started.' These would be the last words he would ever say, as she plunged the stiletto blade into his chest, thrusting upwards to pierce the heart. Death would be instant, not that she cared about that. She pulled on the clown facemask, took the silencer-equipped pistol from her coat pocket and then, pushing the door ajar a fraction, she slipped through, locking it behind her. No-one in the room realised she was there, nor the mortal danger they were in, until they heard the dying gasp of the second policemen as two bullets thudded into his chest.

Adopting a combat position with the pistol thrust out in front of her, she swivelled on her heels and swept the room, looking for heroes. Out the corner of his eye, Yash could see that a cameraman from a US network was still filming. Bloody idiot. The assailant took him out from twenty meters with a shot that smashed straight through his skull, drenching a dozen journalists in a satanic mess of blood and warm brain tissue. Ignoring the screams of horror, she advanced slowly down the aisle towards the platform, still holding the gun out in front of her.

Patience Saddleworth was screaming hysterically. 'Please don't, please don't, please don't.' Beside her sat her father, rooted to the spot, his face a mask of confusion. And now the young woman was raising the pistol, pointing it at Saddleworth's forehead, standing close enough to taste his breath.

'What do you want? Who are you? Why are you doing this?' The woman stayed silent, remaining perfectly motionless with the gun inches from his head. Waiting, just waiting until the shit ran down his leg. And then she turned slightly, no more than four degrees, and blew Patience Saddleworth's brains out.

'This wasn't supposed to happen'. Yash was sure that's what Saddleworth had whispered. His last words before the assassin shot him between the eyes, then disappeared through the fire exit at the back of the room.

This wasn't supposed to happen. What had he meant by that?

***

Within minutes, naturally, it was all over the news. The brutal murder of the Home Secretary and his daughter was bound to shock the country and it did. Since the press was not aware of the existence of the Cathedral Close photograph, early speculation was that this was a planned terrorist outrage aimed at the heart of our democracy, almost certainly Islamic in origin. Outrageous in planning and audacious in execution, it had clearly been arranged so that it was played out live in front of the worlds' media. There was condemnation about the lack of security at the event, which many said was another symptom of the general incompetence of the security services.

In the barrage of comment and analysis which followed, the words of a little-known Chronicle columnist went largely unnoticed. *'This wasn't supposed to happen'.* But Maggie Bainbridge read them with horror, instantly recognising what they signified. Everyone at that dinner was going to die. Meaning Philip Brooks and Dr Tariq Khan were in mortal danger. And their families too.

Now she had only one thought in her head. She had to get to Ollie and make him safe.

Chapter 29

'Shit, that was close.' Jimmy had the pedal nailed to the floor as he accelerated away from the junction, the engine screaming up to maximum revs. He had barged through the crossover at nearly sixty miles an hour, smacking into the rear flank of a big Lexus and narrowly missing being T-boned by the refuse truck proceeding lawfully at ninety degrees with the green light. The wing of the Golf was now hanging on by a thread, throwing up a kaleidoscope of sparks as they powered along, headlights on full beam and horn blaring.

'Sorry about the no-claims Maggie.' He knew it wasn't the time for jokes, but she looked as if she was close to passing out. 'We'll be there in ten minutes, but please when it's time for a change, can you trade this wreck in for something quicker.'

She responded with a weak smile. He could tell the tension would be gnawing at her stomach like a bad curry. *We just have to get there, we just have to get there.* There was a loud bang as the trailing wing smashed against a lamppost and detached itself, flying through the air and taking out the plate-glass window of a charity store.

'Whoa, lost a bit of weight there,' Jimmy exclaimed. 'All helps.' He reached across and took her hand, giving it a squeeze. 'It will be alright.' God, how he hoped that would turn out to be true.

They reached her Hampstead home - he knew she still thought of it as hers, even after all this time - without further incident, as he brought the Golf to a screeching stop with two wheels on the pavement. They threw open the doors and sprinted up the path. Suddenly Jimmy shot out an arm and shouted. 'Wait Maggie!' The front door was ajar, creaking quietly in the gentle breeze. This didn't look right. Helmand all over again, the old instincts kicking in.

'Maggie, you just stay here.'

'But Jimmy...'

'For god's sake Maggie, do as I tell you. Get back on to the police and find out where the hell they've got to.' No time for niceties, he didn't want another dead rooky on his conscience. Gingerly, he edged open the door and went in to the hallway. *Shit.* He could smell it. Cordite, and recently fired too. The smell of death.

'Philip!' he shouted. 'Philip Brooks!' No response. Every door in the hallway was closed tight, making the sweep doubly difficult and doubly dangerous. A professional job, no doubt about that.

'Philip!' He kicked open the nearest door, allowing it to slam against its brass doorstop before entering. A comfortable living room furnished with two soft leather sofas and a huge wall-mounted television. Fresh flowers in a crystal vase. Tasteful reproductions on the wall. *Nothing here.* Two more rooms yielded similar results. Three more to go. But wait a minute, what was that? The faintest of cries. He stood stock-still and listened hard. A child's voice. *My mummy, I want my mummy.* Please god, no! He dashed to the end of the hall and kicked open the door. Christ, he had seen some shit over in Afghanistan, but nothing like this. Spread-eagled on the terracotta tiled floor in a pool of blood lay Angelique Perez, two bullets holes drilled neatly through her forehead. Her white silk blouse, now blood-splattered, had been ripped away, exposing her breasts above her black silk bra. Her flower-patterned skirt had been pulled down to her ankles, and a pair of knickers lay discarded beside her. Whether she had been raped before or after her murder was impossible to tell.

Philip Brooks' body was slumped face down across the kitchen table, an exit wound clearly visible on the back of his head. Jimmy had seen this so many times before. A pistol rammed into the mouth, and then the killer would wait and wait, wait until the shit literally ran down the victim's leg before blowing his head off. Was Perez forced to watch her lover's execution, or was Brooks forced to watch her being raped? It turned his stomach just thinking about it.

But where was Ollie? Surely it was his voice he had heard, it must have been, but where the hell was he? Rapidly, he surveyed the big kitchen. What was that in the corner? A door, maybe a pantry or something. He leapt over and flung it open. There, tied to a wooden chair was little Ollie Brooks. A bloody swelling had almost closed his right eye and his cheek showed the weal marks where he had been struck with force. The bastards, the evil bastards.

And then, to his horror, Jimmy saw the package. Attached to one leg of the chair with cable ties. A package that he instantly recognised. Eight or more coloured wires emerging from the top, most likely leading to a trigger or timer. His eyes traced along the line of the wires as they snaked around the chair-leg and up the backrest. From there, they had been fed down the neck and along the arm of Ollie's jumper. Yes, it was a trigger all right. A trigger that little Ollie Brooks now held in his tiny hand.

The boy had been staring at him, paralysed with fear. And no wonder, because what the boy had witnessed didn't bear thinking about. Jimmy kneeled down in front of him. 'It's Ollie isn't it? I'm Jimmy, I'm a friend of your mummy's and I'm here to help you. Is that ok?'

The little boy nodded slowly then mumbled, 'I want my mummy.'

'She'll be here soon, I promise.' He wrapped his fist around his hand and squeezed gently. At least it was a trigger, not a timer. And then, the ghastly thought. What if it was both, he wouldn't put it past these bastards. Hopefully the police would be here in a minute and then they could get his old mates from the bomb squad on the case. But what if it was also a timer? Of course it will be, that's exactly what they would do. Shit.

Hearing footsteps behind him, he spun round, but it was too late to stop her entering the kitchen, as if he could do anything about it in his current situation. She stood frozen to the spot, unable to take in the scene of utter carnage that filled her field of vision. She staggered towards the wall before throwing up.

'Maggie, just close your eyes and get the hell out of here. Now!' She turned round in the direction of his voice, bringing her son into view. 'Ollie, Ollie, my Ollie!'

'It's a bloody booby-trap Maggie. A bomb. Please don't come any closer.'

'I'm not leaving Ollie. I need to be with him, whatever happens.' Of course she was never going to leave her son to his fate, what mother would? But maybe, just maybe, her presence offered a tiny glimmer of hope.

'Look Maggie, Ollie's holding a trigger in his hand. If he opens his fist, then that's it, the bomb goes off.'

She gasped and covered her mouth with her hand.

'I know, it's a shock,' Jimmy said, 'but I need you to help me. It's the only chance we've got, ok?'

She nodded but her eyes radiated fear.

'His little hand must be hurting so I need you to take over from me so I can take a closer look at the device. I need you to speak to him and tell him how important it is not to open his hand. Just for a second. Just when we're doing the switch. Is that ok?'

She sobbed but was able to wipe the tears from her eyes with her sleeve. 'Of course.'

Kneeling down, she planted a soft kiss on her son's forehead. 'Darling, I need you to be a big brave boy. You're very good at counting aren't you?'

'Yes, mummy I am.'

'And what's the biggest number you can count to my darling?'

He gave a weak smile. 'To infinity and beyond.'

'Infinity and beyond. That's amazing my love. So when I say go, start counting and don't stop squeezing your hand until you reach infinity. Can you do that for me?'

'Yes mummy.'

Jimmy gave her a silent thumbs-up. 'Just move your hand over mine. Once Ollie starts counting I'll slip mine out of the way and you can take over.'

She nodded. 'Ok, Ollie, are you ready? To infinity and beyond. One-two-three- go.'

Deftly, Jimmy slipped his hand away to be replaced in an instant by Maggie's. *Mission accomplished.* He kissed her gently on the cheek and whispered 'It's going to be all right.' He kept telling her that. He just wished he believed it. Now all he needed was a pair of scissors and a massive dose of luck.

And then he remembered that he had the number of Private Alex Marley tucked away in his phone book. Thank god, she answered on the first ring. *'Sir, long time no speak. It's great to hear from you again. What are you up to, enjoying civvy street?'* As upbeat as ever.

'Well actually you might be interested to know I'm standing in a hundred-grand Hampstead kitchen trying to figure out how to disarm another bloody IED. I need your help.'

Instantly the cool professional soldier kicked in, her voice taking on an urgent tone. *'Roger sir, can I have a summary of the situation?'*

'Looks like a standard IRA Semtex package, eight-wire device with a trigger and probably some sort of internal timer wired up as a booby trap. Seen anything like it before?'

'Yes, I think we have sir. Eight wire, did you say?

'Yeah, that's right.' He shot an encouraging glance at Maggie.

'That's fairly good news then sir.'

'It is?' He had to admit that he wasn't seeing much upside at that moment.

'Yeah, so they would have used two wires for the timer circuit and two for the trigger. That means there are only four decoys.'

'Hang on a minute. Does that mean...'

'...fifty-fifty chance sir. Much better than the two out of eight that we normally get.'

'And that's supposed to be good news?'

'Yes sir. I'd best let you get on. Over and out.'

So that was what it now came down to. The lives of Maggie, her son and his own resting on a fifty-fifty throw of the dice, or more accurately, a fifty-fifty snip with a pair of scissors. But as Marley had said, nothing to do but get on with it.

'Scissors!' he barked. 'Where are they kept?'

'I used to keep them in the top drawer. Just left of the hob,' Maggie shouted.

He'd forgotten this was no longer her home. He just hoped Angelique hadn't had a reorganisation. Yanking open the drawer, he rummaged around in the untidy pile of utensils. There they were, thank heavens for that. Two steps and he was back in the pantry, where Ollie was still counting in a lilting rhythm '...sixty-five, sixty-six, sixty-seven...' He hoped to hell he would reach one hundred.

He dropped to the ground, laying on his stomach so that he was eye-level to the device. Eight wires, colour-coded, but the problem was only the bomb makers had the key to the code. He shuffled up close, squinting hard to focus on the gap where the wires emerged from the buff-coloured padded envelope. It was hard to be sure, but was there the tiniest of gaps between the first two wires and the remaining six? He looked again. Yes, it was only a fraction of a millimetre but there was a definite gap. He spun onto his back, pulled out his phone and called Marley again, spitting out the question.

'Would we expect the wires to the battery to be next to one another?'

Her reply was instant. *'Yes sir, it's the only way they could route them. Problem is, you usually can't tell which two by looking.'*

But maybe today, they had got a lucky break. Trouble was they wouldn't get to know if he was wrong. And now it was the moment of truth.

'Maggie, I'm going to cut the wire. You know what that means. You should say your goodbyes to Ollie. Just in case.'

But there was nothing to say. He knew she loved him more deeply than any love in the history of the universe, and saying it wouldn't make it any truer. Besides, it was all going to be fine. Fifty-fifty. Given the shit she had been through in the last eighteen months, surely this time the fates would take pity on her.

'We're good. Cut it Jimmy.' She closed her eyes and rested her cheek against Ollie's.

This was it. Decision time. He had no idea where it came from, but bizarrely he began to hum a familiar lilting tune. *Que sera sera, whatever will be will be.* Red and green, it had to be these two. Cut either, or both, and you cut the power to the detonator. Bomb disarmed, job done. He positioned the blades over the two wires, being careful to move the others well out of the way. *Come on man, just do it.* Unless you want the timer to do it for you anyway. He tightened his fingers on the grip and squeezed hard, looking away, as if that was going to make any difference. *Snip.* And then nothing. Glorious, sweet, life-affirming nothing.

He ripped the package off the leg of the chair and slid it along the floor until it rested against the back wall of the pantry. Wrapping his arms around the chair, he picked it up with Ollie still tied to it. The boy was still counting '... ninety-eight, ninety- nine, one hundred.'

Jimmy beamed a huge smile at him. 'A hundred. That's amazing mate, you can stop now. Come on Maggie, time to get out of here.' As if she needed to be told. They struggled down the hallway, reaching the front door just as the shriek of sirens announced the arrival of the Met, led by Jill Smart and Frank Stewart.

'Christ what's happened here?' Frank asked. 'C'mon, let me help you with the boy.' Gently, they laid the chair down on the driveway.

'Wouldn't rush in there if I was you,' Jimmy cautioned. 'Bit of a mess. And you need to call the bomb squad fast.'

Maggie was feverishly trying to free her son from his bonds, but not making much progress. From the depth of a trouser pocket, Frank retrieved an old-school flick knife.

'Allow me madam.' With a couple of expert slashes, Ollie was free.

There were of course hugs and kisses and tears and thank-yous, and chilling cold sweats when they each contemplated what might have been. For Jimmy, there was overwhelming relief that he hadn't lost another one. For Maggie, the weird realisation that the murder of her husband of eight years had triggered no emotion whatsoever. For now at least. Perhaps the eighteen months of sheer hell had shredded her capacity to feel anything, but whatever it was, right now she was glad he was dead, and Angelique too. Meanwhile, little Ollie was still counting. To infinity and beyond.

The ambulances had arrived to take them to the Royal Free. For Maggie and Jimmy, the injuries were merely psychological, as if that wasn't bad enough. Ollie would need a couple of stitches above his eye and an x-ray of that cheek to make sure there were no broken bones. As to the impact on his little mind of the unspeakable horrors he had witnessed, that would have to wait until the hoards of councillors and psychologists were sent in to do their work. Tonight, for the first time in over eighteen months, he would sleep under the same roof and in the same room as his mummy, and for both of them, it was a heavenly bliss that could not be described in words.

For the professionals of law-enforcement, late on the scene but relieved that events had turned out well, there was now only one priority, as voiced poetically by Detective Inspector Frank Stewart.

Where the fuck was Dr Tariq Khan?

Chapter 30

You could do a lot of things in Department 12B that you couldn't do over at Paddington Green nick. Things like giving two amateur investigators a fake pass to Atlee House and a quiet desk in the corner.

'Does Jill know about this?' Maggie asked as Frank led them down the warren of corridors to the depressing open-plan space they had newly-christened the Operations Room. DCI Smart had decamped to Paddington to head up the case leaving Frank behind, 'nominally in charge of the office' as she had described it.

'Yes, of course,' he lied. 'Tough case like this, we need all the resources that we can lay our hands on.' That much at least was true.

'Did you see her on the news last night? Did a good job I thought. A telly natural.' After the horrifying murder of Saddleworth and his daughter, no stone was being left unturned in the search for the missing Dr Khan, and DCI Smart had decided that a direct appeal to the public was called for. As well as the televised police press conference, photographs of the missing scientist would be plastered on every vacant wall from Lands End to John O' Groats, although logic suggested that he would be holed up somewhere in the North West, close to where he grew up, it being an established fact that fugitives from justice were generally picked up close to their own manor. Not that Khan was exactly fleeing justice, but broadly speaking the same rules applied.

Now Frank was revealing that he had that morning spoken with a detective constable with the Gloucestershire force who had been sent to interview Khan's wife. Contrary to his expectations, Mrs Khan had not denied knowledge of her husband's whereabouts, but was adamant that she would never reveal the location where he was hiding. When asked, politely according to the officer's account, to hand over her phone, she had consented, adding something along the lines of did they think she would be so stupid as to make that sort of school-girl error. Subsequent review of her phone logs, both mobile and landline, had revealed no calls to or from his phone since he had disappeared. Similar scrutiny of those of his three teenage daughters had also drawn a blank. Social media, the same. This was one disciplined operation.

'Take her in to a quiet interview room and water-board her' had been Frank's helpful advice, the slow-witted yokel DC responding in all seriousness that they didn't do things that way in their neck of the woods.

'Doesn't she realise the danger they are all in?' Jimmy said. 'I'd be shitting myself if I was them given what has been happening.'

'The local plod says she's in complete denial about all of it. But they're posting twenty-four-hour surveillance at the house and also keeping tabs on the kids' school. Don't worry, they are taking this very seriously.' He sounded more convincing than he actually felt.

Eleanor Campbell swung by their desks, noisily sucking up the dregs from a *grande* strawberry milkshake. She pointed to the new occupants of the corner desks.

'Who are these two?' Frank might have known that little miss I'm-not-doing-anything-   until-I've-got-the-form-signed-in-triplicate would sniff out anything irregular.

'Work experience students.'

'Does Jill know about this?'

The lie was much easier the second time around. 'Of course she does Eleanor. Naturally.'

'I can like easily check.'

Maggie stood up and reached out her hand. 'Maggie Bainbridge. You must be Eleanor Campbell. Frank has told me so much about you. All good, I hasten to add.'

'Oh has he?' Her expression visibly softened.

'Technical genius he says you are.' With a twinkle in his eye, Jimmy looked at her and smiled his devastating smile. 'I'm Jimmy Stewart, it's great to meet you. A real pleasure.' That was the clincher. Eleanor was in, no matter what roguery Frank was planning. She perched herself on the edge of his desk and expertly propelled the empty cup into the waste bin.

'I assume you guys are looking for that Khan dude right?'

'You assume correctly,' Frank said, 'along with the whole of the Met, MI5, MI6 and every other police force in the land. Don't tell me you've started watching the news?'

She looked horrified. 'No way. But Khan is one real sick dude. I've got his three-point-four and it rocks.'

'I think sick is a term of approval Frank,' Jimmy said. Eleanor looked at him suspiciously, unsure if he was taking the piss or not.

'Three-point-four? What's that?' Maggie asked.

'It's his new version. Just beta and so it's pretty buggy but it's got some awesome features.'

'Ah right,' said Jimmy, beginning to cotton on, 'this is some software of Dr Khan's, is that it?'

'That's it. He put it up on the dot-gov secure download site so that we hackers could try and break it. It like takes face rec to a whole new level. It's now got enhanced landmark processing, family recognition search, cell synchronisation and public CCTV integration right out of the box. It's like, wicked.'

Frank furled his brow. 'Has anybody got a bloody clue what she's talking about? Can you run that past us again Campbell, this time in English.'

She threw him a pitying glance. 'There's a limit to how simple you can make it mate, and I think you're way below that limit. But I'll try and give you the idiot's version.'

Frank ignored the insult. 'Can't we just see this magical three-point-four? Like, on a screen?'

'No chance. It's classified. And these two certainly can't.'

Jimmy spoke softly. 'I understand totally Eleanor...' He lingered on her name, '... but it would really help us to understand what it's all about. We won't tell anybody, honest.' Frank smiled as he saw her resistance start to crumble.

'Well ok then. Come over to my lair.'

Her desk was surrounded by a wall of wide-screen monitors, four wide and two deep, like she was running a NASA mission control franchise. Frank guessed that she was interpreting their amazed expressions as envy.

'Great for gaming. Not that I'm into that. As if.' She rattled a few instructions into the remote keyboard and a left-hand screen filled with a face shot of a bearded man of South Asian appearance. 'Dr Tariq Khan in person. Well, not in person, but you know what I mean.' Alongside the image, a table revealed his personal details, date of birth, address, occupation, passport number, bank accounts and much more besides. 'I think he's hacked GCHQ's HR database to harvest some test data. All his colleagues are on there. Bad man.' It was a compliment.

'So, nice and secure then?' Maggie said. The irony was wasted on

Eleanor. She clicked a button and immediately Khan's face was painted with an intricate array of dots and gridlines. 'That's three-point-four's new landmark algorithms. Twice the resolution of three-point-three and nearly up to Chinese standards. And it's got an ethnicity differentiation processor now too. We don't think Beijing can do that yet.'

'Duh?' Frank said.

'Ethnicity differentiation. The old version only worked reliably on white faces.'

'This is awesome,' Jimmy said. 'And what about all that other stuff you talked about, are you able to show us any of that?'

She threw him a glance that said for you, anything. 'Sure. Where did you say this guy was from again?'

'Blackburn. That's in Lancashire.' Frank was pretty certain that Eleanor would never have heard of it.'

'Lancashire. That's in England, right?' A couple of clicks and she was scrolling down a selector box headed *CCTV Integration*. 'There it is, Blackpool'.

'Black-burn.'

'Whatever.' Another click, and a video feed from what looked like a shopping mall appeared on one of the monitors.

'Is this live?' Maggie asked.

'Pseudo live. There's about a ten-second delay for the servers to process the images and make it available to the network.'

'Good to know,' Frank said.

'So just remember this is a beta version, so it might not work, but we'll have a go anyway.'

She clicked a button labelled 'Match' and then leaned back in her chair. A few seconds later red-bordered boxes started to appear above the head of each of the shoppers captured in the video. Inside each box were two numbers, one labelled *Mobile* and the other *Match %*.

'We're running both family recognition and cell synchronisation here. What you see is the number of any mobile device they're carrying, and if they are likely to be related to our reference subject. Red border and a low percentage says they are not. That will be most of the subjects here of course.'

Maggie's eyes widened with astonishment. 'So Eleanor, are you saying that this can pick out whether any of these people are related to Khan? That's mental.'

'Yeah, exactly, like why not? Family members usually share some likeness, don't they? Three-point-four just turns their facial characteristics into data to make a digital match possible.'

'Bloody hell, look at this one.' Jimmy was pointing at a woman who had just entered the scene. 'She's got a green box above her head.'

'Green, yeah, that's a match. Awesome. That's a score of twenty-seven percent. Could be a cousin, looking at the age of her.'

'Christ's sake, this is scary and incredible at the same time,' Frank said. 'It's like bloody big brother, and I don't mean the TV show.'

'This is big brother two-point-zero,' Eleanor said. 'Awesome, isn't it? Like I said, your Dr Khan is one clever dude.'

At that moment, an older man wearing traditional Pakistani dress wandered into view. Suddenly Maggie blurted out 'The mosque. The mosque.'

'What?' Frank said.

Maggie's voice was crackling with excitement. 'Eleanor, can we see the location of any mosques in the area?'

'Yeah, 'course.' She punched an instruction in to the keyboard and a large-scale map of Blackburn town centre appeared. 'There we go, Blackburn Central Mosque on Mary Street.'

'Can we see it on CCTV?'

'Sure. These green dots, they're cameras hooked up to the national online CCTV network. Red ones are stand-alone. We can still get the footage but we need to ask for the DVD.' She clicked on the green dot nearest the mosque and instantly the building came into view.

'Live?' Maggie asked. 'I mean, pseudo live?'

'Yep. Look, trees swaying in the breeze.'

Frank could see Maggie's mind was working overtime.

'What are you thinking?' he asked.

Her eyes were blazing with excitement as the words tumbled out in a torrent. 'Listen to this guys, see what you think. So tomorrow's Friday. That's when the males of the local Muslim community will gather in the mosque for prayers. I'm right, aren't I?'

'Friday prayers, that's right,' Jimmy said.

'So what if we run three-point-four tomorrow on that camera before and after Friday prayers? I guess it's a long shot, but we might be able to find at least one or two of Dr Khan's relatives, maybe more if we are lucky. Because I think if he's hiding in the area, it's pretty likely that someone in his family will be helping him. We get their phone numbers, give them a call out of the blue, and one of them might panic and spill the beans. What do you think?'

'You know what,' Jimmy said, speaking slowly. 'I think this might just work. Definitely worth a shot.'

Frank anticipated that Eleanor might object to the scheme if the proper procedures weren't followed. Deadpan he said, 'Aye, it's a great idea, but I'll need to run it passed DCI Smart first. She'll probably have to get a warrant or something from a judge. But I'll sort it before tomorrow.'

It seemed to satisfy her.

'Yeah, awesome, I'll set it up. Sweet.'

Now they had a plan.

***

Up until now Plan B had been executed flawlessly, but this situation had now become very concerning. Khan had always been at the epicentre of the whole affair, so it was obvious in hindsight that he should have been taken out right at the start. Instead, they had waited to see how events unfolded, and now he had gone into hiding. Inconvenient, to say the least. He was proving to be a very clever guy, and for three and a half weeks he had outsmarted them. But no matter, they were playing the long game. Mrs Khan loved her husband and he loved her, and eventually they would be able to bear the agony of separation no longer. Chances are they had equipped themselves with burner phones, and sooner or later Mrs Khan would be compelled to switch hers on so that she could hear her husband's sweet voice once more. Or maybe drive to a remote pay-phone and call him from there.

An asset had been stationed such that movements into and out of the Khan's modest semi could be monitored. It was a bonus that the police seemed to be taking the threat to Mrs Khan less seriously than they perhaps should. This kind of thing didn't normally happen in Gloucestershire, and they didn't like the fact that it was disturbing their routine. So it was that whilst their chief constable had promised the Met twenty-four-hour surveillance, in reality there was a half-hour gap in the schedule around five-thirty when the afternoon shift knocked off. The asset had observed that most times, the evening shift didn't turn up to about six o'clock, sometimes more like six-thirty. Sloppy.

Naturally the distinguished member had been both pleased and relieved to get the message that finally the target was on the move. One afternoon, Mrs Khan had waited until the surveillance officer had been gone a few minutes before slipping into the family Corsa and racing off. Soon she had joined the Tewkesbury Road heading north-east, the asset, name of Kareem, following undetected three or four cars behind. After four miles, she had swung left onto a minor road that headed towards the Coombe Hill canal and in a few hundred yards pulled up onto a grass verge. With his powerful binoculars Kareem had maintained observation from a safe distance, simultaneously booting up the portable Scanner-Pro cell phone detector to ensure he was ready. He hadn't had long to wait.

Blackburn, Lancashire. That was going to be a nice day out.

Chapter 31

The operation was scheduled to launch around eleven thirty that day. Not only had Jill Smart given her approval, but she had signed off the requisition to allow Frank to drive to Blackburn the previous evening and check into a faceless business hotel on the ring-road. Jimmy and Maggie were there too and in separate rooms, but not on the public purse, although they had suffered the four-hour drive north with him in the Mondeo. Back at Atlee House, Eleanor Campbell was all geared up to run three-point-four's awesome search capabilities.

A team from Lancashire Constabulary's anti-terrorist response squad had been rounded up into a brightly-lit conference room, where they were now listening to the incident commander giving his briefing. Maggie and Jimmy sat quietly at the back, being introduced by Frank as psychological profilers seconded to the case. The commander had accepted the explanation without comment. He probably thought every cop in the Met travelled with at least one of them.

'Guys, this is DI Frank Stewart from the Met. Department 12B isn't that right Frank? Best not to ask what goes on in that unit, I'd imagine,' he joked. If only he knew.

Frank got to his feet and smiled at the room. 'Thanks Commander. So, to cut to the chase, our profilers here think there's a good chance that our Dr Khan could be hiding in perfect sight right here in Blackburn. But as you guys know, conventional enquiries have got us nowhere. We've talked to his wife, we've talked to his father, we've talked to his known associates and got nowhere. Everybody's doing a good job of keeping schtum, but we still think it's likely that he's being helped by a family member, maybe a cousin or someone who's not on our radar. So this is where this stuff comes in.' He pointed to the large screen behind him which was displaying the video feed from the mosque. 'Back in the smoke, we're running some new real-time surveillance technology which hopefully can tell us if any of the attendees at Friday prayers are related to him in any way. We will also get their mobile numbers if they are carrying a device, which of course is highly likely.'

The expressionless faces around the room betrayed their scepticism, but up on the screen a few early worshippers had wandered into shot, their heads trailed by a red box filled with numbers. 'You see, red says these guys aren't related to Khan, but for most of them, we are getting a mobile number. So what do you think to that, eh? Awesome.' It was fast becoming his favourite word. On screen, they saw a member of the public stop, take out his mobile and stare at it, in the way you did when you did not recognise the incoming number. Tentatively, he raised it to his ear. 'He-llo?' The distorted voice echoed around the conference room. A young detective shook his phone in the air and laughed. 'Whoa, this stuff really works.'

'Told you,' Frank said. 'So, we just sit, watch and take notes. Can't say I'm confident, but you never know.' As twelve o'clock neared, the street in front of the mosque became increasingly busy. Many worshippers were dropped off directly outside, their faces invisible to the CCTV, and many more came from the direction of town such that their backs were to the camera. Soon the last few stragglers were making their way up to the front door, but still they had registered no positives.

'Let's not get too despondent folks,' Frank said. 'We'll have a much better chance to clock them on the way out.' An hour or so later, members of the flock began to emerge. *Red, red, red, red, red.* Every box was red. 'Doesn't mean it's not working, just hasn't registered a match yet.' They all hoped to god it was true.

A grizzled DC who looked at least ten years past retirement age piped up. 'This is a friggin' waste of time. I don't know why we don't just send a team up there and question everyone as they're leaving.' The younger woman DC sitting beside him voiced what everyone was thinking. 'Genius John. That would be brilliant for community relations. A squad of coppers swarming all over the mosque.'

'Let's just be patient,' said another, 'not even half of them have left yet.' More than three-quarters of an hour later, there were still no matches. You could almost taste the mood of despondency that seeped through the room, tinged with no little schadenfreude. 'Load of shite, I knew it was,' DC Grizzle said, not quite under his breath. 'Met wankers, they're all the same.' Frank decided to let it pass. This time. The commander was more diplomatic, but it was obvious he shared the opinion of his outspoken colleague. His manner was condescending.

'A bit of a waste of time I'm afraid Frank. We rely too much on new technology these days in my opinion.'

'What, like DNA profiling and CCTV and mobile call records sir? Aye, bring back old-fashioned policing, magnifying glasses, bobbies on the beat, all that stuff.' His bitterness was driven by disappointment, but even he recognised he might have gone too far. 'Sorry sir, I didn't mean to be disrespectful.' Although he did.

'Ok, I think we're done here,' the commander said sharply. 'Now if you don't mind, could you take your... your profilers or whatever they are and let us have our conference room back. You should be able to find a couple of desks in the general office if you have more work to do.'

'Thank you sir.' He beckoned to Jimmy and Maggie to follow him. No way was he going to face the scorn that would be heaped upon them in that cauldron of naysayers. Technology? They'd only just got colour telly up here.

'Starbucks is it?' Maggie said.

'Pub more like. Come on guys.' Jimmy gave a thumbs up and followed them to the front door.

The pub was dull and depressing, and deserted too, a function as much of local financial deprivation as to it being three-fifteen in the afternoon. In the corner, a large TV blared out Sky Sports News. Jimmy had just got to the bar when his phone rang.

'Hi Eleanor, nice to hear from you.'

Frank pulled a face. 'Eleanor? Why's she calling you?'

Jimmy shrugged and covered an ear with his cupped palm. It was apparent he was having difficulty hearing her above the din of the television. 'Sorry Eleanor, you need to say that again. Frank, can you get them to turn that bloody thing down.' There was no-one serving. Frank banged his fists on the bar and bellowed 'Service!' Eventually a bored-looking barmaid appeared, chewing gum.

'What can I get you?'

'Maybe you could turn that thing down.'

'The customers like it,' she said, unsmiling.

'Sorry love but we're the customers and we don't.' Reluctantly the barmaid picked up the remote and pointed it at the set.

'Thank you.'

'You're welcome.' She didn't sound it.

'That's better,' Jimmy said, returning to his phone-call. 'Eleanor, I'm going to put you on speaker phone. Don't go away.'

They found a table by the window and sat down. 'Ok, go ahead.'

'Hi guys.' She sounded excited.

'Hi Eleanor,' they replied in unison.

'So the reason I'm calling you guys, did you know that mosque thing had a back door? Like, you know, a fire escape or something.'

'No, we didn't...' Frank's heart began to race.

'Yeah, so there's a camera covering the back of the place. We missed the live feed, but I found a hack that let me download a recording. It's like awesome how quick it gets onto the servers. They must have a shit-load of tin in that datacentre.'

'Awesome,' Frank said, being rewarded by a scolding look from Maggie.

'So I ran three-point-four against the recording and holy shit, within minutes the alerts were going like mental. I saw seven hits just as a bunch of these guys in nightshirts were all coming out together.'

'Wow!' Maggie was now struggling to contain her excitement. 'And did you get all their phone numbers?'

'Shit to that. So, like in the middle of this group is a guy wearing a funny little hat and dark glasses and a scarf over his mouth and nose. Thinks he's in some sort of disguise or something but three-point-four only needs eleven reference points for a hit. Bang, a big dialogue box fills my screen, bang, bells ringing everywhere, and bang, a message tells me we've got a one-hundred-percent match.'

'Holy shit!' Jimmy exclaimed. 'Did you get his...'

'Number? 'course. 07835 098871. And then we triangulated him to 78 Granville Street. He's there right now. Oh, and I've messaged you the directions.'

***

'That's just three minutes away,' Jimmy shouted. 'Come on, let's get our arses round there now.'

'What, without back up?' Frank said. 'Not a good plan.'

'Well why don't you head back to the station to pick up the car and phone in on the way,' Maggie said. 'Jimmy and I will go and hang around outside the house until the teams arrive. We can't risk missing him, not when we're this close.'

'Aye all right then, but please don't try anything stupid. Wait for us to arrive, is that understood?'

Without answering they tore out of the pub, Jimmy's eyes fixed on his phone, Maggie blowing heavily but determined to keep up.

'It's just at the top of this street,' he shouted back. 'We'd better go carefully when we get there in case we're spotted. I'll wait for you up there.'

She gave a breathless thumbs-up, gritting her teeth and trying in vain to ignore her burning thighs. Granville Street turned out to be a classic northern industrial-era thoroughfare, the narrow street lined on both sides by well-kept two-up two-downs terraced properties which once would have been the crowded homes of mill workers and their families. The mills were long gone, and the homes were now almost exclusively occupied by members of the town's long-established Muslim community. They may have been here since the sixties, but that didn't mean that community relations were always good, so much so that the local council found it necessary to run a large team of 'community integration officers' to maintain an uneasy truce.

Maggie finally caught up with him, panting as she placed her hands on her hips, head bowed. 'I need to get fitter Jimmy, I really do.'

He gave her a sympathetic smile.

'The house is just along there on the left, according to my google maps. Should have a blue door if this Streetview shot is reasonably recent.'

She was beginning to catch her breath. 'So are we going to wait for Frank and the cavalry to arrive or what?'

'Don't see any reason to, do you? It's not as if Khan's going to be surrounded by armed guards or anything. I say we just wander up and knock on the door, see if he's in.'

Cautiously they crossed the deserted street and edged towards number seventy-eight, located about two hundred yards ahead. The street was lined on both sides by residents' parking bays, the majority unoccupied on this work-day afternoon, save for the occasional white van belonging to a visiting tradesman. Suddenly there was screech as a black Mercedes S-class powered out of a side road, clipping the wing of a parked van in the process.

'Bloody hell, he's in a hurry,' Jimmy said. Their eyes followed the car as it sped past them, then with another screech of brakes, pulled up right outside the blue door. Jimmy sensed the threat immediately.

'Maggie, you wait here and don't bloody move ok? Get on to Frank and tell him we've got a situation developing. We need an armed response team fast.'

Two men had emerged from the Mercedes and were now standing at the front door, a finger jamming on the doorbell. Even from a distance, Jimmy recognised the deadly outline of the weapons they were carrying. *AK-47s.* These guys meant business. They waited a few seconds for a response and then with practised synchronization, applied their boots to the door, bursting it open with little resistance. A few seconds later came a gunshot, causing Jimmy's heart to sink. *Damn, we're too late. The last man standing has now been silenced.* But then unexpectedly, the two gunmen emerged through the door dragging a third man by the scruff of his neck, an automatic shoved into his face in case he had any thought of escaping. As they reached the end of the short path, one of the men stopped and then with a sickening thud, smashed the butt of his assault rifle into the face of their captive. Satisfied that he was subdued, they bundled him into the back of the car, leapt into the front seats, and with a roar of the big vee-eight, accelerated violently away from the kerb.

Jimmy sprinted after them without a thought of what to do if he caught up. He'd figure that out when he got there, just playing it by ear as he had done so many times in the army. Except this time he wasn't in an armoured personnel carrier and there wasn't a comforting helicopter gunship hovering overhead.

But then suddenly and without appearing to look, a vehicle pulled out of another side road immediately in front of the escaping Mercedes. It was a white parcel delivery van, the driver proceeding at a snail's pace as he peered at the house numbers, straining to locate the address for his next delivery. The assailants blared their horn to no effect, white-van-man continuing to dawdle along, blocking their path, oblivious to their presence. That was going to prove to be a mistake. Without warning, the passenger door of the car flew open and a gunman leapt out and ran towards the driver's side of the van. He yanked opened the door and gestured for the driver to get down from the cab. Maybe he hadn't seen the gun, but evidently the driver was not in any hurry to comply with the request. That was his second mistake, as a bullet shattered his ribcage and smashed out through the roof of the van. The gunman dragged him from his seat and threw him to the ground, not caring whether he was dead or alive.

That gave Jimmy his chance. He put on an extra spurt and a second later was within touching distance of the Mercedes, gambling on the fact that the driver would be too occupied by events playing out in front of him to glance in the rear-view mirror. Dropping to the ground he crawled along the pavement on his stomach, being careful to keep below the line of sight of the wing mirror, until he was alongside the rear kerbside door. And now everything depended on what the driver had done with his AK-47, because there would be only one chance to get this right. The odds must be at least fifty-fifty that it was just lying there on the passenger's seat. That was the obvious place to leave it. Time to find out if he was right. He started counting down to steady his nerves. *Five-four-three-two-one.* Reaching up, he grabbed the handle with his left hand, simultaneously pulling open the door as he slipped his right hand in to feel for the automatic. Too late, the driver realised what was happening, just as Jimmy snatched the butt-end of the weapon and wrenched it out of his grasp. In a microsecond he was on his feet, thrusting the barrel of the gun through the open door just as the driver tried to escape. In Helmand, he would have simply taken him out, leaving the awkward questions for later, but that was a long time ago. A different life, thank god. The terrorist was looking him straight in the eye, perfectly calm even though he must have supposed he was about to die. Jimmy had seen that so many times in Afghanistan, a faith so certain that death was not something to be feared. He waved his gun to indicate he should raise his hands.

'You'll need to wait a bit longer for your fifty virgins pal. Today's your lucky day, or maybe not.'

Ahead, the second gunman was just beginning to absorb what was happening. He stood motionless beside the delivery van, straddling the dead driver with his AK-47 held tightly across his chest, seemingly weighing up the options. *Fight or flight, what was it to be?* And then without a word, he climbed into the cab and raced off. Thank heavens for that. The last thing Jimmy wanted was a fire-fight on a sleepy suburban street.

Then he remembered Khan, slumped semi-conscious in the back seat after his brutal beating. 'Dr Khan, are you all right sir?' he shouted, not daring to take his eyes off his captive for a single second. 'My cousin, my cousin,' Khan moaned, 'they killed her.' Christ, he'd forgotten the shot. Who were these bastards and who was running them? Now at least they'd got one of them, and soon surely everything would fall into place. He tried to comfort him the best he could.

'Sir, the police will be here soon, and then everything will be ok.' And on that subject, where the hell were they? Because he was stuck here with his captive until they arrived.

'Dr Khan I presume?'

He heard Maggie's voice, a breath of wind brushing his cheek as the rear door was opened. 'I thought I told you to keep away.' But he was bloody pleased to see her.

'You looked like you needed some help mate,' she said wryly. 'You're not the man you used to be. '

'Yeah, thanks. Anyway how does Dr Khan look?'

'He looks like he's about to pass out. His face is a right mess too.'

At last the police squad had arrived, tumbling out of their vehicles and barking out terse instructions. Frank spotted Maggie at the Mercedes and ran over, giving a rueful shake of the head.

'Sorry we're a bit late. That commander needed to do his damned risk assessment before he would send in any of his precious officers. Anyway, there'll be an ambulance here in a minute I think.' Glancing at Khan he said, 'He looks in a bit of a bad way.'

'Excuse me Frank,' Jimmy said, forcing a smile, 'but never mind chatting up young Maggie here, could you slap some cuffs on this guy? Only if you can fit it into your busy schedule.'

'Any idea who he is?' Frank pulled the gunman's arms behind him and snapped the cuffs closed.

'No idea. He hasn't opened his mouth once. Looks middle-eastern but I can't tell.'

Frank beckoned to two armed officers. 'Over here boys, take this guy off my hands.' They led him away to the detention van, sullen and silent.

'Maybe they'll run three-point-four on him, that should tell us who he is.' Two female paramedics were now tending to Khan's wounds, offering soothing words as he winced with the pain of the stinging antiseptic. 'Soon have you in hospital sir, it's only five minutes away.'

'My cousin. What's happened to my cousin...'

'Shit,' said Jimmy, suddenly remembering. He took one of the paramedics to one side, speaking quietly. 'There was a shot. Inside. It might be pretty messy, I should warn you.'

'We've seen everything in this job sir,' she answered, taking no offence. 'But thanks.' She tapped her colleague on the arm and nodded towards the front door.

***

Khan had been kept in the Royal Blackburn hospital overnight under heightened security and then flown by RAF helicopter down to Northolt air base, where he was questioned at length by DCI Jill Smart and a nameless officer from MI5. Later on Saturday, Khan's family had been driven up from Gloucester under police escort for an emotional reunion. Afterwards, it had been decided to keep them all on the base for a few days until the authorities could assure their immediate safety.

Now it was Monday morning, and Smart was making a rare visit back to Atlee House to brief the team. Not that she had found out much.

'He wouldn't say anything. He's absolutely beside himself with fear, mainly for his family it should be said. But also, despite everything that's happened he's still terrified that his secret will get out.'

'His family still don't know about the Cheltenham Spa incident then?' Maggie asked.

'Apparently not. And he wants to keep it that way.'

'What about the cousin?'

'She's going to be ok, thank goodness. She's got a pretty bad shoulder wound, but it's not life-threatening. That was a huge relief for Dr Kahn and his family as you can imagine. But he's very grateful for the part that you lot played in his rescue.'

'He kind of rescued himself,' Jimmy said. 'It was all down to his own three-point-four software, wasn't it?'

'There is something else,' Smart said. 'He wants to talk to you Maggie. Says he has some information that's for your ears only. They're all travelling back to Gloucester this afternoon but maybe you can get over there later this morning.'

Despite its use as a convenient arrival and departure point for royals and government ministers, the base was no oil-painting. Spread around the site were a hotchpotch of ancient buildings in various state of disrepair, most with the corrugated roofs and ugly metal-framed windows that dated them to the fifties or even earlier. An RAF policeman had driven Maggie from the entrance gatehouse to a block out near the perimeter, ushering her into a small meeting room then standing guard outside the door. The room was provided with a small formica-topped desk and two wooden chairs. Dr Tariq Khan sat at the desk tapping into a slim notebook computer, his head heavily bandaged and an extravagant purple-black bruise spreading from his left cheekbone to the eye-socket. He stood up to greet her.

'Mrs Brooks, we meet again. But my apologies, I'm told you are now Ms. Bainbridge.'

She smiled at him. 'Call me Maggie, please. How are you feeling after your ordeal?'

'I'm ok actually. It frightened my wife and kids when they saw my face but it looks a lot worse than it feels. Please sit down here beside me. I've got something to tell you. And to show you.'

He took a sip of water from a plastic cup. 'They never fully told me what it was all about you know. I knew they wanted to get her freed, but I never knew why. They just used my...my little indiscretion to force me into it. I had no choice, really I hadn't.' She wasn't sure if he was expecting forgiveness from her or not.

'Who were *they* Dr Khan? Who is it you are talking about?'

'Both of them. Saddleworth. And Brooks, who was your husband I believe.'

'And all of them now dead.'

'Exactly. So you can understand why I was so frightened.'

'I understand, totally. But you said you had something to tell me.'

'Yes. You see, they did talk of you many times. Your role was clearly important, although I did not know how or why. I was hoping you might be able to tell me. All I knew was it was something to do with disclosure, they used that term a lot.'

Have you thought about disclosure? She remembered that phrase, casually dropped into conversation by Philip. So innocuous but setting off a chain of events that had devastated her life and taken that of her beautiful niece Daisy. And little Tom Swift and all the other tragic innocents. Christ, how she had been played. *Totally played.*

'I... I wasn't part of it. Not knowingly at least. We've both been used, haven't we? And yet we still don't know why.'

'That's what I wanted to show you Maggie,' he said quietly. 'I think I might have worked it out. In fact I know I have.'

She recognised the distinctive light-blue launch screen as soon as he started it up.

'We all love your three-point-four,' she said brightly. He gave her a faintly scornful look.

'Three-point-four was ok I suppose, but this is three-point-five. My latest version. A hundred times better. This takes family recognition technology to a whole new level. As you will see.'

'Awesome,' she said, without irony.

* * *

It had been a complete foul-up, no-one could argue with that. That's why the distinguished member had insisted that they go to all the trouble and expense of using professionals, exactly to avoid this sort of occurrence. They should have killed Khan on the spot rather than dragging him off for a pointless interrogation. Now he would be guarded twenty-four-by-seven and they would never be able to get to him.

But on the other hand, think about it rationally. Even if Khan had told everything he knew, it wouldn't have mattered. Because really he knew nothing. He didn't know why he'd had to write that report or who was really behind it either. No, on reflection, they were still quite safe and he could concentrate on cementing his legacy. It was stupid really, because by the time they came to write the history books, you were long dead, too late for you to give a damn about what they said about you. But you did it anyway. They all did, all his predecessors. It was your legacy and it was important. And quite definitely, he was safe.

Except what he didn't know was that Maggie Bainbridge had worked it all out. Why it was done and how it was done and who did it. *Everything.* From start to finish. And now she was coming for him.

Chapter 32

It took them just eight minutes to make the journey from Atlee House to the Savoy, the path through the drizzly evening rush-hour eased by the flashing blue lights and penetrating siren of Frank's commandeered patrol car. As they screeched into the hotel's canopied drop-off zone, two armed officers bounded over, nervously pointing their automatics at the windscreen. Frank brandished his credit card-sized ID pass through his open window.

'Steady on pal, we're police.' One of the officers gestured with his gun. 'Ok sir could you just get out of the car, nice and slowly, and make sure I can see your hands at all times.'

'God's sake man.' It was frustrating, but he knew he would be doing exactly the same thing if he was in their position. Slowly, he opened the door of the BMW and slid out as gracefully as a man of his physique could manage.

'Look, here's my ID. DI Frank Stewart, Department 12B of the Met.'

The officer took the pass and examined it carefully, then looked up at Frank, still covering him with his automatic. Evidently he was satisfied that the photo was an adequate likeness.

'That looks in order sir, and are you able to vouch for the others in the motor car?'

'Aye, aye, they're pukka, no worries on that score. Now you guys need to come with me right now.'

The PC was uncertain whether to comply. 'But sir, we're under strict orders not to let anyone in.'

'We're not worried about people getting in now lads,' Frank replied. 'It's people getting out we need to worry about. Come on, move it!'

Now Jimmy and Maggie were by his side, and a moment later they were sprinting down a long plush-carpeted corridor towards the ballroom which was hosting the peace conference.

'You don't think they'll really try and make a break for it do you?' Maggie gasped.

'Not all of them, but we're only interested in one person, aren't we?'

As they expected, there was further armed presence outside the ballroom, two female officers stationed either side of the elaborately-panelled oak doors of the room. From inside they could just make out the muted tones of Prime Minister Julian Priest delivering his closing speech to the assembled media. 'A significant breakthrough'...'the dream of a Palestinian state within our grasp'. He could have written it before the conference was even arranged. He probably did.

Frank flashed his ID at the officers. 'Has anyone entered or left here since this session started?'

'No sir, not this way. There are four fire exits as well but they're all alarmed and guarded too. But Chief Super Clarke is in charge sir, she's inside at the moment, I can get her on the radio if you like.'

'No, I think we'll keep it low-key for now. We're just going to slip in at the back of the room, nice and quietly.' He gestured to Jimmy, Maggie and the police officers to follow, opening a door just wide enough for them to squeeze through. The room was packed to capacity with reporters, the TV journalists accompanied by camera and sound crews, all anxious to get a hearing when the session was opened up for questions. A few turned round to see what was happening at the back of the room, momentarily disconcerted by the arrival of yet more armed police. Julian Priest though was unmoved, continuing to deliver his speech from behind the official HM Government-crested podium which had been placed in the middle of the long table. Behind the table sat the key figures of the government's hopeful peace initiative. Maggie did a quick mental roll-call. Philomena Forbes-Brown, over-promoted to the Home Office after the murder of Gerrard Saddleworth, looking bored and disengaged, struggling to stifle a yawn. Robert Francis, the new Attorney General, appointed to sweep up the mess left over from the Alzahrani foul-up.

Then there was Lillian Cortes, the twenty-nine-year-old firebrand Democrat congresswoman and darling of America's emerging radical left, sitting alongside Otaga Mombassa, an obscure and very junior UN official from Nigeria. Both had been parachuted in in a desperate attempt to lend the conference a semblance of international credibility. To the left of Julian Priest, the beautiful Fadwa Ziadeh, and to his right, her son Mohammed.

And at that moment Maggie could see it, in crystal-clear high-definition, just as if she had been looking at a finely-realised family portrait painted by an old master. It didn't need the help of Dr Khan's super-sophisticated three-point-five software, because in the flesh, the resemblance was as striking as it was startling. Mohammed Ziadeh shared the delicate cheek bones and wide mouth and full lips of his mother, but there was no mistaking from whom he had inherited the piercing green eyes, close-set under a fine Roman forehead. It was from the man who a few seconds earlier had finished his speech and now sat alongside him. *His father, Julian Priest.* Now too, Maggie recognised what Khan's sophisticated algorithms, developed to be as reliable as DNA matching, had already unveiled. The sibling likeness was obvious and undeniable. Dena Alzahrani, the Hampstead bomber, the woman who had ruined her life and that of so many other innocents, was Mohammed Ziadeh's twin. Now the motive behind the whole ghastly conspiracy could be and would be revealed.

Slowly and purposefully, Maggie began walking towards the platform. 'Where is she Priest? Where is she? We know she's your daughter. So where have you hidden Dena?'

An audible gasp reverberated around the room as stunned media hacks struggled to process the accusation. There were murmurs of surprise as some recognised the interlocutor to be the notorious defence barrister from the Alzahrani trial. The BBC's sharp young political correspondent was the first to react, struggling to believe she was actually about to ask this crazy question.

'Is it true what Mrs Brooks says, Mr Priest. Is it true? Are you Dena Alzahrani's father?'

But it could not be denied, for now everyone in the room could see it with their own eyes, and in the outside-broadcast control trucks, sharp-reacting producers were zooming in on the faces of Priest, Fadwa and Mohammed Ziadeh and piecing together collages that added the notorious image of Dena Alzahrani for the benefit of their millions of viewers. And he did not try to deny it. With a sudden surge of rage, he upended the table, sending water jugs, glasses, mobile phones and laptops flying in all directions, unleashing a maelstrom of confusion. Lillian Cortes was now in tears as her much-anticipated grandstanding event turned into a PR disaster. Otaga Mombassa had been joined by his burly private security detail and was remonstrating furiously with a stunned Forbes-Brown, sitting with her head in her hands. And there, centre-stage was the Right Honourable Julian Peregrine Priest, eighty-seventh Prime Minister of Great Britain and Northern Ireland, with his hands tightening around the throat of

Maggie Brooks.

'You interfering bitch. I told Philip he should have dealt with you but he wouldn't because of that damned brat of yours. Well now I'm going to do the job for him.' She gripped his wrists in an effort to free herself but he was too powerful. The room began to spin and she realised that she was beginning to lose consciousness.

It took Jimmy only a fraction of a second to react. He bounded onto the stage and placed a crushing arm-lock around the throat of Priest, tightening it until he slumped back into his chair.

'It's all over for you now pal. Frank, get over here and take this bastard out of my sight.'

He gave him a thumbs-up, 'I'll take it from here bruv.' He grabbed Priest by the arm. 'We can make this as easy or as difficult as you want sir, it's up to you, but it would be best to avoid handcuffs, don't you think? Not a good look for the cameras.' Broken, Priest could only nod his silent consent.

They had been joined by Chief Superintendent Jennifer Clarke who had emerged from undercover deployment amongst the journalists.

'Who are you exactly?' she asked, looking puzzled.

'DI Frank Stewart ma'am. I'm working the Cathedral Close murders.'

'And is all of this true? Is Priest really that terrorist's father?'

'We think so ma'am, almost certainly. That's what it was all about. He was desperate for her to be freed.'

'And all these murders? Was he responsible for them too?'

'Aye, we're pretty sure he was. He didn't carry out the killings himself of course, but we're certain he ordered them. Iranians, we think, revolutionary guards. We caught one of them up in Blackburn and he should help us track the rest of them down. But we can work out the exact charges when we get him to the station.'

'Understood Inspector, and very good work here.' She barked an order to a uniformed officer. 'Get the media out of here and lock down this room. This is now a crime scene.'

Now only Fadwa Ziadeh and her son remained in the room, sharing some private joke, calm and unmoved despite the turmoil of the last few minutes. Safe in the knowledge that they were immune from prosecution because of their diplomatic status, and probably smart enough not have taken any active role in the crime. Conspirators undoubtedly, but participants probably not. Clever bastards.

'So you're Maggie Brooks?' she said, her voice laden with venom. 'I was so hoping to get to meet you. Philip told me so much about you during his little trips to my country. Pillow talk, that's what they call it, don't they? He was a very good lover. So caring and considerate. You were very lucky to have had him for a few years. Although in the end I think he found you, well, just a little dull.'

Maggie found it easy to ignore the provocation.

'Where is Dena?'

'My beautiful but stupid daughter? Her name is Hasema and I assume she is still in Cairo at the moment, or perhaps she is already on her way back to Gaza. She flew out yesterday on her brother's passport you see, on your excellent British Airways, business class naturally. An easy disguise. My children, they look so alike, of course.' Maggie knew from Dr Tariq Khan that the border force scanners would have been unable to tell the difference between the twins. They were still running three-point-one.

'Do you really care about Palestine, that's what I want to know. Because to me, it looks just a big game to you, a bloody lifestyle choice. So where is it next for you Fadwa? Gstaad, Davoz, Rio, after we have you deported of course.'

She smiled. 'Stockholm actually. So nice in midsummer, don't you think? But you're wrong Maggie, I do care, I care very much. And one day we will achieve our destiny and have our homeland returned to us, but it won't be through killings and hatred. That way is the fool's way.' It was said with such passion and conviction that Maggie could not help but believe it.

'So you must be so disappointed in Hasema. All that hate and anger in such a beautiful young woman.'

'I'm afraid Hasema is young and foolish, and was so easily led astray by her stupid grandfather and his cynical Iranian supporters. She has her father's blood you see, and we all know what a fool he is. But I love her of course, and Julian loves her too and so she had to be rescued. And dear Philip, he arranged it all so beautifully. He played you Maggie, just like he said he would.'

She was conscious of Jimmy's presence, his arm around her shoulders, hugging her close to him. He kissed her gently on her forehead. Perhaps it was only a platonic brotherly kiss, but she didn't care. It was still nice.

'Don't rise to it Maggie, she's not worth it. You have only good things to look forward to now.'

And it was true, there could be no doubt. Perhaps her reputation could be restored and she might be able to go back to the Bar - but did she still want all of that now? Because the truth was, she had enjoyed the last few weeks more than she could have ever imagined, and the thought of not having Jimmy and Frank Stewart in her life already seemed impossible. And Asvina was already talking about another case, some famous soap-star who had tired of her husband. But now it was too soon, too raw to make these kind of decisions. Now she must concentrate on the one thing that mattered above all others. Soon she would have Ollie back with her and everything would be wonderful again.

* * *

'Eighty-eight quid for a steak, and it doesn't even come with chips? Ridiculous.'

This time they had rejected Frank's favourite Shoreditch pub in favour of a lunchtime table for three at the rather more upmarket Ship just around the corner. A few minutes earlier, a good-looking waiter had reeled off a list of complicated-sounding specials before presenting each with the eye-wateringly expensive menu.

'It's chateaubriand,' laughed Maggie, 'and it's for two. And besides, I'm paying, so you don't need to worry about the price.'

Jimmy adopted a tone of mock concern. 'Oh dear, I've had a look, and they don't seem to have sausage rolls on the menu today mate. Do you want me to choose something for you?'

'Oh aye, and you're mister sophistication, are you?'

'Boys, boys, we're here to have a lovely time and to celebrate our great success. Let's not behave like little school boys in the dinner-hall.'

'Sorry miss,' Jimmy smiled.

'Aye sorry miss,' Frank said.

After much discussion, food and wine was finally ordered, accompanied by three very large gin and tonics procured at the insistence of Maggie. Frank dealt with his in just two swigs.

'All right then, you two smart-arse private dicks. I want to know the full story from the beginning, sparing no detail.' He raised his hand to draw the attention of a white-shirted waiter who was just passing. 'Pint of Doom Bar please mate. Right Maggie, sorry, where were we?'

'I hadn't actually started yet. But I think it all goes back nearly twenty-five years ago to Palestinian Solidarity. That was the pressure group founded by Philip's brother Hugo. It was a deeply fashionable cause back then for any left-leaning politician...'

'Still is,' Jimmy said.

'Indeed, and as it is now, it was a great thing to have on your CV when you were trying to make the candidate short-list in one of these fashionable metropolitan seats. That's what attracted the likes of Saddleworth and Priest, and a host of others too who didn't manage to climb the greasy pole and have now slipped into obscurity.'

'Slipped into obscurity down the greasy pole. Very good Maggie,' Jimmy smiled.

'Purely accidental, honest.'

'And that's when Priest and Fadwa hooked up I assume,' Frank said. 'She looks pretty amazing now, so god knows what she looked like in her twenties.'

'Irresistible by all accounts, and as the daughter of Yasser Ziadeh she was also at the centre of the fight for Palestinian self-determination. Intoxicating for these young idealists.'

'Or opportunists,' Jimmy said.

'Exactly. So before long, Fadwa finds herself pregnant and gives birth to twins. She was always headstrong and so she refused to name the father, but there was a lot of speculation at the time that it was Julian Priest. We don't know of course what the subsequent relationship between Priest and Fadwa was like, but we can imagine the likely difficulties just taking into account the geography. And it's hard to think of either of them settling down to cosy domesticity.'

'So just a shag, not a big love affair then.'

Maggie gave an amused look. 'Yes, I suppose that's one way of describing it Frank.'

'But Priest must have kept some contact with his children over the years?' he asked.

'Yes, he was still quite heavily involved with Palestinian Solidarity, and was a regular visitor to Gaza. So yes, he did keep in touch. But I don't think he was going to birthday parties and school sports days or anything like that.'

'So why the hell did he risk everything to get involved in getting Dena freed?' Frank said. 'That seems really dumb to me if he didn't really give a shit about her.'

'Pretty simple,' Jimmy answered. 'We think that Fadwa threatened to expose him as Dena's father if he didn't cooperate. Can you imagine the storm that would be stirred up if the Prime Minister is exposed as the father of the notorious terrorist?'

Frank nodded. 'Aye, and so Priest ropes in his old mates to help him out. But why did they agree to help him, that's what I don't quite understand? I would have just told him to bugger off.'

'We know now from Fadwa that Philip was Priest's fixer. He was given the job of working the whole thing out,' Maggie said. 'That was typical Philip. He would have weighed up that helping Priest would give him some bargaining chips which he could cash in at some unspecified time in the future. And although it's hard to stomach, I was the first piece in the jigsaw. It made sense to have someone he thought he could influence defending the case.'

'You see Frank, I talked to that Clerk at Maggie's Chambers,' Jimmy said. 'He admitted he'd been paid by Philip to pass the brief to her. Didn't see anything wrong with doing that, he just thought Brooks was trying to help his wife's career.'

'Yes, at that stage I don't think Philip had any particular plan worked out,' Maggie said. 'But in the back of his mind he knew he could use the Miner's Trust situation to get Saddleworth to do anything he wanted.'

'So it was blackmail then,' Frank said. 'Or coercion to be exact.'

'Indeed,' Maggie agreed. 'Gerrard almost certainly knew that Priest was Dena's father, and probably the last thing on earth he wanted was to be caught up in this conspiracy. But Brooks played the Trust scandal card and so he had no choice but to cooperate.'

Frank shook his head in disbelief. 'So now I suppose the big question was how to get the jury to deliver a not-guilty verdict. The bloody government trying to get a murdering terrorist freed, I mean you couldn't make it up.'

'Yep Frank, but that's what happened. And then my shit-face husband Philip has the brainwave that engineering a mistrial might be a whole lot easier than trying to convince a jury of Alzahrani's innocence. There had been so much focus on all these failure-to-disclose-evidence scandals that he knew every judge in the land would be hypersensitive to even a hint that it was happening in one of their trials.'

'That was it,' said Jimmy. 'Now Brooks and Saddleworth had to come up with some scheme to engineer a mistrial and that was not as easy as it looks. I think at first they were hoping for some technicality around Alzahrani's human rights, you know given Philip's background, but I don't think they were getting far.'

'And then Saddleworth the blackmailer remembered the Khan affair,' said Frank. 'That was a gift right enough.'

'It was,' agreed Maggie, 'and in fact you uncovered it yourself Frank. The devout Muslim family man cautioned for using rent boys, the affair swept under the carpet because of his importance to national security. Of course, as Home Secretary, the file would have passed through Saddleworth's office. And naturally, Khan is going to do anything to stop his family knowing about his little indiscretions.'

'So,' said Jimmy, 'Khan looks at the official report and says there's nothing wrong with it, only eighteen percent chance it could have identified the wrong person, what do you expect me to do? Saddleworth says, what we expect you to do is rubbish it, that's what we expect you to do, unless of course you want your sick habit of putting your hands down the pants of young boys splashed all over the papers. Oh, and as it happens, we've been talking to Penelope White of the Chronicle about your story. She would absolutely love to put your photograph on her front page.'

'That's why she was at the dinner you see,' Maggie added, 'just in case he has a last-minute change of heart. Although I'm not sure Gerrard had told her the full background.'

'That's right. So of course Khan has no choice. He writes a counter-report that says there's a high percentage chance that the identification was wrong. Scientifically, it's a heap of crap, but it delivers exactly what Saddleworth wants. Because now he is able to go to the CPS and bring up this rather inconvenient difficulty that has emerged just before the start of the trial.'

'So the CPS were involved in it too?' Frank asked.

'Yes, but they didn't know about the conspiracy. Elizabeth Rooke their boss is guilty through negligence, that's all. I expect the way it was raised was that Saddleworth says to her something's come up, some mad scientist guy who works for the Home Office has written a report, probably not that serious, but I thought we'd better run it past

Cameron, see what he thinks. He knows that the last thing Rooke wants is to delay the trial, which would be a PR nightmare for her department, and so she says, go ahead, not really knowing what she's agreeing to.'

'So they arrange the dinner,' Frank said.

Maggie nodded. 'So they arrange the dinner. Right from the start, there's already pressure on Cameron from the CPS to sweep the whole thing under the carpet. Five minutes in, he realises that the geeky Dr Khan will be hopeless if he tries to put him in the witness box.'

'Yeah, we think that's probably what happened,' Jimmy said. 'So there's a discussion, Khan gives a complicated and confusing pitch, Cameron asks some questions but still can't make head or tail of it. He knows that Rooke just wants it to go away, and so after two or three bottles of rather nice Beaujolais and a call or two, they collectively decide that on balance it's best to leave things as they are.'

'Aye, I see it,' Frank said. 'Cameron has fallen into a bloody great bear-trap without even knowing it, because now that he's seen the report, the non-disclosure scam is in play. He knows it exists but now he's in on the decision not to use it. That's bloody clever, I've got to say.'

'Exactly,' Jimmy agreed. 'The trap is set, and the only person left to snare is Maggie.'

She gave a rueful smile. 'And how easy was that? By some ridiculous coincidence, a report turns up right at the end of the trial that could change everything for me. Too improbable for words of course, and I should have smelt a rat, but I was so bound up in my own dreams of glory. What a stupid idiot I was. And I remember now so clearly how interested Philip suddenly becomes about how the trial is going. Of course, I tell him about the report and surprise-surprise, he casually says, have you thought about using a disclosure angle? *Have you thought about disclosure.* That's all it took. And I fell for it one hundred percent.'

'But the judge was told you had got the report much earlier than you actually had it, wasn't she?' Frank said. 'That's why you got reported to the Bar Council. So how did that happen?'

'That was Philip's doing too. He spoke to Lady Rooke at the CPS. He said that I had told him I'd got it, you know, just as part of casual husband and wife conversation.'

'Weeks before you *actually* got it?'

'Exactly,' she said. 'What a hero he was, don't you think?'

Frank nodded. 'Aye he was, and bloody evil too. But there's something else I don't get. Why did Cameron have to be killed if he didn't know about the conspiracy?'

Maggie held up her hands and sighed. 'I'm afraid that was my fault again. Dr Khan told me that Philip panicked when he found out we had that photograph. Within minutes, he'd called everyone up and told them to keep quiet. Of course, Khan and Cameron who are all in the dark say, keep quiet about what?'

'And that's what signed his death warrant,' Frank said. 'A real tragedy. Priest decided it was too risky for any of them to stay alive and told the Iranian hoods to take care of all of them.'

'And they murdered that poor young waiter too,' Jimmy said ruefully. 'Presumably they were worried he had overheard something.'

Maggie nodded. 'Yeah, I know, in some ways that one was the most shocking of all. All Priest's doing, and he was our sodding Prime Minister.'

Jimmy laughed. 'Aye, but I don't think he'll be running for re-election any time soon.'

Frank let out an exaggerated yawn.

'Well it's all as clear as mud to me. But you know what guys, I say we've had enough talk. I'm already bored stiff with all this Cathedral Close stuff. So how's about another round of these G-and-Ts before our puddings come?'

'Did someone say something about G-and-Ts? Yes please.'

Surprised, they spun round to greet the tall willowy figure of Asvina Rani. It was the first time Jimmy had seen her both out from behind a desk and not wearing her glasses, and he could not hide his appreciation of her loveliness. Frank meanwhile was looking at him with a non-too-subtle expression that said 'who the hell is this and how do you know her?'

'This is Asvina,' Jimmy said, reading his thoughts. 'Our patron. The lady who brought us Saddleworth verses Saddleworth.'

Maggie had leapt to her feet to envelop her friend in a warm hug. 'Asvina! I didn't expect to see you here. How did you find us?'

'A very nice girl at your office told me where you were. Elsa I believe her name is.' They noticed she was carrying a crisp white foolscap envelope. Gently, she freed herself from Maggie's embrace and began to wave the envelope above her head. There was an unmistakable air of triumph about her.

'So then Miss Bainbridge, I happened to be in front of a family court this morning, with magistrate Mrs Evelyn Black presiding. We were there to hear a petition, which I raised on your behalf, that Oliver Jonathon Brooks, aged seven, should be removed from the care of Camden Council Social Services to the care of his mother Mrs Magdalene Jane Brooks. I did not ask you to attend Maggie because quite frankly, and I say this as your best friend, I could not trust you not to get aggressive and not to get emotional and not to say a four-letter swear word, even under your breath, if an official made a statement you did not agree with.'

Maggie had collapsed back in her seat and now tears streamed uncontrollably down her face. Jimmy tilted his head and gave her a thumbs up. 'She knows you, that's all I can say.'

Asvina smiled. 'As it happens, a stern and rather overweight woman who called herself the Assistant Deputy Director of Children's Services did make many statements that I did not agree with, and she made them with considerable force and at considerable length. However, you will be pleased to hear that I did not get aggressive, I did not get emotional and above all, I did not say a four-letter swear word, not even once.'

She handed the letter to Maggie, her voice the faintest whisper. 'Why don't you open it?'

Ollie was coming home.